Angel Vindicated

VIOLA ESTRELLA

Cerridwen Press

A Cerridwen Press Publication

www.cerridwenpress.com

Angel Vindicated

ISBN 9781419960222
ALL RIGHTS RESERVED
Angel Vindicated Copyright © 2009 Viola Estrella
Edited by Helen Woodall.
Cover art by Dar Albert.

This book printed in the U.S.A. by Jasmine-Jade Enterprises, LLC.

Electronic book publication May 2009
Trade paperback publication November 2009

With the exception of quotes used in reviews, this book may not be reproduced or used in whole or in part by any means existing without written permission from the publisher, Ellora's Cave Publishing Inc., 1056 Home Avenue, Akron, OH 44310-3502.

Warning: The unauthorized reproduction or distribution of this copyrighted work is illegal. Criminal copyright infringement, including infringement without monetary gain, is investigated by the FBI and is punishable by up to 5 years in federal prison and a fine of $250,000.
(http://www.fbi.gov/ipr/)

This book is a work of fiction and any resemblance to persons, living or dead, or places, events or locales is purely coincidental. The characters are productions of the author's imagination and used fictitiously.

Cerridwen Press is an imprint of Ellora's Cave Publishing, Inc.®

Angel Vindicated

Dedication

൭

To all the beautifully flawed people who always give their best but still seem to make mistakes.

To my hubby, Mark, for kindly overlooking the majority of my mistakes. Love you!

To my fabulous critique partners, Patrice, Helen, Tricia and Monica, for catching my mistakes. Thank you!

And to my editor, Helen, for looking past my mistakes and giving this baby a chance. I'm honored to be a member of your frog pond.

Trademarks Acknowledgement

൭

The author acknowledges the trademarked status and trademark owners of the following wordmarks mentioned in this work of fiction:

Aerosmith: Rag Doll Merchandising, Inc.

Baywatch: Baywatch Production Company

Buick: General Motors Corporation

Coca-Cola: The Coca-Cola Company

Cocoa Puffs: General Mills IP Holdings II, LLC

Denver Broncos: Empire Sports, Inc.

Diet Coke: Coca-Cola Company

Doritos: Frito-Lay North America, Inc.

Dracula: Marvel Comics Group

Escort: Ford Motor Company
ESPN: ESPN, Inc.
Geo: General Motors Corporation
Hustler: LFP IP, LLC
Jack Daniel's: Jack Daniel's Properties, Inc.
Jaguar: Jaguar Cars Limited Corporation
Martha Stewart: Martha Stewart Living Omnimedia, Inc.
Mr. Clean: The Procter & Gamble Company
Nike: Nike, Inc.
Nordstrom: NIHC, Inc.
Oldsmobile: General Motors Corporation
Silverado: General Motors Corporation
Star Wars: Lucasfilm Entertainment Company Ltd
The Cheesecake Factory: Cheesecake Factory Assets Co. LLC
TiVo: Tivo Brands LLC
Volkswagen: Volkswagen Aktiengesellschaft Corporation

Chapter One

Some of my fellow Angels find it hilarious that my middle name is Virtue. Abigail Virtue Angel. It was printed right on my Creation Certificate. My mother was always an optimist. She said when I came out red-faced and bawling with my wings spread out to the heavens she knew I'd need an extra boost of encouragement.

Angels don't misbehave, she'd always say. Angels were virtuous.

Sadly, for my mother, I haven't been able to live up to that goddamn middle name. No matter how hard I've tried. I've made mistakes. I've sinned just like a human. I once even gave in to a demon's seduction, if you can believe that. He was only a half-demon but that didn't matter. He was one hundred percent pure evil.

And I was put on this earth to stop evil.

My first target tonight was sitting at the bar with a mug of draft beer in front of him, munching on an unlit cigar while scratching his ass. I recognized his nicely shaped posterior from the picture in his file. Demon #3761. His file also said he lived in a studio apartment in this same building and he didn't own a vehicle. Seeing how most demons love to drink and were too lazy to travel far on foot, I figured he'd be here. I was right. Imagine that.

This particular demon already had one strike against him for using his power of persuasion to convince a convenience store clerk to stage a robbery, steal money from the safe and give half to him. I was to issue him a second strike for conning a human into starting a pyramid scam. Pathetic. These overgrown hellions had too much time on their hands. And it was my job to remind them to knock it off.

I walked across the dimly lit, nearly empty room and stood behind him. My shoulder blades—where my wings sprouted when in use—twitched, as they loved to do when in the presence of a demon. The older the demon, the more my wings begged to be released.

"Peter Piper?" I asked, trying not to laugh. Some of the names these guys came up with for themselves were comical.

He swiveled around on his barstool and sniffed the air around my mouth. He had a perfect nose, high cheekbones, full lips and sensual brown eyes. One thing the demons had going for them was their attractive features and muscular bodies. Deceptively gorgeous. Otherwise, the guy in front of me looked like a used car salesman with his thrift store polyester suit tailored for a man half a foot shorter. Not to mention the cheesy Christmas tree tie he wore in the middle of October.

Piper sniffed again and then sneered. "Angel?"

"Yep. Abigail Angel but you can call me Abby." I glanced around to see if anyone was watching us. There was one man slumped over the counter at the other side of the bar, daydreaming over his Jack and Coke. A couple of guys sat at a table in the far corner of the room. One was passing an envelope to the other. Probably a demon behind that transaction as well but there wasn't anything I could do about it now. It wasn't my job to police the humans, only the demons.

The bartender, who looked like a lumberjack on steroids, looked my way. "Get you a drink?"

"Sure. I'll have a Shirley Temple with extra cherries and a wedge of lime."

Both Piper and the bartender chuckled.

"What?" I said with my best PMS glare.

"Nothing." The bartender went in search of some cherries.

I turned back to Piper. "You're in violation of Code Three, manipulating a human into acting on greed. You know the drill."

There were seven codes for each of the seven deadly sins—lust, gluttony, greed, sloth, wrath, envy and pride. Each time a demon was involved in corrupting a human to commit a sin the demon was in violation of a code.

That was where I came into the picture.

Most humans weren't aware of my existence, so an explanation may be due. Three types of Angels occupy this earth. Guardian Angels, Angels of Death and Law Enforcement Angels, otherwise known as Demon Control agents, all under an organization called Angels, Inc. I was in the line of law enforcement. Yep, little ole me, Abigail V. Angel. I kept the demons in line. At least I was here to try.

It wasn't as if I had a choice. I hadn't woken up one day and decided I wanted to save the human population from avoidable sin. I hadn't raised my hand and said "pick me" when they were passing out *reasons why you'll never have any type of normalcy*. Nope. I was born an Angel, raised an Angel and I will die an Angel. Eventually. There were some advantages, including having an extended life. I would live a healthy existence for eternity as long as I didn't get myself murdered or run over by a bus. I'd never be sick and I was immune to diseases. And—this was the best part—I'd always look like I was twenty-four years old.

So all I needed to do was avoid moving vehicles, falling pianos, sharp knives and guns.

Yeah, right. Did I mention I was in Demon Control?

"Fuck off, bitch," Piper said and threw his lukewarm beer in my face.

I hated this part about my job—when they put up a fight. Which usually didn't happen unless I was there to give them their third strike. Because you know what three strikes meant, right? *You're outta here.* Or for demons it meant they get deported back to Hell. Right where they belong if you ask me.

I used his tie to wipe off my face. "I wish you hadn't done that, Peter."

"Oh yeah?" He stood up and towered a foot taller than me. "What are you going to do about it? Pray for me?" He smiled, showing teeth that hadn't been brushed in months. Yellowed, thick with tartar, plaque and last night's dinner. Nasty. So much for the gorgeousness.

I held my breath and continued. "If you want to do this the hard way I'll probably kick you in the balls and pin your ass to the ground." Like I mentioned earlier, I wasn't the most virtuous Angel. But when dealing with a demon, an Angel had to do what an Angel had to do.

Unfortunately, I needed to touch him to give him his warning. One thumbprint to the heart. It would imprint into his skin and would only be visible to Angels. Don't ask me who made up these stupid rules. I vaguely remembered learning at Angel Academy about a pact between the powers that be, appropriately called the "Powers That Be Pact". Essentially it said Demons were allowed to roam the earth as long as Angels were in control. When a demon got out of hand, Demon Control Angels stepped in.

"Feisty little sprite, aren't you?" Piper said.

"I try my best. Now, why don't we get this over with so we can both get on with it?" I reached under his suit jacket.

He backed up. "Not so fast. I've had enough of you elfin bitches trying to run my life."

Elfin? Okay, that was a little insensitive. No, Angels weren't overgrown mongrels but we weren't elves either. On average, we were five and a half feet tall. And we were all of the female persuasion. It became evident several years ago that men didn't make the best Angels. Too much testosterone and not enough patience had led to multiple reports of demon mistreatment.

There were still a few male Angels of Death. It didn't require a lot of control to take a life when a human's time came. But for the most part, men had been removed from active duty at Angels, Inc. This meant we females had to work twice as hard to save our image.

I lunged forward at the demon and he turned, jerking back wildly to get away from me. Then he ran for the door, knocking over chairs in the process.

"Oh, come on," I yelled.

This was getting a little screwy. Never have I had to chase a demon for a second offense. They simply didn't care enough to run unless there was the threat of deportation.

"You need some help, lady?" the bartender asked, with Shirley Temple in hand. "Did he take your purse or something?"

I was half tempted to lie so the big, burly guy would do the footwork for me. But rule number one in Demon Control was don't let the humans get involved.

Freaking humans. They didn't know how good they had it.

"No. I'm fine." I hurried after Piper. "Go ahead and put that drink on my tab."

"You don't have a tab," he yelled, as the door closed behind me.

Downtown Denver was where my division of Demon Control was situated. Denver and its surrounding areas was where we usually found our offenders. It had it all the perfect locations for potential sinning — bars, strip clubs, banks, sleazy hotels, ritzy hotels and the State Capital.

I pursued Peter Piper as he cut across Blake Street and ran a few blocks to Lawrence. The roads were mostly deserted since it was past midnight on a weekday. He wasn't running very fast and I was gaining on him without much effort. Which led me to believe he wasn't as athletic as the other demons I'd encountered...or he was luring me somewhere.

Hmm. I slowed to a stop and watched as he turned into an alley between two buildings. A dark alley. I backed up against the brick wall and listened closely.

Steam rose from a manhole in the middle of the street and the roads glistened from a recent rain. I could hear a woman laughing a couple of blocks away. A car drove past, splashing water onto the other side of the street.

I peeked around the corner down the alley. The shadow of his body was a quarter of the way up the eight stories. No noise but the sound of Piper climbing up the side of the building, his feet scraping against the brick.

"What are you doing, Peter?" I asked. There wasn't any point in trying to sneak up on him. Not only could demons scale the sides of buildings, they also had exceptional hearing.

Me? I could hover. Not fly. Hover. My translucent wings had a span of seven feet when fully engaged but sadly, they only allowed me to levitate. Twelve feet up if I concentrated hard enough. And I could probably match his strength if I could just get my hands on him. Unfortunately, the powers that be didn't think we Angels required much to keep the bad guys in line.

No answer from Piper other than a snort, a hack and the sound of phlegm splattering on concrete.

So I guess I'd meet him at the top. Say hello, give him his strike and be on my way. Although, after the crap he was putting me through tonight, I ought to give him his third strike.

I opened the door to the apartment building, didn't see any type of security so I took the eight flights of stairs up to the very top. The door to the roof needed a little shove but other than that, there were no problems. Too easy, the little voice in my head was saying.

I hated that little voice. It never shut up.

Piper was pulling himself up over the wall with grunts and groans. I helped him out by grabbing his coat and dragging him to the rooftop. Then I straddled him, ripped open his shirt and lifted up my hand to press my thumb to his chest.

He laughed. "Stupid bitch."

I heard the sound of footsteps scrambling behind me and the next thing I knew I was staring up at the stars, the moon and four nice-looking men. Demons. Damn it. This couldn't be good.

"Hi there," one of them said. He had shoulder-length, golden-blond hair, tanned skin and blue eyes. His shirt was unbuttoned, revealing his muscular chest and one tiny thumbprint. "Must have gotten the wind knocked out of you." His voice was smooth and deceivingly relaxing.

I tried to sit up but the second demon pressed his foot down on my chest.

"No need to get up," Blondie said. Apparently, he was the leader of the pack here and the other guys were his goons. Including Peter, who was looking increasingly nervous with each passing second.

"What do you want?" I had nothing to give them. Unless what they wanted from me was physical. But any demon knew that if he messed with an Angel there would be hell to pay. Literally.

More often than not, after a demon was deported it only took a few months before he was permitted back onto Earth. You know, overpopulation and all that crap. The severity of their crimes determined how long they had to serve time in Hell.

Killing, raping or maiming an Angel meant you were there for eternity.

"I'm glad you asked." The leader narrowed his twinkling blue eyes at me. "We have a message we want you to take back to the rest of the Angels."

"Okay. What is it?" Let's get this over with then. There was a piece of cheesecake in my refrigerator calling my name. Not to mention I had Monday night football recorded on TiVo. And it was Wednesday.

He chuckled and kneeled down next to me. Two of the goons, one of them Piper, grabbed my wrists and pressed them to the gravelly rooftop. I didn't resist. There was no way I could take all four of them.

"This is quite a treat." He tugged on a lock of my hair. "I've never seen an Angel with red hair before."

I tried not to show my disgust that the fiend was touching me. My unusual looks had caused me more trouble than I'd like to admit. Red hair, brown eyes and pale skin for an Angel was extremely rare. It made me stand out when all I wanted to do was blend in.

"You seem pretty calm, Abigail Angel. Aren't you afraid of us?" His warm breath swept across my face. At least this guy brushed his teeth.

I shrugged. "You all appear to be smart guys. You probably know the rules so what would I fear?"

He smiled, all gleaming teeth and straight lines. "Sweetheart, there is much to fear." He nodded to the goon on my left and I felt his foot kick into my side with enough strength to make me ball my legs up in pain.

I took deep breaths to gain back some control, ignoring the deep bruising the steel-toe boot had left right below my rib cage. I centered my stare on Blondie. "What do you want?" I asked again.

Satisfaction covered his face. "You see, the rules are about to change. What I want, Abigail, is for you to spread the word. Demons will no longer be policed by Angels. We refuse to be controlled. And if you attempt to do so, then we'll take action." He slid his finger down my t-shirt, through the space between my breasts. "Do you understand?"

"Yes." What else could I say? It was one against four and these guys weren't playing by the rules. They wanted to change the rules. My best bet was to get the heck out of there and warn Demon Control about our new little problem.

"Good." He seemed surprised by my answer.

So was I, to tell you the truth. But, hey, I was no hero. I was just an Angel trying to do her job and get through the day.

They all stood and freed my wrists. I tried to get up too but before I could rise to my knees, Blondie backhanded me, throwing me back down to the rooftop.

"Shit," I yelled. The sting was worse than my side. I wasn't used to pain. Other than a scuffle with a demon now and then, Angels had always been above getting knocked around.

I removed my hand from my throbbing cheek and noticed the goons were all laughing. However, Blondie looked pretty serious, like he might want to hit me again. I stayed down.

"I warn you to take this threat seriously," he said. "If you don't, Angels *will* be punished. And the blood will be on your hands."

Chapter Two

I waited until the demons were well out of sight before I slowly made my way back to the bar to get my car. I'd rescued a soft blue 1972 Volkswagen Super Beetle from the scrapyard. The interior still needed reupholstering. The seats were torn and the dashboard was cracked but I'd get to that soon. It was my baby.

No, not all Angels were mechanically inclined. Most didn't know how to change a tire. I was different in that aspect, I guess. I wouldn't say I was smarter. In fact, Angel Academy was tough for me. History was the worst. Who really cared why Eve picked the freaking apple from the tree? Maybe she was hungry. Maybe she was PMSing. You don't put food in front of a woman and say, "don't touch", especially when she was craving it. That was just wrong.

My car was still in the same spot, unharmed. I supposed the demons wanted me to have a way to spread their idiotic little message. Fools. I wasn't totally surprised they were rebelling. It was only a matter of time. And they *were* programmed to do the wrong thing.

I turned over the engine and started down the street, making sure no one followed me. I drove in the wrong direction and then came back around, going out of my way to be safe.

Angels, Inc. Denver Demon Control was located in an old factory on Twenty-Second Street and *I'd tell you but then I'd have to deport you*. It had a parking lot attached that we made some money on, more so during baseball season because we were only a couple of blocks from Coors Field. And now I've told you too much. Boy, I had a big mouth. I'll blame it on the excruciating pain at my side and my throbbing cheek. Those pricks. Who did they think they were?

Anyway, the Demon Control garage entrance was located in the back of the building just past the lot. Only Angels and Demon Control employees, who were mostly male Ex-Angels, were allowed in the garage. I drove up to the scanner, punched in the secret code and put my thumb to the scanning device. The computer thought about it for a moment before the metal gate rolled up in front of me, allowing me through.

I pulled into my designated parking space and then took the secure elevator to the second floor, the hub of Demon Control. The first floor was used as a cover for any unsuspecting pedestrian who happened by. If they were to look through the windows, they'd see machinery. Lots of complicated, boring machinery. And if that didn't deter their curiosity, there was an Ex-Angel employed to sit at a desk by the front door to answer any questions as vaguely as possible. It helped that the Ex-Angel looked like a regular Joe. Nothing special to remember or tell your friends about.

Floors three through six were where the Angels and Ex-Angels lived. Each of those floors consisted of a dozen studio apartments. Floor seven at the very top belonged to the head honcho Angel, otherwise known as MOG or Messenger of God. Through her visions, MOG was the only one who knew precisely which demon had done what and when. I didn't understand the whole deal. I'd heard she was given God's power to see all but only in Northern Colorado.

There were other MOGs and Demon Control Angels stationed in other parts of the U.S. and around the world. Of course, I'd be able to give you more info on that if I hadn't been daydreaming in class that day. Sorry. Angel Academy was co-ed back then and I'd sat next to a beefcake. It happens, you know.

The elevator doors opened to a bustling office with cubicles, computers and yawning employees. There were no windows to bring us attention from the outside. Just solid white-painted brick walls. Boring. No one ever accused Angels of being creative.

I started down the gray-carpeted aisle to the back of the large room but I was stopped by my friend Judd, who was sitting at his desk with online poker up on his computer screen. Judd was an Ex-Angel and my best friend. He used to be a Law Enforcement Angel until they phased men out of the program. Judd hadn't been happy about going from street work to deskwork. He'd been good at hunting down demons. Too good, some would say, giving three strikes all at once instead of one at a time. It hadn't made sense to him why we should keep the demons on earth. Naturally, the Powers That Be Pact explained that all but I guess he wasn't paying attention in class that day either.

Maybe that was what allowed us to be such good friends. He was different from the other Angels and Ex-Angels. He didn't try to be good to the point of insincerity. His actions and words were straight from his heart…and sometimes lower regions.

"Hey, what happened to your face?" He dropped his huge foot in the aisle so I couldn't get through. Male Angels were much larger than their female counterparts and Judd was no exception. He was six and a half feet of lean muscle. Sort of attractive too. Not the same way a demon was. Not supermodel attractive. Just normal, everyday, sandy blond hair ruffled, deep blue eyes, needed a shave, sexy attractive. Not that I was looking.

"Fell." I shrugged his question off. The last thing I wanted to do was give him a reason to think women couldn't handle the demons. He did enough complaining about men losing Angel status as it was.

"That sucks. You know your face and your chest get all pink when you lie, right?"

I rolled my eyes at him. "I gotta go talk to Lois."

"I knew it." He let his foot fall with a thud. "I want to hear all about it later when I come over. You still have the football game recorded?"

"Yep."

"Cool. I'll bring the pizza. Eli's bringing the beverage of choice. What do you got?"

"Um, my television and my presence." No way was I sharing the cheesecake.

He gave me a crooked smile, trying to be cute. "I'll go for that."

"Lovely."

There was a time when I would've blushed at Judd's sad flirtations. When I'd first starting working as an Angel over ten years ago, at the age of eighteen after graduating from Academy, I'd been incredibly naïve. I'd gone out on dates—yes, with Judd too. I'd dressed up in heels and dresses. I'd teased. I'd flirted. I had even slept with a few after the third date, breaking a couple of Angel rules in the process, hoping I'd find a keeper. Or a way out of serving my time as an Angel.

The rule was when an Angel married she'd be relieved of her Angel duties. She'd then be allowed to live a "normal" human life. The extended life was no longer an option but most felt it was worth it. And, of course, this was how new Angels were created. Children—now only female children—who were born of us were sent to Angel Academy at the age of five. I supposed it was the equivalent of boarding school for humans.

Anyway, all of this—marriage, babies and the white picket fence human life—were what most Angels strived to have. Otherwise, we were stuck living under Angels, Inc. quarters, under Angels, Inc. rules. The only problem was getting a male Angel, now Ex-Angel, to agree to marry you. And, frankly, I'd tired of trying to prove myself worthy to the dwindling lot.

I knew better now. Men, no matter what species, were no good. I'd given up on my pitiful hopes for finding Mr. Right and other than friendship, men were off limits. Period. I would no longer waste any time trying to get in their good graces only to be rejected. Honestly, I'd rather spend eternity chasing down demons. It was a heck of a lot easier.

I ignored Judd's suspicious stare and headed toward Lois' office. Some might say Lois was special…in a psychotic, paranoid and judgmental sort of way. The woman was mean. And she was MOG's second-in-command. She knew how to throw a scripture from the Bible at you and make you feel like you'd die and go to Hell tomorrow if you didn't do what she said stat.

I thought MOG put Lois in charge of the office so she wouldn't feel the need to go out into the human world where she'd probably be sent to the loony bin for yelling, "The apocalypse is coming!" from the street corner. Yeah, Lois was that scary.

Before I could make it to her door, it swung open and she stepped out, glaring at me through black, thick-framed glasses she didn't need—a woman who looked twenty-four and dressed sixty-five. All polyester slacks, ruffled blouse with a tweed coat.

"*What* happened to you?" she asked with a disapproving look. Every Angel and Ex-Angel in the vicinity stopped what they were doing to stare at me. I hoped Judd wasn't watching.

"I got beat up by some demons," I whispered.

"Whatever did you do to deserve that? Did you fall into one of their *beds* again?"

I was never going to live that down. One moment of passion with a half-demon hottie and I was labeled a slut for eternity. Did I mention I used to be naïve? "No. I need to talk to you about—"

"Hold on." Lois stuck her finger up for me to wait and listened into her earpiece. "Yes, MOG," she said and turned to me. "MOG wants to see you immediately. She sounds *very* upset."

"Great. Thanks." I turned and headed toward the elevator, stepping over Judd's outreached foot this time. What was he? Twelve? He really needed a hobby.

The elevator played human gospel music. I hummed an Aerosmith tune to drown it out.

I wasn't too concerned about MOG. I'd met her a few times before and I was pretty sure Lois was exaggerating when she said MOG was upset. The holy Messenger of God didn't get upset as far as I could tell.

The doors opened to a small reception area much classier than our tiresome office a few floors down. The overhead lights were dim, casting a glint on a golden granite desk. Pauline, MOG's receptionist, sat behind the desk with her hands clasped together in front of her. Her long blonde hair fell in loose curls over her shoulders—a common hairstyle for Angels both blonde and brunette.

There was nothing on the desk in front of her. No computer. No papers. No writing utensils. Nothing to occupy her time. It seemed her only job was to smile. But the narrowing of her big blue eyes negated any chance that her smile was genuine. For me anyway.

I wasn't offended. Not many of my fellow Angels liked me much. It didn't bother me though. I didn't really care for them either. Most of them were *too* good. Too pristine. Or maybe I just had too many flaws for an Angel. Who knew? One thing was certain—I'd take down the bad guys any day of the week but I refused to pretend I was anything other than Abby Angel. Even with all my imperfections.

"Go ahead and go in, Abigail. MOG is waiting for you." Pauline's voice was angelic. Go figure.

I nodded, not wanting to assault the small serene room with my own huskier voice and ambled through the knobless door that had swished open for me.

The first time I met MOG I'd been surprised by her appearance. She hadn't worn a robe or a toga with gold piping at her waist as I thought an almighty messenger of God would. There hadn't been a visible aura around her. She hadn't radiated holiness and perfection. Nope. MOG's only outfit seemed to be a tie-dyed t-shirt and holey bellbottom jeans. She had long straight brown hair pulled back by a washed-out yellow bandana and she'd been barefoot. She'd looked like a hippie straight from the 1960s which had led me to believe that was when she'd reached her prime, her twenty-four years of age that she'd never look older than.

Today she dressed no differently as she glided gracefully across the thick shag carpet toward me. "Abigail," she said with a calming smile. "Come in and sit with me. We must talk."

I smiled back, not able to help myself. My cheek stung so I stopped and did a quick glance around the room. I'd seen the seventh floor only once before on a tour through the building right after I'd moved here from the Academy. Everything seemed the same. The large windows were tinted black so we could see out but no one could see in, just like in all the Angels' studio apartments. The walls were red brick, unpainted. There was a king-sized bed far off in the corner partially blocked off by a rainbow of lace curtains hanging from the ceiling. Oversized beanbags were scattered across the carpet in random spots. A refrigerator and a small table with one chair were in another corner and a large mahogany desk sat along the center of the far wall covered with little glass bottles of who-knows-what. There really was nothing else to describe except for the slight smell of what could only be marijuana.

Huh. So the clothes weren't all that MOG kept from the sixties.

She pulled me down on a beanbag the size of a loveseat and turned to me with intense brown eyes. "Are you okay? I saw what happened. It looked painful."

I shrugged but was embarrassed she'd seen me fall into that trap. I'd forgotten that MOG was able to view demons when they behaved badly. It was her only purpose at Demon Control.

"Are you sure?" She gently swept her soft hand down my cheek. "Such a beautiful face. I hate to see my Angels pained in any way."

Before I could respond, she jumped to her feet and floated to the desk. "I have just the thing." She searched through the bottles finally finding one that seemed to please her. "Here it is. This will take care of that nasty bruising."

I tensed at the thought of putting an unknown substance on the face I'd have for the rest of my hopefully long existence. "Or we could just pray about it?" I suggested and regretted my words immediately. I hoped she wouldn't know that I hadn't prayed since my Academy years when we were required to stop and kneel down before every class.

She laughed. "Are you frightened of my concoctions, Abigail?"

MOG was the last person—er, being—I wanted to offend. "I'm a fast healer anyway," I said. Most Angels were. "Those demons must've got in some good shots, that's all."

She blinked, undeterred. "No need to be scared. I promise I won't harm you. Besides, prayer is nice but this—" She shook the bottle half full of some sort of thick tawny liquid. "This is the miracle we're looking for."

She sat back down before I could blink. She had a lot of energy and enthusiasm for a woman who sat alone in beanbag chairs viewing visions all day long. I wondered if it was lonely watching other people live the lives she could only observe.

I stiffened and cringed as she spread the liquid on my cheek but realized quickly it didn't hurt. Actually, it was cool and soothing. Not bad.

"Now lift up your shirt so I can get your side."

I did as she said. No one else would have known my side had been bruised hidden underneath my t-shirt. No one who hadn't seen it happen, that was.

"You must have heard their threat then?" I asked.

"Yes, I did." She dabbed my side one last time.

"What are we going to do about it?"

She waved the question away. "There's nothing to do. We aren't going to worry about some silly demons and their idle threats. I assure you we're in no danger."

"Really? Can you see the future too?"

A smile brightened her wholesome face. "No, dear. Of course not. In fact, most visions are delayed, backed up one after the other. I hadn't viewed your attack until you were in the office. The system is somewhat flawed, I'm afraid. And it's quite a disappointment I can't pinpoint exactly where your attackers are located. Well, not unless they do something awful again. But it's neither here nor there."

I was surprised at her nonchalance. Maybe she didn't hear the threat as well as she thought...since the system was flawed and all.

"The blond one, the leader, said that Angels *will* be punished if we continue to police them." I tried to mimic the demon's deep voice to jog her memory but it came out all wrong.

She laughed at my sad attempt and tried her own, finishing what the demon had said to me. "And the blood will be on your hands."

My mouth dropped open. Maybe she'd smoked one too many doobies? "I don't think it's a funny situation, MOG."

"Oh, Abigail." She straightened her face and looked disappointed I hadn't laughed along with her. "You'll see that there's nothing to worry about. Really. We've been through this many times before and nothing ever comes of it."

"Before?" I had no idea Angels had been in jeopardy before tonight.

"Several times in the past and the threats were never played out. Demons are funny that way. They get bored and like to amuse themselves by toying with an Angel occasionally. But they know better not to go further than that. They know Angels, by the hand of God, control this earth."

"But—"

"Abigail, do you know what happens to a demon if he takes an Angel's life?"

"He goes to Hell for eternity?"

"Yes and do you have any idea what Hell is like for them?"

I shook my head. I'd always wondered, though, what happened after the third strike, after the Hell Spirits rose from the ground and lugged the demon, kicking and screaming, back to the underworld.

"Picture living in your worst nightmare with no end in sight. Could you imagine that? I couldn't. There's simply no way they'd put themselves in that sort of danger."

"But we need some sort of precaution, don't you think?" I understood where MOG was coming from but Blondie's alarming words were still fresh in my mind.

"What do you suggest?"

"What if we went out in pairs?" I bit my lips shut after the words had come out. Did I really want to have a tag-along? Especially one whose perfection irritated me to the nth degree? "Never mind," I blurted out before she could respond. "You're right. I'm sure everything will be fine."

She patted my hand and smiled. "Of course. However if you think having a partner would make you feel safer?"

"No. I'm fine. Honestly."

"Why don't you take the rest of the night off? Heal and come back tomorrow evening refreshed?"

"Okay. I just want to check on a few things before I leave though. Would you mind if I investigated Peter Piper a little more? Maybe I can find something in his online files that will give us a reason why he'd revolt."

She looked bored by the idea. "Fine. Go ahead. If that would make you feel better."

"It would." I stood up and realized my side didn't hurt as much anymore. "Thanks for the...uh, medicine."

"No problem, Abigail. Be careful out there."

"I'll try."

I waved to Pauline, who was still in the same spot with the same insincere smile and then headed back down to the office. I wasn't sure why I couldn't let this warning go...and why MOG so easily could. It was very possible the demons who had attacked me were simply amusing themselves. It was even more likely they'd realize their blunder and come to their senses. The danger of spending an eternity in any of my nightmares would scare *me* straight, that was for sure.

But still...

Judd was on the phone with the pizza place when I walked up to his cubicle. "Extra pepperoni on the second one." He peered at me from the corner of his eye and mouthed, "What?"

"I need you to look up some stuff for me." The desk clerks were at our disposal for whatever info we needed to obtain to do our job on the street. Usually I didn't bother Judd. *Usually* I let him play his little computer games while I troubled another desk Angel. But I didn't want any of this to get out and start a panic. I trusted Judd the most to stay calm.

Judd rolled his eyes and gave his attention back to the person on the phone. "I'll pick them up... Phone number is 1-800-Nunyabusiness... Sure thing... See you then." He set the phone down and swiveled his chair around to face me. "Does this have to do with why your face is turning into a pumpkin?"

"No. Well, kind of. MOG put this on me. It's some sort of medicine."

He pouted his lips. "That's so cute. Did mommy make it feel better?"

I ignored him. "Peter Piper. Could you look him up for me please?"

"What do you need to know?"

"I need all the information on him that's not in his standard file. You know, the stuff I didn't get the first time around."

"Because?" He leaned back in his chair and put his hands behind his head.

"Because I need to locate him."

"You couldn't find your target with the info in your file? I'm not impressed, Abby."

I tried not to grind my teeth together. "I *did* find him. That's how this happened." I pointed to my cheek.

"Please tell me you didn't let a demon take you down. This is exactly why men shouldn't have been taken off the streets." He sat up straight and clenched his hands on the armrests. "You have no idea—"

"Shut up, Judd. I didn't let *a* demon take me down. It was more like four."

"You got ambushed?" he asked too loudly. "Those mother fuckers."

"Shhh." I didn't see any other way around telling him the whole story, so I did. I leaned down and whispered every embarrassing detail.

"You're kidding?" he said when I was done. "And MOG said to ignore it?"

"For the most part but I want to investigate it a little more. I'd feel like crap if an Angel got hurt because I did nothing."

He nodded his head and gave me approving look. "Understandable. His name was Peter Piper?"

"Yeah."

Judd turned back to his computer and typed in the name. I released a breath. Why I let Judd get to me was ridiculous. So what if he'd been screwed out of a career I still had? It wasn't my fault men couldn't do the job Demon Control had demanded. It wasn't my fault Judd was sitting at a desk while I roamed the streets for demons.

"Here it is," he said, breaking me from my thoughts.

I looked over his shoulder at the monitor. One line popped out at me from all the rest of the words on the screen. PREVIOUS EMPLOYMENT—KELLER TEMPORARY EMPLOYMENT AGENCY. OWNER—SIMÉON KELLER.

Oh shit.

Judd read down the list, unaware of the warmth creeping up my neck. "Looks like Piper's been in trouble with human law enforcement as well. What a loser." His finger scanned down the monitor and I hoped to MOG that he didn't notice the name that was giving me so much anxiety. "He was lawfully employed up to two weeks ago by...huh. Why does that name sound familiar?"

He looked over at me. I was sure he could see the heat now burning my cheeks.

"Siméon Keller," he said and grinned cunningly. "The half-breed who got Abigail *Virtue* Angel into the sack. How could I forget? So tell me, Abby, are you going to investigate this to the fullest? I think it calls for some *deep* undercover work, don't you?"

"Just print it out for me, would you?" I said and left his cubicle. Sure, I'd made mistakes but why was it that *this* one haunted me like no other?

Chapter Three

ೞ

My puny apartment wasn't big enough for the two guys who were sprawled across my floor and couch. But I didn't mind so much. Judd and Eli would leave after the game was over and I'd be alone again with nothing to do but think of the very memory I wanted to banish from my brain—the day Siméon Keller had seduced me.

I'd heard demons have a special power of persuasion to get humans do to unsightly acts. Something in the tone of a demon's voice and the depth of their eyes could convince a human to do almost anything. A *human* was putty in a demon's hands. But I was an *Angel*, immune to the powers of evil. How in the world had I let that happen?

Almost five years ago, I had gone to his office to issue him a first warning for violating Code One, Lust. He'd convinced a married woman to sleep with him instead of her husband on her wedding night. I'd wondered what was so special about this half-breed to make a human woman behave so foolishly...until I saw Siméon for the first time. Then I understood. He was more alluring than any full demon I'd ever seen.

My heart still sped up at the memory of his unusual features—a heart-shaped face with olive skin framed by ink black straight hair. He had silver eyes, not gray but a shiny silvery hue that I couldn't help but gaze into. Eyes I couldn't forget. And I wasn't one to remember a face, especially a demon's.

He'd smiled when he saw me walking through his door and immediately unbuttoned his shirt for me. He'd known who I was and why I was there, as if expecting me. I'd crossed the room slow and unsure. My mind racing. How could a creature so evil be so appealing? How much of the man before me was human? What was his story? Half-breeds were as rare for demons as my hair color was for Angels. How did he become this way? And what was to become of him in his afterlife? I had so many questions but knew my place wasn't to ask them, only to give him his strike and be gone. On to the next.

To this day, I still don't know what it was but something had kept me there.

Staring up into his eyes, I raised my hand and clumsily brushed my fingers across the muscles on his chest. "Sorry," I mumbled and my cheeks blazed. There I was, a member of law enforcement, apologizing for doing my job. Ridiculous.

His smile faded as he reached for my hand and helped me. He actually *helped* me press my thumb to his heart. "No apology needed." His voice was silk, smooth and pleasing to my ears.

He kept his hand clasped with mine even after the strike had clearly been imprinted on his skin. I couldn't seem to pull away, intrigued by what he would do next, what words would leave his lips.

"You're like no Angel I've seen before," he said after his gaze examined me thoroughly. His pupils were large, the silver disappearing into blackness. "Absolutely stunning."

I wanted to argue with him, I remembered. I wanted to tell him about how most men didn't agree with him. At least not to the point of committing to an ongoing relationship. Even if an Ex-Angel decided to marry, it wouldn't be to someone as abnormal as me. I'd come to that conclusion, anyway.

But I didn't tell him anything. Instead, I breathed in his words, letting them absorb into my lungs. There were few times in my life when I'd been complimented. It felt nice. Nice enough to melt into his grasp. I couldn't push him away. Not yet.

"What's your name?" he asked.

"Abigail."

"Beautiful." His free hand cupped my cheek while his other held me close to his chest.

Taken aback by his affection, I froze. Even on the few dates I'd been on, no man had ever appeared so engrossed with my presence. I liked it too much. It fed my ego. It empowered me if only for a moment. I couldn't turn away from that. I was too weak.

"Can I kiss you, Abigail?"

I nodded oh-so slightly. Then his lips were on mine. He tasted so good. Not just good. Delicious. If I could've identified the exact flavor, I would've bottled it and ingested it on my own so I wouldn't have ever needed to crave his kiss again. But since that day I'd never come across it. He owned it. And it was very wicked of him to have allowed me to sample him in the first place. Had he known I'd have that reaction? Had his taste been the venom that paralyzed my willpower?

Because from that second on my mind was not my own.

I had no idea who started taking off my clothes but I hazily remembered them falling to the floor. Our hands searched each other's bodies and then I felt his fingers on my bare skin. He caressed me so gently, so completely, that my legs faltered.

He clung onto me, not letting me fall and then lifted me effortlessly onto his desk. With a swoop of his arm, he knocked down everything in my way. The computer monitor, his telephone, papers, everything — they all crashed to the floor.

I looked up at him, shocked by his disregard. He shrugged, grinned and kissed me again, down my neck to my breasts and back up. Breathless, I reclined against the cold, smooth wooden desktop and I watched with both eagerness and anxiety as he stripped off his own clothes.

In less than a heartbeat, he was inside me and I was ecstatic. As though the mere seconds it took to happen had been too long. I clung to his strong arms and enjoyed every thrust until my insides were quaking with pleasure.

When we were both satisfied, he continued to kiss my lips and my body until my senses started to come back to me. Only then did I realize what a huge event I'd just allowed and how incredibly foolish I'd been.

"I have to go," I said, my body trembling. "I'm sorry but this shouldn't have happened. I have to go."

I shoved him away, not having the courage to watch his response. Quickly, I dressed and scrambled to the door.

A question ate at my gut and I wasn't able leave until I asked, "How did you do it? I'm an Angel. What power do you, a half-breed, have over me?"

He was silent for a moment and then I felt him behind me. His fingers grazed my shoulders and instead of my wings begging to be free, they stilled, dormant.

"Your power is your own." A low murmur in my ear. "Believe it or not, Abigail, you desired a *half-breed* as much as I desired you." He pushed a lock of my hair away from my heated cheek. "How does that make you feel? Dirty? Immoral? *Evil?*"

I left without another word, sick to my stomach. Angry and humiliated that not only had I let a half-demon seduce me but I'd also let him fool me. Because for the briefest time I'd thought maybe, possibly, he'd had some good in him.

I'd never been more wrong and I vowed I'd never look into Siméon Keller's silvery eyes again.

"What are you thinking about?" Judd asked, jolting me out of my deep thoughts.

I sat at the edge of my love seat with Judd beside me. Eli stretched out on the floor in front of us, giving all his attention to the television.

"Nothing," I said. "Just watching the game."

"Liar. You were fantasizing about me again, weren't you?"

I blew out a breath and realized my cheeks were clammy and cold with perspiration. Why did I still let that day with the half-breed rule my emotions?

Judd's smile disappeared. "If you weren't an Angel, I'd think you were getting sick. Why are you paler than usual?"

"I'm just tired. It's been a long day."

"You want us to leave so you can get some rest?"

"I'm not going anywhere until the game's over," Eli mumbled.

Eli was more a buddy than a friend, if that made sense. He came around when there was something in it for him, whereas I couldn't get rid of Judd if I tried. The difference might have had to do with Eli being an Angel of Death or AOD. He didn't live in our building, the Demon Control building. He didn't run in our same circle. And his mind was programmed differently. Judd and I were all about getting the bad guys and deporting them back to Hell. Eli was all about sending humans to heaven.

Judd and I were born and raised Angel right here in Denver. Eli was born and raised Angel in Puerto Rico and was transferred here after graduating from Academy. He had black eyes, short dark brown hair that he combed to the side and a goatee he trimmed meticulously. His clothes were always ironed and his crisp dress shirts were never seen untucked.

Judd was the opposite, always wrinkled and ruffled but for some reason he always smelled really good. His musky aroma definitely made up for his haphazard appearance.

Me? My unruly copper hair needed anti-frizz products galore and my pale freckles couldn't be camouflaged by any amount of foundation. My wardrobe consisted mostly of jeans, t-shirts, jerseys and sweatshirts. And at the moment I was wearing a tank top, sweats and blue and orange striped Broncos socks. My typical pajamas. Comfy.

Neither man seemed to mind that I was a flawed Angel and I didn't mind most of their imperfections. This made for comfortable companionship. It wasn't a marriage like some of the Angels were able to pull off but it was all I needed. Friends, pizza and beer and Monday night football on early Thursday morning.

Eli rolled over onto his back and looked up at me. "Sorry. I'd leave but I have a heart attack waiting to happen down the street." He glanced at his watch. "It's just after three a.m., so I got another forty-five minutes. You don't mind, right?"

"Geez, Eli," I said. "Do you ever stop working?"

"I wish." Eli sat up and started on a familiar rant. "I got a quota to fill if I want to keep my job. AODs don't work in shifts like Demon Control does. A human dies and we have to be there to show their pansy asses where to go."

Judd put his hand up for Eli to stop. "I'm really sick of your whining, dude. At least you still have Angel status. At least you're not stuck in some dumbass office waiting for eternity to be over. You know, sometimes I wonder if switching sides and becoming a demon would be better than this insignificant deskwork as an Ex-Angel."

"But you hate demons," I reminded him. Was he seriously considering selling his soul to become one of them?

"I know," he said with an edge to his voice. "They disgust me. But at least that side gives men the respect we deserve." His dark blue gaze did a once-over of my face and must have noticed my utterly bewildered expression. He put his arm around me and forced a grin. "I'm kidding, Abby."

"Didn't sound like a joke, dude." Eli stood and checked his vibrating pager. "I'm out of here. Broncos are never going to win this one, anyway. And there's a pedestrian accident at Sixteenth Street Mall. Possible fatality." Eli kissed me on my good cheek, pounded Judd's fist and left.

The room was silent for a moment. Judd avoided my stare. Easing his arm away from me, he pretended to stretch.

I studied his face. I knew every crease, every expression, every annoying tick. He was my best friend. Actually, pretty much my only friend. How could he even consider joining forces with our enemy?

Finally, he blew out a breath and met my eyes. "I really was kidding," he said. "You don't need to look at me like that."

"Like what?" I was curious.

"Like you think I'm going to abandon you."

"What?" I tried to act shocked. Maybe he knew my face a little too well. "If you really want to do something stupid like go around soulless and depraved for the rest of your life then that's fine with me. I'll smile as I deport your ass to Hell."

"Hey, maybe if I'm a demon I'll have a better chance of getting you in my bed. Or should I say 'across my desk'?"

"That's not funny." I'd been on one date with Judd back when men weren't off limits but it never went anywhere. Not even a kiss. He hadn't asked me out again, so I figured we were better off as friends. But that didn't stop him from constantly flirting and badgering me.

"You're right," he said. "It's hilarious. So are you going to go see this half-breed? Ask him about Piper?"

"I don't know." I grew anxious just thinking about it.

"I'll go with you if you want. I'd love to see the reason behind your temporary insanity."

"Never."

"Why? You going back for seconds? Don't want an audience?"

"No, Judd and I'd really love to stop talking about this. It was a *mistake*."

"But how did it happen? You've never given me any details. I had to hear all this shit through the tainted Angel rumor mill. Cutting out all the slut comments I dwindled it down to *it happened on his desk and you seemed to thoroughly enjoy it*. What I want to know is what did he say to get you there? Did he entrance you? Was he like Don Juan, or what?"

"Knock it off, all right?" I pleaded.

"Come on, Abby. I'm just curious. We're friends, right?"

Usually, Judd didn't push the subject. He'd been content with my vague excuses before but from the look on his face, it appeared he wasn't going to stop until I told him something more than he already knew.

"The truth is," I sputtered out, "I don't know what happened. If I could explain it then I could defend my actions but I can't. All I can say is when I walked into his office I felt like it was different from any other time I'd gone to give a warning. I thought *he* was different. And there was this irresistible pull between us I can't really explain. But now I realize I was completely wrong and apparently I have to pay for my error for the rest of my life."

"Irresistible pull, huh?" Judd's lips twitched up to a smile.

I sighed. "Did I just give you more fuel for the fire?"

Judd chuckled and took my hand in his, clasping them in the rough texture of a man who'd worked hard as an Angel. "Sounds like it bothers you more than it should. Why don't you do yourself a favor and go tell the guy off?"

"You mean face my fears?"

"Do you fear him? Or do you fear what you'll do with him?"

"Neither," I lied.

"Prove it then."

Chapter Four

I had an hour before my four p.m. to one a.m. shift started. And I was exhausted. I hadn't slept all day. Instead, I'd thought of a hundred reasons to avoid Siméon Keller. But now, despite my efforts, I was on an elevator up to his office.

Keep it professional, I told myself. My only goal was to uncover what he knew about Peter Piper and then I could be on my way. Fears faced. End of story.

He probably wouldn't even remember me. It was almost five years ago. I was sure there'd been numerous naked women on his desk since then. Right? I wasn't the only idiot? Blah. Who was I kidding? I was certain I was the only *Angel* who'd been foolish enough to fall for the half-breed's seduction.

I clenched my trembling hands as the elevator doors opened. What was I so afraid of? I wasn't going to let it happen again. I was smarter now. Not so naïve. Those days were in the past.

The receptionist didn't look familiar. Thankfully, she wasn't the same woman who worked here before when *it* happened. She didn't acknowledge me as I walked up to the desk. Instead, she typed at her keyboard with a ferocity that was somewhat humorous. If Judd were here I would've had the nerve to laugh. But I hadn't told him I was coming. Better he hear it from the tainted rumor mill after MOG watched the scene go down.

Ugh. I forgot about MOG. She was going to love this. I hoped she was too busy with other visions. I was under the impression she typically only viewed demons who were up to no good. Which made me wonder if she'd located my attackers yet. I'd have to visit her first thing when I got to the office.

First, I needed to get through this meeting.

"Excuse me," I finally said.

"Yeah?" She didn't look up at me. No smile. Nothing. She was like the anti-Pauline with short, spiky black hair, loads of makeup and a scowl permanently attached to her red lips. What a strange human. She appeared to be no older than twenty but her demeanor aged her another decade.

"I need to see Siméon Keller." His name sounded oddly plain coming out of my mouth. There was nothing plain about the man.

"Do you have an appointment?"

"No. Do I need one?" Maybe luck was on my side today.

That got her attention. Her pierced eyebrow vaulted up her forehead. "Uh, yeah. Mr. Keller's a very busy man."

"Oh. Sorry about that. Some other time then." I backed up a couple of steps and then froze when I heard his voice call out from a speaker on the desk.

"Send her in, Harley," he said. "She doesn't need an appointment."

I glanced up at each corner of the room to see four cameras staring back at me. Oh, shit. He remembered.

Harley rolled her eyes. "You heard him." She shot her thumb toward the mahogany-stained door that looked more like the entrance to a high-priced lawyer's office than a demonic temporary employment agency.

I twisted the hefty knob and eased the door open. My eyes found him right away. He was sitting at his desk. A different desk, thank the heavens. And he was staring at his computer screen, ignoring me just as his receptionist had. His ink black hair was longer, reaching his shoulders, I noticed straightaway as I closed the door behind me. It was incredibly sexy, I thought and immediately gave myself a mental slap on the forehead.

Keep it professional, Abby!

I took in the room around me to keep from staring. His office had been remodeled since I'd been here. The bookshelves and desk were a dark mahogany just like the door. The burgundy and gold Oriental rug on the floor covered most of the hardwood. Two sleek black leather chairs sat in front of his desk.

"Have a seat, Abigail." His crisp silver eyes flickered over my body briefly as he stood.

Suddenly I became acutely aware of what I was wearing as I dropped down into one of the leather chairs. I hadn't dressed up for the occasion but it was somewhat nicer than my usual. Instead of a t-shirt or sweatshirt, I wore a forest green fitted v-neck sweater and replacing my faded jeans was a pair of dark stretch jeans. And, naturally, I had on my Nike running shoes. I was going to work soon, after all. Who was I trying to impress anyway?

He followed my lead and sat back down. It gave me the chance to assess his duds. Charcoal leather pants and a ribbed white sweater that clung to his lean muscles. Yep, more alluring than any full demon I'd ever laid eyes on.

"It's good to see you again." His voice was as smooth and pleasing as I remembered. "It's been too long but I'm afraid I'm confused by the nature of your visit. I don't believe I've done anything lately to require your presence." He grinned toward the last part. Red, soft, powerful lips.

"No," I blurted out. "I mean, that's not why I'm here." I leaned toward his desk and noticed his eyes dip to my chest. I should've worn a t-shirt. An extra large one.

Slowly, deliberately, he met my eyes again. "Why then?"

I could feel my entire body heat up. I probably looked like a big red freak of nature.

Get a hold of yourself, Abby. He was evil. A demon. Not worth the provocative thoughts dancing through my mind.

"I'm looking for someone you used to employ. His name is Peter Piper and last night he escaped a second warning."

"And?"

"And I hoped you'd be able to give me some information about him."

He cocked his head, braced his hands on the desk and bowed toward me to look at my bruised cheek. It couldn't have been too noticeable. With MOG's medicine and my healing power, it should be mostly gone.

"Did this Peter Piper hit you, Abigail?" He went on to examine the rest of my face and down farther.

"No," I said, thankful there was a large piece of furniture between us. Afraid I'd be in his lap right then if there wasn't. "No, he didn't touch me." *His buddy did but Siméon didn't need to know that.*

He sat back down. "What happened to you then?"

"I fell." *I was such a bad liar. Judd was right.*

Siméon smiled, showing me a perfect set of teeth and a dimple on his left cheek. "Aren't Angels bred to be honest and noble?"

"I *am* those things." Most of the time.

"Really?" He tsked. "That's disappointing to hear. I thought you were different."

I didn't ask what gave him that idea. I already knew. I also knew the half-breed sitting before me was the devil in disguise and was being very good at avoiding my purpose for coming here.

"Peter Piper. Would you mind?" I pointed to his computer monitor. "Unless you know him personally. I'll take any information you can give me."

Truth was Siméon didn't have to share any of his knowledge with me. Angels didn't have the authority to force a presumably innocent demon to do anything they didn't want to. When male Angels had worked on the streets, they'd blatantly ignored that rule. Just another reason why they were forced to work behind a desk. Me, however, I wasn't as aggressive.

Siméon pressed a few buttons on his keyboard and then stood again. I could hear his printer zipping out papers from a separate table in the corner. He collected them and then came to sit by me. I scooted back in my seat and crossed my legs *and* my ankles. *It* wasn't going to happen again. You could only call something a mistake if it happened once. Two times and I'd be validating what every Angel at Demon Control thought about me. Forget that.

"Here's what I have on him," he said. "I like to keep a detailed file on whoever I work with." He sifted through the stack of papers in his hands, scanning down each page. There must have been at least a dozen pages of type. But I resisted leaning in and trying to make out the print. If that was his goal then he failed.

Several minutes passed before Siméon looked up from his reading. He gave me a warm grin and plunked the pile of papers on his desk. It was sorely obvious he was teasing me and it irritated me to no end.

"Well?" I asked, grinning back, hiding my annoyance. "Are those for me?"

"I'd love to know more about how you were hurt."

"Going to keep a file on me too?"

"Will I be working with you?" His eyes did a quick scan of my body.

I thought maybe he was kidding but his expression showed no signs of it. "No," I said. "I'll get out of your hair as soon as I get what I came for. Now, can I have that file?"

Not waiting for an answer, I reached for his desk where the papers sat. But he blocked my path by leaning toward me. Just as quickly, he slid his hand to the outside of my thigh. His caressing touch was warm even through the denim of my jeans.

"That doesn't seem fair," he said. "If I give you something what do I get in return?"

I thought I stopped breathing then. He was too close. I avoided eye contact in case he really did have some sort of mystical control over me. But it was becoming sadly obvious his pull on me was the fault of my own weakness. I was attracted to him.

Evil or not, I craved his touch, his taste, his body.

Chapter Five

ೞ

"I have to go." I stood up and escaped his hand, angry about his proposition but even more furious with myself for entertaining it even in the slightest. The file on Piper wasn't worth it. I needed to get away from this man before I did something I regretted.

Siméon rose to his feet and smiled down at me. He was taller than I'd remembered. There was at least a foot of difference between us. It made me feel petite and feminine when all I strived to be was strong and resilient. I had no doubt I could defend myself against a demon his size but the stupid little voice in my head told me Siméon wouldn't try to hurt me.

Not physically anyway.

"What is it with you and leaving me?" he asked, showing the sexy dimple on his cheek. "You always *have* to go. Why don't you stay?"

I gathered up all my anger and threw it at him. "If you think I'm going to have sex with you in return for...for anything then you are a...a...never mind." I gave up. How could I yell at him when he was smiling at me like that?

He chuckled. "I think I gave you the wrong impression when I touched your thigh. I shouldn't have but I find it's very difficult to keep my hands off you. Even after all this time. What I meant was if you aren't going to tell me who harmed you, then I won't be sharing any of my information."

"Why do you want to know?" I tried to hide my embarrassment. He hadn't been propositioning me? I'd been so sure of it.

"My business is to help demons. I give them a chance for lawful employment so they don't have to stoop to using humans. I thoroughly interview them before I recommend them to businesses. For that reason, I feel I'm responsible for their behavior. If any one of them has harmed an Angel, especially you, then I want to know about it."

"Oh." I let that sink in a moment. "So you try to keep them out of trouble?"

"I try to keep them from being deported, yes."

"What about you? Do you try to keep from being deported?"

He took a step closer to me and brought his warm hands to frame my face. "When I'm not corrupting Angels."

Holy cow. I could've been in the parking lot by now. I could've been in the safety of my VW, listening to *Aerosmith's Greatest Hits*. But, no, I'd stayed to argue and question and find out more about this mysterious being. And now, here I was, inches from his body, staring up into his mesmerizing eyes.

"That was a mistake." I sounded like a broken record.

His mouth quirked up to a grin as he traced my bottom lip with his thumb. "What? Our little tangle on the desktop? If I remember correctly you enjoyed every second of it."

"I did not. Not in any way." *Liar, liar, pants on fire.* "I was repulsed, actually. It was the worst experience of my life."

He dropped his hands to his side. I hated that I missed the warmth of his touch.

"Repulsed?" he asked. "That's a strong word. You're not suggesting, then, that I forced myself on you, are you? The repulsive, evil half-breed that I am."

"No but I—"

"You could've finished me off back then if it was that horrible an experience. I was waiting for it, you know. For you to come back in a blaze of regret and strike me down to Hell for eternity. But you didn't. You avoided me instead."

Angel Vindicated

"I was humiliated."

He opened his mouth to respond but shut it again and gave me a puzzled look. "How so?"

"I was there to give you a warning, Siméon. Then I was on top of your desk naked. That doesn't happen to other Angels. Other Angels don't let themselves get seduced by demons."

"I'm half human."

"They don't get seduced by humans either."

"Has it happened before? With other demons?"

"Of course not. I'm not a slut." Ugh. That sounded a little too defensive.

He grinned. "How many humans?"

"Zero."

"How many Angels?"

"That's none of your business."

"More than six?"

"No," I said too quickly.

"More than five?"

"Why do you care?"

"Five then." He tapped his finger on his chin. "So I'm one of five? That surprises me a little considering how easy it was to get you naked. Not that I'm complaining."

"Actually, I've only been with three men, you jerk. Including you." MOG help me. Why was I standing here arguing with a half-breed who could testify I was a true redhead?

"Did the other two enjoy you as much as I did?"

My mouth fell open in shock. "I-I'm not here to discuss my sex life. What is wrong with you?" Why did I ask? I already knew what was wrong with him. He was a fiend, a mongrel, Satan's little helper, wreaking havoc wherever he

47

went. I made a move for the doorknob but he held the door shut with one large hand.

"I apologize, Abigail." He spoke softly in my ear with his front pressed against my back. "I only want to know more about you. You intrigue me. But I understand if my questions are too personal. I'll try to behave."

"What do you mean I intrigue you?" I had to ask. Yep, I was so hard up I was fishing for compliments from my enemy. How pathetic.

I felt his mouth brush against my shoulder as he inhaled. "Your smell is of an Angel but slightly different. Spicier, maybe. Your hair is the color of fire, wild, free and sensuous." He collected my spiraled locks into a ponytail with his hand and then swept the tips of his fingers down the back of my neck. "And your skin is pale and delicate with…freckles. It's imperfect but charming. No, more like enchanting. You enchant me, Abigail." He said the last part as if he'd found the final piece to a puzzle and I sighed.

Heat rushed through my body as we remained motionless. I didn't want to move, not being able to remember the last time a man had touched me so affectionately. With such desire. It was sinful, I knew, to lust for this half-breed, to want his touch and to crave his taste. It was wrong. So very wrong.

"You're right about other Angels," he said. "I don't know a single demon or half-breed who's been able to seduce one. Not that any would want to. Most Angels disgust us. In fact, you're the only one I've been attracted to."

My senses came back to me like a sledgehammer to the chest. Did he think I needed to be reminded of the enormity of my mistake? Did he not know my affair with him was a big reason why I didn't fit in with the rest of the Angels? I turned to glare up at him.

"What did I say?" he asked.

"I'm leaving. I really shouldn't be around you anymore."

"You're attracted to me too. Why can't you admit it?" It wasn't really a question though. He knew. He braced my waist and drew me toward him. "Oh, wait. I know. If you admit you desire a half-breed, then you're somehow admitting you're inadequate. Right?"

"You don't know what you're talking about," I lied. He couldn't be more right.

"Because you believe half-breeds are inferior and not worth an Angel's time or affection. Is that it, Abigail?"

His lips were so close to mine, his warm breath lingered at my nose, reminding me of the delicious taste of his mouth. I sniffed the aroma in and gulped it down. Pathetic. Really, really pathetic.

With whatever brain cells I had left I muttered, "I have to go. *Now*."

"Of course."

Before I knew what was happening next I was being escorted to the elevator. His hand was on my back as he gently guided me along the hardwood floor. I couldn't hear his shoes but mine were squeaking noisily, covering the sound of Harley's continuous keyboard tapping.

Such a stupid thing to concentrate on, Abby.

He pressed the down button and turned me by my shoulders so he could look at my face. "Be careful," he whispered. "Peter Piper isn't dangerous by himself but he's idiotic enough to follow someone who is. Do you understand?"

"Why don't you give me more information then?" I was surprised he'd come to that conclusion by simply looking at Piper's file. What kind of notes did this guy take? And how could I get my hands on them?

"Have dinner with me tonight and we can discuss it."

"I wouldn't even if I could."

"You're working?"

I didn't answer. I may have wanted to lick whipped cream off his body but I didn't trust him to know any more about me than he already did.

"Lunch tomorrow, then?"

"Not going to happen."

He drew in an annoyed breath and pulled a business card out of thin air. "Take this. Call me if you change your mind, day or night. Or if you feel like you might be attacked again."

I narrowed my eyes at him. "What would you do about it?"

"Prevent it from happening, of course."

Chapter Six
☙

I left Siméon's building with my cheeks hurting from smiling too wide. It was insane that I'd gotten a rush from just talking to him. Then again, I'd spent five years wondering what a conversation with him would be like. We hadn't wasted much time talking the first time around. But my point for the visit hadn't been to satisfy some weird fantasy...although strangely it had. The point *had* been to get info on Piper. And to prove to Judd I wasn't afraid.

I hadn't gotten any new data on Piper. And my fears had been faced but only to instill a new one altogether. I'd successfully avoided Siméon Keller for five long years. Now, it seemed I'd unintentionally given him a reason to want to contact me. Who knew he'd respond that way about his ex-employee getting into trouble? Or that he'd care who'd hurt me?

My VW was waiting for me at the curb where I'd left it. I got in and checked my face in the mirror. Still smiling. Apparently, the new fear hadn't kicked in for me yet. Did I *want* to see Siméon again? Was I out of my mind?

Probably on both counts. Blah. I wondered if there was some sort of Angel therapist out there somewhere. Maybe she could talk me out of my stupidity. Maybe she could prescribe some sort of medication I could take to make me good. You know, get the bad thoughts out of my head. None of the other Angels ever had this problem. Why did I?

Siméon's building was a few miles west of the football stadium, about ten miles from where Demon Control was located. Traffic was already a mess, so the drive was fifteen minutes longer than I'd anticipated. I avoided road rage by singing at the top of my lungs to Aerosmith's *Angel*, my all-time favorite song. Those guys really knew how to write lyrics.

When I finally got to my parking space, I cut my engine and pulled out Siméon's card to take a better look at it. On the front, his name, office, fax, cell phone number and email were printed in silver lettering on a black shiny background. Appropriate. I flipped it over and noticed a phone number and address in ink with the word "home" above it.

My mind went directly to envisioning what Siméon's home might look like. More importantly, his bedroom. I imagined if it was anything like his office, it was masculine with dark wood, leather and sleek lines. Sexy. Everything about the man exuded sex, so why would his residence be any different? He probably had red or maybe black silk sheets on a big huge four-poster bed. I wondered if he'd ever tied anyone up to those posts. I wondered if —

A knock on my window startled me out of my guilty thoughts. I looked up to see Judd staring down at the card in my hand. He didn't look happy.

"Where have you been? And why haven't you been answering your phone?" His voice was muffled through my closed window.

I glanced at the little clock attached to my dashboard to see it was thirty-five minutes after my shift was supposed to start and then further down to where my cell phone sat uncharged on my passenger seat. Shit. I hadn't been thinking about the time at all. My visit with Siméon had lasted too long.

Judd opened my door and waited for me to get out. "Abby, I could wring your neck. You got beat up last night and today you decide to be late, making me think it might've happened again or maybe even something worse. I think that's a pretty shitty thing to do to a guy."

"Sorry, Judd. I lost track of time." I stepped out and wrapped a quick hug around his stiff body. I guess this was his way of saying he'd been worried about me.

He slammed my door and headed to the elevator. I followed behind amused by his reaction. Since when did Judd get mad at me for being late? I was always late. And so was he. He had no room to be angry with me.

I pushed the number two button and the doors closed, locking me in the elevator with Mr. Pissed-off-for-no-good-reason. He stood against the opposite wall with his arms crossed. I noticed for the first time that he was clutching a manila folder in his hand.

"What's that?" I asked. Judd didn't usually walk around holding anything other than a can of Coke.

"Siméon Keller's file. I was about to hunt you down. Figured you went to see him."

"Huh. Well, you were right but you didn't have to worry."

"I wasn't." He met my eyes finally.

"Whatever. You wanted to be my big, bad hero, didn't you?" I teased. "You wanted to save me from the evil half-breed, didn't you?"

He cracked a smile. "The only person you need saving from is yourself. What am I going to hear from the rumor mill this time?"

"Absolutely nothing. I was very good."

"For once."

I ignored that. "What got you all keyed up if you weren't worried about me?"

"There's something going on at the office. Lois called an emergency meeting in ten minutes."

The elevator doors opened on cue. The usual dull ambiance in the room was replaced by the buzzing of whispers. Everyone was probably trying to figure out what the meeting would be about. I was kind of curious myself considering what had happened yesterday.

I trailed Judd to his cubicle. Our discussion was *not* over.

"And you didn't want me to miss it?" I held back a laugh. This was so unlike Judd.

"Actually I thought the meeting was going to be about you and the reason why you weren't here." He sat down and dropped Siméon's file into the tin trashcan by his desk. "I overreacted, I guess."

"You guess?" I snagged the folder back out and sat cross-legged on the floor. "Why don't you just admit you care about me?" I opened it and started reading through. The last time I'd looked at Siméon's file was five years ago.

"And give you a big ego? I don't think so."

"Judd, your momma didn't hug you enough as a child," I joked absently as I read.

Siméon hadn't had a strike since the one I'd given him. Interesting. Most demons went through three strikes like they went through *Hustler* magazines.

What also grabbed my attention was that his home address we had on file didn't match the address on the back of his card. Maybe our system wasn't as efficient as we thought. We did rely heavily on the information MOG gave us. Other than notes we took and reported from the streets, she was our only source. And from what I heard from her yesterday, her visions weren't entirely reliable.

I flipped the page, remembering what I'd found intriguing about his case before. Siméon aged while full demons did not. Although it was obvious he aged slower than humans did. The records showed he was born sixty-nine years ago but he appeared to be in his early thirties. There was a note to have his photo taken after every deportation. I wondered if there was more about that in his extended file. What I wouldn't do to get my hands on that.

I went back to the first page, the one with his most recent photo on it. He wasn't smiling so his dimple didn't show. However, his eyes were just as piercing and his lips... I traced my finger over them. His lips were—

"Abby, please do not tell me you're fantasizing about a goddamn demon while sitting less than two feet from me." Judd scowled down at me in disgust.

I closed the file. "I'm not. I was wondering about his age, that's all."

He rolled his eyes at me. "Horrible liar. What is it with you and this guy?"

I stood and picked Siméon's card from my back pocket. A distraction was in order. "Here. Why don't you update his address? Looks like he has a new one."

Judd took the card from my hand and examined it. "You know you could give him a strike for not reporting a change of address."

"He did. It's right there in front of you." Demons were supposed to report any address change. It had been part of the Powers That Be Pact but with all the other menacing things demons did, Angels rarely enforced the rule. It was silly, really.

Before he could argue Lois' voice boomed from the speakers. "All Angels and staff must report at once to the meeting room."

Judd handed the card back to me. "I'll update it later. After you give him his strike. You have to follow the rules, Abby."

What did Judd know about rules? He never followed any.

"You're being a real putz today," I informed him.

"And you're being irresponsible and foolish." He maneuvered around me. "I'm going to the meeting. See ya."

I waited until he was down the aisle before I lurched into his chair and typed in Siméon's name on the search engine. I was just curious about the guy. It was research about half-breeds, really. There wasn't anything irresponsible or foolish about wanting to know more about your targets. It was part of my job.

I printed out every bit of data Demon Control had on him, stuffed the papers into the manila folder and headed to the meeting.

The room was packed by the time I got there, so I stood next to Pauline against the wall in the back. She gave me one of those phony smiles and I returned the favor. It surprised me that she'd left her post as MOG's receptionist for this thing. As I looked around I realized almost every Demon Control Angel and Ex-Angel from every shift was in here. Great. Something big had happened or was about to.

I scanned the room for MOG but she wasn't in sight. I still needed to ask her if she'd located my attackers. If Judd hadn't distracted me with his temper tantrum, I probably would've remembered to go see her.

Lois stood at the front of the room and cleared her throat, sending a hushed wave of silence. She looked out at everyone over the top of her thick-rimmed glasses.

"Bless you all for coming," she said. "I apologize in advance for MOG's absence. She's unable to be here due to more pressing circumstances."

I noticed Judd sitting in the third row. He turned to scan the room until he met my eyes and then gave his attention back to Lois. No smile. No funny crude hand gestures. Nothing. Apparently my best friend had become my babysitter overnight. I didn't like it one bit.

Lois continued her overly rehearsed speech. "I'm deeply saddened by the reason we are all gathered here today. And it's my great displeasure to inform you that two of our Angels have been seriously injured in the line of duty."

A collective gasp filled the room. Judd eyed me again. Heaven and MOG only knew what exactly the man was thinking. *I* hadn't been seriously injured. But I was anxious to hear who was and how. And if it was because of my lack of finding and deporting my attackers. My stomach turned over at the thought.

Lois went into a long-winded sermon about demons being vessels of wrath and any of them who harmed an Angel will be doomed to suffer God's fury.

Would she just get to the point?

"And ye shall keep the charge of sanctuary." Blah, blah, blah. "That there be no wrath any more upon the children of Israel."

What? I raised my hand, regressing to my Angel Academy years when I'd needed every scripture translated for me.

Lois ignored me. "Our two beloved Angels who've worked hard and selflessly during their dayshift position have lost their only weapons. Their thumbs sliced by a gang of foul, revolting demons. We shall stay strong like warriors. We shall continue on our task to protect this earth from sin. We *shall* overcome."

I raised my hand higher and waved it. If I understood correctly Lois was saying two Angels were attacked and had their thumbs cut off. What I wanted to know was if MOG knew if *their* attackers were *my* attackers.

Lois sighed. "Later, Abigail," she muttered and lifted her chin to continue. "MOG has ordered as a precaution that Angels go out in pairs until these heinous sinners meet justice." She spewed out another few scriptures and then released everyone but the evening shift Angels.

Judd didn't move from his seat so I went to sit by him. He was grinding his teeth and narrowing his eyes at the table in front of him. He only did that when he was thinking about how much he missed street work. I bet he was boiling over to get out there and stomp some demon ass.

Lois finally approached me while the room bustled with Angels leaving and/or finding a partner. "We're not discussing what happened yesterday, Abigail. MOG has given me explicit instructions to stay the course."

"But could I talk to her to see if she's located my attack—"

"Shhh. We don't need to upset the Angels any further," she said under her breath. "MOG has no new information. And that is why she's in deep visionary mode and cannot be bothered. Do you understand?"

It didn't sound like a question. She walked away terminating my chance to inquire about anything else. I guess I'd have to do my own investigating.

I turned to Judd. "I know these are the same demons. And it's all my fault for allowing MOG to convince me it wasn't a real threat."

"I'm going with you."

"Where?"

"I don't give a shit what they say. I'm going to be your partner and we're going to find these fuckers."

I smiled at him. There was the Judd I knew and loved. However, I highly doubted MOG or Lois would allow him out on the streets for any reason. I wasn't going to be the one to burst his bubble though.

The room started calming down and I looked around to see pairs of Angels holding hands. How freaking adorable. I was pretty sure if I took Judd's hand he would think I was losing my mind. Not that I wanted to hold his hand.

I strummed my fingers on the table impatiently wondering which Angel Lois would put me with considering I didn't see any leftovers standing around. Judd wasn't even supposed to be in the room. All the other Ex-Angels had gone back to their assigned jobs. It didn't look like Judd intended to move from his spot.

"Pauline," Lois called out. "Over here." She pointed to me.

"What?" Judd stood and his chair loudly clanked into the table behind him. "Are you nuts?"

Lois' glasses dropped to the tip of her nose. "Pardon?"

"Pauline has no street experience. You can't send her out there with Abby. You might as well tie them up and throw them to the demons."

I was insulted. "Excuse me? I don't even need a partner. I'll do just fine on my own."

"I'm going with you." He turned to Lois. "*I'm* going with Abby."

"No. You're going back to your desk. And Pauline is pairing with Abby."

"Fuck that," he said, causing another round of gasps.

Lois inhaled a sharp breath. "Young man, either you go to your desk or you'll be detained in your apartment for the remainder of the shift writing MOG a letter explaining why you feel it's appropriate to disrespect a senior Angel. Then we'll let her decide what she'd like to do with you. I heard we're in need of a janitor."

I could hear Judd's knuckles crack as he stormed out of the room. He was fuming and I couldn't blame him. He was right about Pauline. She had zero experience when it came to law enforcement. Having her with me was going to be no help.

"Okay then." I looked at Pauline who didn't seem too thrilled about the prospect either. "Let's go see what cases they have for us. You up for it?"

She forced a grin. "Should be exciting."

I led the way to the Demon Case Distribution Station, otherwise known as Bertha's cubicle. I didn't need to describe Bertha. Just think of Pauline but maybe five pounds heavier and two inches shorter. Same blonde hair. Same blue eyes. Yeah, they all looked alike.

Bertha was our Angel for sorting out the demons and their actions from MOG's description of her visions. MOG typed out a narrative of the felonious scene, including names, locations and actions and then emailed it over to Bertha. Back in the day, it was all on paper. Not fun. Then Bertha located the demon's file, added MOG's testament, printed it out and left them on a rack for the street Angels. Bertha was one busy lady. I never bothered her unless I really needed to.

I pulled out the file on top and showed it to Pauline. "Ever done this before?"

She shook her head. She wasn't much of a talker, which was fine with me.

"I take three to six cases, depending on if one of them is a third strike. Those guys tend to run so they take longer. I flip through the file to see who I've got and if they're in the same vicinity. You don't want to go after a guy in Estes Park and then have to drive all the way over to Brighton for the next one. Takes too long. Thankfully, the majority of them are right here in Denver."

I opened the file and skimmed through. "Huh. A director of pornography. This one should be fun." I tucked it under my arm and pulled another file. "This demon is up for his third strike. I remember giving him his second. Most of his strikes are for causing bar fights. He finds it amusing when the humans knock the crap out of each other." I grabbed the next folder in line and my heart did a cartwheel. It was a file on Siméon. "Damn it."

Bertha peered up at me. "What?" she asked, sounding put out.

"Was this from MOG?" I showed her the file.

"Nope. One of the Ex-Angels reported it. Is there a problem?" It sounded more like a dare than a question.

"No. It's fine. I'll take care of it." I turned to Pauline, trying to hide the fact that I was furious with my *ex*-best friend. "We'll take these three for now. Don't want to overload you on your first night out."

Not to mention I wanted to have time to investigate. How I'd do that with Pauline tagging along was beyond me. Maybe if Siméon didn't hate me for giving him a bogus strike he'd still be willing to discuss what information he could give me over lunch tomorrow. I'd do just about anything to solve this mess before any more blood was on my hands.

Chapter Seven

Siméon,

I am back in town as you might have heard. I would like to meet with you as soon as possible. There is much we need to discuss. Please give your answer to my courier so that we might set up a time and place.

~SSS

* * * * *

The weatherman said tonight was going to be chilly and windy. I didn't take much stock in weather prediction in Colorado since it could transform from a sunny sixty degrees to a havoc-wreaking blizzard in less than a day. I'd seen it happen before and it wasn't pretty. The trick was to be prepared for the worst.

I handed Pauline the three demon case files and told her I'd meet her in the parking garage. Then I went to my apartment to grab my fuchsia ski jacket. Fuchsia is a bold color for a gal like me, especially with my blaring red hair but when I noticed this particular jacket marked down seventy-five percent at the sporting goods store last spring, I'd snatched it right up. An Angel's spending budget was trifling, so I shopped the clearance racks as much as possible.

The best thing about this jacket was its deep pockets that substituted for having to lug around a purse. I stuffed them with my wallet, keys, lip balm and hand cream—the weather was so dry out here—and my dead cell phone. If I could only remember to plug the darn thing into the charger in my car. Not that it was of any consequence. I hardly ever used it anyway. Judd was the only one who ever called me and I wasn't talking to him for at least another twenty-four hours. He needed to pay for what he'd done.

I decided to leave Siméon's extended file that I'd printed out on Judd's computer at home. There was no point in bringing it along if Pauline was with me. She probably wouldn't understand my reasoning for wanting to research half-breeds, Siméon in particular. So I dropped it onto the kitchen counter, hoping I could read through it after my shift.

Pauline was standing by my car when I got off the elevator, which answered my question about whose car we were taking. I remembered she drove an early nineties model Ford Escort, so I was fine with driving.

She had the case files clutched in her hands and her lips pursed tightly together. I bet she was nervous. I couldn't blame her. This was her first time out on the streets and a gang of evil thumb stealers was on the loose. Not exactly the most opportune time to be trained in Demon Control.

I unlocked the passenger door for her and hopped in on the driver's side. We both plugged in our seat belts and I peeked over at Pauline to see that her perfect bronze tone had completely drained from her complexion leaving her as pale as me.

"We'll be fine," I said. "I heard those injured Angels didn't stay together." I was such a liar. "So all we need to do is keep close. They might mess with one of us but definitely not two."

"Okay." Pauline's cheeks started to gain some color so I forgave myself for fibbing. Sometimes it was necessary, right?

When I turned the engine over Steven Tyler's high-pitched squeal blared from my speakers. I flipped the knob to mute but not before Pauline jumped and white-knuckled the door handle.

"Sorry," I said and she let out a haughty breath.

Lovely. This was going to be a long night if I couldn't listen to music.

Our first stop would be the pornography director since this was only his first strike and odds were he wouldn't fight us. I had Pauline recite the address for me. The demon named Harry Bigone had a house just east of Colorado Boulevard on East Colfax. He ran his so-called business out of it. So there was a very good chance we'd find him there.

"That's it right there," Pauline said with a lilt of excitement in her voice as she pointed at a two-story beige brick house.

The neighborhood appeared to be fairly decent. Too bad this guy was mucking it up. That was what demons did, I supposed. They brought out the worst in humans and the earth we all lived on. It was a damn shame.

I parked across the street in case Harry saw us and ran. Unlikely but with everything that had been happening lately I didn't want to take any chances.

Pauline took in a deep breath as we crossed the street together. If I were her I'd be asking a million questions but I guess she was the type to learn by observation. Or maybe she was simply scared out of her mind.

I decided to help her out by answering any questions she might be have been asking if she weren't so petrified. "This guy should be easy. It's his first strike this time around. We'll go in, press a thumb to his heart and be gone."

Pauline nodded.

"His past strikes have been mostly for profiteering and sexual exploitation of a human like this one." I tapped the folder Pauline was clutching. "He's a pervert, for sure. And perverts aren't usually fighters. But sometimes they try to grope if they're feeling frisky."

"Grope?"

"Yeah, don't worry though. Just keep your distance and you'll be fine."

We cut across his yellowed lawn, the dead grass crunching under our feet. It was dusk and there was a light on inside behind the sheer red curtains covering the window. When we reached the door, I knocked once.

The door swung open and a voluptuous blonde with big hair, missing teeth and no clothes smiled at us. I kept eye contact because I *really* didn't want to see anything else.

"Who's there?" a man called from farther inside the house.

"A couple of girls," she said while scratching her lower regions. "You didn't tell me you hired more."

Beside me, Pauline let out a small, terrified gasp. She stepped back and I grabbed her arm before she could run. Demon Control rule number two, Never falter in the line of duty.

Demons flourished when they sensed panic, especially if it was coming from an Angel. What was Pauline thinking? Freaking and bolting would be the worst thing to do. And this woman wasn't even a demon, just a hideous human.

I pressed on. "Is Mr. Bigone available?" I asked, giving his last name a hard "e" at the end.

"Come on in, sweetie," the hussy said. "What's this about?"

I hauled Pauline in with me and shut the door behind us. The front room was decorated with every animal print imaginable and a few animals' heads hung jarringly from each wall. I guess this was some human's definition of sexy. I thought it was creepy.

"Just a visit," I said. "My partner and I have seen Mr. Bigone's work and think he's a genius." May MOG forgive me for my deceitfulness. At least it was easier to lie to people I cared nothing about.

"Your partner? Oh, you mean you're a couple?" She seemed excited by the idea.

"You got it." I played along by pinching Pauline's stiff, flushed cheek and finished the act off with a smoochy sound. "Isn't she a cutey?"

The woman clapped her hands together in delight. "Harry is going to be thrilled. He's never had a fan come to his business before. Come on back. He's in the studio wrapping up a scene."

She led us into what would have been the dining room in an alternate, less perverse universe. There were red velvet drapes hanging from the ceilings, covering all the walls. On top of a double-sized bed in the corner of the room was a naked young woman on her hands and knees, preparing for a mutant penis man to penetrate her backside. The thick air assaulted my nose with the stench of unprotected sex, rank body odor and undeniable evil.

My stomach churned with nausea. I could only imagine what poor Pauline was feeling.

Harry Bigone called out, "Cut!" behind a handheld digital video camera and turned toward us, his nose sniffing the air in our direction. "Ten minutes, people. Go freshen up, get a drink, take a piss, whatever. I need to speak to these two ladies for a second."

"They're fans, Harry," the blonde woman said.

"Great. Get out. I'll sign their tits or something and send them on their way. We're on a tight schedule here."

Harry unbuttoned his lavender polyester shirt even before the room was empty. Like all demons, he was an attractive guy. He had shoulder-length brown hair and movie star eyes. And like all demons, his nasty attitude negated his outward appearance. Moreover, he smelled like his momma didn't teach him how to wipe his ass properly.

"You fucking Angels need to start making appointments, all right? I'm in the middle of shooting a fucking love scene here and you ruin the whole thing. It's going to take another goddamn hour to get that guy hard again."

I ignored him and stepped forward to press my thumb to his hairy chest crusted over with a white substance I couldn't identify, nor did I want to. "This one's for violating Code One and Code Three, Lust and Greed. You persuaded an underage teenager to act inappropriately for money."

"Fuck that. She was eager to take her clothes off and get to it. Your fucking Codes are ridiculous."

"Really? Does that make you want to rebel against the system, Mr. Bigone?" I asked, testing the waters.

"Rebel?"

"You know, join a gang and take out the Angels?"

"What?" His eyebrows squished together. "Do you think I'm fucking stupid? I got a goddamn business here, lady. I don't got time to even think about you bitches."

"You know any demons who've talked about revolting?" It didn't hurt to ask.

He blinked at me. "Fuck no."

"Just checking. If you come across anything of that nature, don't hesitate to call our hotline." I smiled and headed out the door, dragging Pauline with me.

She looked green by the time we got to the car. I opened her door for her and assisted her inside before getting into the driver's seat.

"If you have to vomit let me know and I'll pull over. Vomit smell is the worst kind. You can never quite get it out."

She nodded. "How do you do it?"

"You get used to it." I grabbed a sanitizing hand wipe from a container in my glove compartment and scrubbed my hands with it. Angels were immune from diseases but the thought of having Harry Bigone's cooties on me wasn't all too appealing.

"He was repulsive," Pauline said and gagged a little bit. I handed her a hand wipe.

Yep, repulsive was the best way to characterize Harry Bigone. I thought about Siméon and how I'd used that word to describe how I'd felt about my affair with him. It wasn't even close to being true. Siméon wasn't like these other demons. Far from it. He was decent and clean. Plus, he smelled *really* good. I turned to Pauline and wondered if she'd feel the same way about Siméon or if she'd see him as just another vile creature, proving that there really was something wrong with me.

I didn't want to find out. "We'll go locate the bar fight demon next. What's his name again?"

Pauline opened the file. "He calls himself Mikey Tyson."

I stopped to get a cherry cheesecake to go from the Cheesecake Factory before heading to the city of Golden where Mikey lived and liked to hang out. I'd offered Pauline a piece but she'd declined. Too many calories, she'd said. So I'd told her to drive so I could eat. What could I say? Cheesecake was my passion. One might say it was almost as good as sex. A harmless replacement, if you asked me.

After we reached Golden, we passed in and out of a couple of bars before heading down Washington Street, the main strip filled with boutique shops and restaurants—a tourist's paradise. There were several bars and taverns in this city but only a few Mikey hadn't been kicked out of. We passed under the large arching sign that read, "Howdy Folks! Welcome to Golden" and then we took a left, heading down a street that shadowed Coors Brewery.

I parked along the sidewalk and we started toward the last bar on our list. The distinct smell of barley filled my nostrils as we crossed the street and I wondered for the umpteenth time how the residence of Golden could get used to it. I supposed it was a small price to pay for living at the foothills of the majestic Rocky Mountains. Absolutely beautiful.

Angel Vindicated

Despite the frigid weather, there was a crowd of people gathered on the outdoor patio, drinking and having a grand time. I glanced around but didn't notice my target.

"You see him?" I asked Pauline.

She shook her head, so I led the way inside the rowdy bar filled with drunken women and lucky men.

That was when I spotted him.

He sat at the bar with a cute young waitress standing between his legs. She was giggling and smiling. The dim-witted human didn't have a clue she was flirting with a malevolent creature from Hell. Behind them the bartender was red-faced and glaring at my target. I was sure Mikey was stirring up more trouble to start a fight. Playing at people's weaknesses was his specialty.

"Why don't you guard the front door," I said to Pauline. "If he gets past me and attempts to escape then follow him outside and tackle him down. Our goal is to steer clear of witnesses."

Pauline raised an eyebrow at me.

"What? It's okay if you think you can't handle the situation. You can wait in the car if you want."

She sighed. "I'll be fine."

To be truthful, witnesses weren't a huge problem. Humans were oblivious to any Angel or demon extraordinary activity, including when an Angel deported a demon. Whether it happened in a crowd of people or in private, humans simply had no idea of what was happening. Their minds weren't at that level and couldn't conceive such an unearthly act of Spirits rising from the ground. Nor could they fathom demons and Angels ignoring gravity by climbing walls or levitating several feet in the air without assistance.

Nevertheless, I always used caution. Just in case. Humans were constantly evolving. How long would it take for one to notice? To see past the haze and realize there were events going around them that superseded their realm of thinking.

I suppose you could compare it to the poltergeists that roamed the earth. A rare human could spot one. A rare human would notice. Or the psychics who could tap into the future and the past. They had superior abilities. I was sure it wouldn't be long before the act of demon deportation was sighted.

I wanted to avoid that, as I was sure most Angels and demons did as well. The less humans knew about us the better.

Mikey saw me coming. He didn't have to sniff my scent to know I was an Angel. We'd crossed paths a couple times before so he was well aware of why I was here. He pushed the waitress to the side and set his baby blues on me. Mikey looked like a young Brad Pitt from his *Thelma and Louise* days. Cute but ornery.

"I'll be back," he told the young woman.

"Or not," I said. "Want to take a walk with me outside?"

"Not really." He stood, threw a bill on the counter and strode past me.

I trailed close behind, maneuvering around people and furniture and watched as Pauline allowed him to pass her through the door, stumbling over her feet in the process. I could see how her job as MOG's receptionist was a much better fit.

Once outside, as I expected, Mikey ran...and fast. I yelled at Pauline to get the car and then I took off on foot after my target. He crossed the intersection, dodging cars and proceeded toward the Coors Brewery building. I kept my sights on him. I wanted to detain him before he reached the massive structure. If he made it inside there, he'd have a good chance of escaping. I'd taken a tour of the brewery once and knew it had many floors and many hallways to get lost in.

Mikey took a sharp turn before reaching the parking lot and headed down a narrow street flanked by the brewery and a mountainside. Crap. I didn't want to lose him in the mountains either. There was something about the deer and their big huge eyes that freaked me out.

I was getting closer to him but before I could grab him, he leaped up and grasped onto the side of the building. A demon's skill to scale a flat wall never ceased to amaze me...and make me green with envy. Why did they get this power? What was so special about them?

Mikey was out of my reach so I used the only skill *I* had. I sprouted my wings and I hovered off the ground until I was able to grab his ankle. I gripped on and forcibly yanked him down before he could start kicking at me.

He fell to the concrete platform below with a blow that knocked the air out of him. Before he could get back up, I dropped down, pinning his arms to the side with my feet and ripped open his t-shirt. I didn't hesitate as I pressed my thumb to his chest right next to the other two thumbprints.

Immediately, a whirl of hot wind blew up through the cracks in the concrete followed by inky-colored smoke that heated my skin and rushed through my hair. Hell Spirits. They swept up like an ominous tornado, swirling in the sky right above our heads.

I glanced down at Mikey who was staring at me with reddened eyes and flaring nostrils. "All Angels are going down, Abigail," he said, his voice thick with malice. "He will see to it."

"Who's he?" Damn. I should've interrogated him before giving him his strike. There wasn't much time.

"Oh, you'll find out, Abigail." He laughed and I noticed some of the black smoke enter his mouth, causing him to choke.

"Does he have blond hair?"

"You dumb bitch, if you were smart, you'd already know. It's right in front of you." More choking. "I hope you die of your own ignorance."

Startled by his words, I scrambled off him and landed on my ass on the ground, my wings crushing up against the wall behind me.

The Hell Spirits developed menacing fingers, hundreds of them that enveloped his entire body, taking him screaming into nothingness. I closed my eyes, still unable to witness the act after ten years of Demon Control duty. When I opened them, there was an eerie stillness, the smell of burned flesh…and the sound of my VW screeching to a halt.

Pauline bounded out of the car and helped me to my feet. "Are you okay?" she asked.

I nodded. "All in a day's work, right?"

She smiled and blew out a breath, seeming relieved.

I brushed myself off, willed my wings back into my shoulders and bypassed Pauline on the way to my car. I wanted to get the heck out there, pronto. I'd never get used to the savagery of demon deportation. Not now, not ever.

I decided not to tell Pauline about Mikey's last words. She'd seen enough tonight to scare her right back behind her golden desk on the seventh floor. After she got in the car, I asked her about that, partly because I was curious but mostly to get my mind off the way Mikey's scream sounded as he was forced back to purgatory.

"Why are you on the streets instead of your usual position?"

"I'm not exactly sure," she said. "MOG came out and dismissed me until further notice. When I asked why all she said was she'd send for me when she needed me again."

"That's odd, don't you think?"

Pauline nodded.

MOG was one mysterious being, that was for sure. I'd need to talk to her about what Mikey had said. *If you were smart, you'd already know.* It didn't make sense unless it was Blondie from the rooftop. My instinct told me it wasn't. He was just one of the minions. A demon powerful enough to start a revolution wouldn't be dumb enough to do the dirty work. No, he'd stay safe while his men fought for him. So far it appeared they were willing to.

We drove back to Denver via Colfax Avenue. I figured it was the shortest way to Siméon's house, our last stop. It was close to midnight when we got there. I parked in front of his driveway and looked around. His one-story, red brick house was in the middle of the nice Edgewater neighborhood across the street from Sloan Lake. The lights from downtown Denver shimmered across the body of water. During the day this lake was alive with recreational activities—boating, tennis, softball, soccer, you name it. I'd driven around it hundreds of times but never actually stopped to enjoy it. Tonight it was pretty quiet. Only the sound of cars driving on a nearby street could be heard.

Pauline cleared her throat. "Um. This is Siméon Keller. It says he's a half-demon." She had the file open on her lap.

"Yep. And he's a low threat, so if you want to stay in the car I can take care of this."

A dim lamplight showed through his partially opened wooden blinds. If the lights were on it probably meant he was still awake. I wasn't sure if that was a good thing. It was so ridiculous that I had to give him this strike. But it was better that I do it rather than another Angel.

"Shouldn't we stay together though?" Pauline asked. "Remember? The injured Angels didn't stay together."

"Right." Me and my big mouth. "Come on then."

Chapter Eight

Either Pauline didn't know this was the half-breed I'd been seduced by five years ago or she wasn't saying anything. I was relieved in any case. I knew about all the rumors that went around. I knew what the Angels thought of me. Words like whore and harlot had been whispered in the break room, across the office, while walking past me on my way to my apartment. Pauline hadn't been one of the whisperers but I could tell she was no fan of mine.

An Angel who slept with a demon gave away any hope that we were perfect. In a single act, I disproved that we were any different from the demons we hunted. What could they do other than call me an outcast? I was the reject, the exception to the rule. So they could still claim to be holy and righteous. Whatever. I knew who I was and I'd never alleged to be anything else.

Pauline followed close behind me on the way to the door. She seemed so dainty and fragile in her yellow knit sweater. No one would ever presume she had the strength of an Angel to throw a grown man across a room. I wondered if she'd ever used force on anyone, or knew that she had that ability. Gym class in Angel Academy had been where I realized my strength. Probably that was where she would have too.

I took a deep breath and rang the doorbell. A full minute passed before I heard his feet pad to the door. I waved at the peephole and moved over so he could see I had company.

The door swung open, showing Siméon in black silk pajama pants that hung low on his hips and an unbuttoned matching pajama shirt. Pauline let out a small gasp and dropped her head down. I bit my lip and stared. It wasn't like he was naked after all.

He frowned as he motioned for us to enter. "You come in pairs now?" he asked and shut the door behind us. "Is this business or pleasure?" His eyes were set on me but he was doing me a favor by not calling me by my name, acting as if he didn't know me personally.

I panicked anyway and my cheeks heated up despite the cold temperature in the room. With the naturally high-temperature body of a demon, Siméon didn't need the heater running on this cold autumn night. He was already warm.

Not knowing what to say, I shoved my hands into my jacket pockets and stood there speechless. I needed to get him alone somehow so I could explain that this strike I was about to give him wasn't my idea. Because for whatever reason, I didn't want Siméon Keller to hate me.

Pauline was staring at me, waiting for me to say something. Her blue eyes narrowed together as if she were trying to decipher why I was behaving so strangely. It was only a matter of time before she figured it out.

"Can I use your restroom?" I blurted out.

"Yes," Siméon answered immediately.

"You can't wait?" Pauline raised her eyebrows at me.

"No. It must be the Diet Coke I had with my cheesecake. Went right through me."

"But—"

"I'll show you where it is." Siméon motioned toward a hallway past the living room. He turned to Pauline. "Make yourself comfortable, Angel. You'll be on your way soon."

I bolted into the hall before Pauline could object. It certainly wasn't common for an Angel to ask to use a demon's restroom in the middle of giving him a strike and I was sure Pauline would question my sanity—but it was my only option.

With his hand on my lower back, Siméon guided me into a very large, very exquisite bathroom with a large tub, a two-headed shower and a vast double sink vanity with a black granite countertop. I looked all around and noticed big fluffy towels hung on the towel bar and plush rugs on the tile floor.

The door clicked shut behind me and I turned to look up at him.

"I'm assuming you didn't really have to go?" he whispered and stepped toward me.

I shook my head. Here I was, once again too close to Siméon Keller. His shoulder-length hair fell across his cheeks as he looked down at me. I could feel his hands on my hips underneath my jacket. The little voice inside my mind was silent, letting me have the floor.

Good-for-nothing voice.

"What is it, Abigail?"

"I'm so sorry," I said. "I gave Judd your new address to update in our system and the big jerk said you were in violation of not reporting your new address, because you know the rule where a demon has to call into Demon Control to inform us if he moves residences?" I didn't wait for his answer. "I had no idea Judd was going to do that, because, really, it's asinine. It's not like you were hiding from us or anything. You just forgot, right?"

His somber expression didn't change. "So you're here to give me a strike?"

"I'm really, really sorry."

A slow smile curved his lips. "I'm having déjà vu. Do you apologize to every demon every time or just me?"

I relaxed a little. "Just you."

He grasped my hand and pressed it to his bare abdomen. His skin was warm as usual, soothing my icy fingers. Slowly, he slid my hand up to his chest where he pressed my thumb next to the other thumbprint I'd given him. It blazed red and then yellow as it imprinted.

One more strike and he'd be going through the same agony I'd just forced on Mikey. I didn't want to think about that.

"There. That's done," he said. "Now tell me why you have a partner? You don't usually have one, do you?"

"No. It's a precaution. Two Angels were maimed today while on duty." I'd tell him all he wanted to know as long as he told me all he knew. And I hoped that he would.

"The same demons who attacked you?"

"Maybe. We don't know. I was hoping you could help me find my attackers. You seem to have a lot of information on demons."

"I do and I'm glad you decided to take me up on my offer. Come back over when you're done with your Angel duties. When will that be?"

"You're my last case."

"Abigail?" Pauline called down the hallway.

"Be right out."

Siméon flushed the toilet to cover our voices and took his stance in front of me again. I didn't know why he insisted on standing so close. I braced my hands on the counter behind me to avoid running them across the rigid muscles on his stomach again.

"How about tomorrow at lunch?" I asked. "It'll be easier for me."

He shook his head. "Tonight. I want to see you tonight."

"How am I going to explain leaving at this hour? Usually, I go right to my apartment."

"You live in the Demon Control building?"

"I can't tell you that." Shit. I was giving away information without even realizing it.

"They keep a tight leash on you then?"

"Sort of, I guess." It was more Judd's reaction I was worried about. He'd probably stop by my place to watch television for an hour or so after our shift was over. What would he think if I was nowhere to be found?

Why did I care? I was mad at Judd, I reminded myself. He was a putz to me today. And he forced me to give Siméon a bogus second strike.

"Never mind," I said. "Give me an hour."

"Good choice." He kissed my forehead. "Come hungry. I'll feed you."

Damn. If only Siméon were an Angel, er, Ex-Angel. Or even a full human. Why couldn't I have dark sexual thoughts about any of those guys? Oh, wait, I already tried that.

I walked out into the living room and saw Pauline sitting with her legs crossed on Siméon's big, cushy leather sofa. Her foot was going a hundred miles an hour until she spotted me and stood.

"Where have you been?"

I held my stomach and made a face. "Must've been bad cheesecake. Sorry I took so long but I saw Mr. Keller in the hallway and gave him his strike. We can go."

On cue Siméon walked out, his silk pajama shirt still open, showing Pauline I'd done my duty.

"You clogged up my toilet," he said with a straight face. "What kind of sick Angel are you?" So the half-breed had a sense of humor. Cute.

I bit my lips shut to keep from laughing and turned to Pauline. "Let's go."

* * * * *

Pauline tapped her fingers on the file folders she held in her lap as I drove back to Demon Control. It was the most noise she'd made all night, which told me she had something on her mind. I hoped to MOG she hadn't figured out the connection between Siméon and me.

She cocked her head toward me. "I was wondering," she started to say.

I gulped.

"Do you and Judd... Are you two a couple?"

"Me and Judd?" Had I heard that correctly?

"Yes. You're always together, so some of the Angels assumed you had some sort of, uh, intimate relationship."

I knew all about what the Angels assumed. "He's my best friend. Nothing else."

"It's just a friendship then? He's available?"

"I suppose." I'd never thought of it that way. Judd hadn't shown interest in any of the Angels in years. He always complained they were too high maintenance. He didn't have the patience to take them out on a date because they'd always want to discuss marriage and having babies. And he wasn't ready for any of that. Typical.

"Does he ever talk about anyone?"

"Not really." I thought about it some more. "Although he does have a thing for Pamela Anderson. He's got all the *Baywatch* episodes on DVD. Watches them all the time and in slow motion once in a while. It's kind of disturbing when you think about it."

"Pamela Anderson. She's the one with the long blonde hair." Pauline tugged on a lock of her hair. "And pretty blue eyes." She batted her eyes. "And..." She looked down at her chest. "Well, she's very lovely. She could be an Angel."

No way. Pauline was *not* comparing herself to Pamela Anderson.

"Do you have a crush on Judd?" I blurted out after the light clicked on in my head.

"Um...well... He seems very nice."

Judd was so not nice but he was *my* Judd. What was Pauline doing having a crush on him? And for how long?

"That's it?" I asked. "You think he's nice?"

Pauline cleared her throat. "As you might've noticed some of the Ex-Angels have gotten a little unhealthy since being forced behind a desk."

"You mean they have love handles. Yeah, I noticed that." Judd wasn't like that. He did a lot of sit-ups and ran every day. Now that I thought about it, he was possibly the only male in Demon Control who had stayed fit. Judd was a catch.

Damn.

Pauline clasped her hands together on her lap. "I guess you could say I have a crush on him. He's very attractive."

"Yeah, he's okay," I said. "But you know he curses, right?"

She blushed. "I've heard, yes."

"Hmm." Why was I worried? Judd didn't like Pauline. He thought she was a frigid robot. And why did I care anyway? Even if Judd decided to date her, it wouldn't stop us from being friends. Right?

Until they got married, had kids and joined the world of humanity, leaving me behind.

"He drinks beer too," I added. "And he has a temper. Sometimes he can be a real putz."

I walked with Pauline through the parking garage, up the elevator and into the office. She didn't mention anything else about Judd. What was she going to do? Ask him out? She barely spoke to *me*. I couldn't imagine her being bold enough to proposition a man.

Judd wasn't at his cubicle when we walked by, luckily. I had a few reasons for not wanting to run into him now but mostly I didn't want to get caught leaving for Siméon's house at one in the morning.

I showed Pauline where to drop off the files we'd just updated and noticed Judd in the break room fervently shaking the soda vending machine while cursing under his breath.

I gestured toward him and mouthed the word "temper" to Pauline. She just shrugged and stared starry-eyed as Judd continued his baby fit. Ugh. Maybe they deserved each other.

"Well, see ya tomorrow night," I said. "Going up to bed now. I'm exhausted." I yawned excessively and stretched my arms.

Pauline ignored me and walked into the break room. I was half-tempted to go in after her but knew I needed to get back to Siméon's house. Hopefully, he'd have some answers for me. Something. Anything to clue me in on who was attacking Angels and why.

I ran into Lois on the way to the elevator. "MOG find out anything yet?"

"No," she said, agitated. "Don't ask me again. I'll let you know."

"You got it." I hopped on the elevator and walked to my studio. The halls were clear. Most of the Angels were either still on shift or asleep.

Good. I'd get in and out before any of them noticed me.

My minuscule apartment consisted of a small living room, a kitchen area, a bathroom with the bare essentials and a divider wall separating a space for my bed and dresser. Really pathetic. This was another reason Angels aspired to get married and leave this joint. Our living conditions were anything but luxurious.

I could handle it though because no matter what Judd said, *I* wasn't high maintenance. All I needed was right here. Although I wouldn't mind having a big bathtub like Siméon's. I'd light candles all around it and sink into the steaming hot water, relaxing my muscles after a long night of chasing down demons. Yeah, that would be nice.

My bathroom only had a one-person shower. Siméon had a tub and a shower both large enough for two. I wondered if he'd ever bathed with anyone, if he'd ever made love to anyone in that tub or anywhere else in his home. He was a gorgeous man, not to mention a highly skilled seducer, I'd learned firsthand. It wouldn't be surprising if he'd had a woman screaming out his name in every corner of that house at one point or time.

Ergh. For whatever reason, imagining Siméon being affectionate with other women made me anxious. I shook the thought out of my head and freshened up, taking a quick shower, brushing my teeth and applying my usual makeup with a finishing touch of lip gloss. I didn't bother putting a brush through my hair because it would only frizz up if I did. Stupid hair. It looked okay as long as I used enough hair products to keep it under control. As it was, it hung down my back in spiraled locks.

I threw my green sweater off and tossed it in the hamper. He'd already seen me in it twice today. Instead, I opted for the only other sweater I owned, a pale pink knit that fit snug against my body, giving my unsubstantial rack a chance to get noticed.

Not that I wanted Siméon to notice my body. Nope…

Okay, maybe a little. Oh, I was an awful Angel. The worst. And if I wasn't careful, I'd end up spread-eagle in that big bathtub with the half-breed making *me* scream.

To take precaution, I didn't change out of my granny panties. There was no chance I was taking my pants off for him with those on underneath. My rule tonight was no sexy panties, no sex.

I was good to go.

Chapter Nine

※

My hands trembled as I rang Siméon's doorbell. It was half past one in the morning and I was exhausted. The icy wind was whipping into me and I was freezing. Moreover, my anxiety level was through the roof and I was questioning my current state of sanity.

Before I could call to mind my reasoning for being here, he opened the door and gave me that heartrending smile, dimple and all. And I relaxed. Somewhat.

He'd changed out of his night clothes and into a pair of jeans and a white button-up shirt, untucked with his sleeves rolled up to his elbows. So innocuous, it was difficult to keep thinking of him as evil, my enemy. Why I existed.

"Abigail, come in," he said and gestured toward the living room.

I stepped inside far enough for him to close the door. The heat from the fireplace instantly warmed me. He must've started the fire for my benefit. He certainly didn't need it. I was fully aware of that fact when the feverish temperature from his fingers grazed my neck as he pulled my jacket off me. The simple touch made my skin prickle. I blew out a breath, attempting to calm myself as he turned to hang my jacket on the coat rack.

Boy, was I in trouble.

"That's a lovely sweater," he said, briefly dropping his attention to my breasts.

"This old thing?"

He smiled and grabbed hold of my hand, drawing me further into the living room. The coffee table was set for two with a plate of sushi rolls in the center. Oh boy. Call me what you will but any food that wasn't thoroughly cooked scared the heck out of me. I was a coward when it came to trying new cuisines, I'll admit it.

"Sit with me," he said. "You'll enjoy this. It's one of my favorite recipes."

"Thank you but I'm not very hungry. And I really have to get back soon or…"

"Sit, Abigail. I promise to help you find the bad guys when we're done eating. But not until then."

"Blackmailing Angels is evil."

"Maybe but not accepting a carefully prepared meal is rude." He sat down on a cushion, resting his arm on his bent leg, waiting for me to join him.

"Pig-headed, aren't you?" I plopped down on the opposite side of the table and eyed the offending food. Some sort of raw fish with rice wrapped up in seaweed.

"That's why we get along so well." He picked up a pair of chopsticks and pointed them at me. "You know how to use these, right?"

"I'm more of a fork and spoon kind of girl."

He arched one black eyebrow at me. "But you've eaten sushi before, right?"

"Uh, more of a pizza and burgers kind of girl too. I like to stick to the tried and true. Know what I mean?"

"A sushi virgin. I'm honored to feed you your first." He used his chopsticks to drop a roll onto my plate and then filled our glasses with white wine. "You can use your fingers if you like. I prefer that actually."

Why did every word that came out of his mouth sound sexual? I studied his expression to see if it matched his tone but he only grinned back at me.

"Just taste it," he said. "You might love it."

"I might vomit." I gasped at my own words. "I'm sorry. Sometimes things fall out of my mouth, making me sound like a complete ignoramus. I'm sure it's delicious—"

A heartfelt laugh erupted from Siméon and I couldn't help but giggle along with him. I'd never heard a demon laugh so sincerely before, which made me think he was more on the human side. He was such a fascinating creature...and beautiful to watch.

His amusement faded as he set his eyes on me. "Consider this, Miss Ignoramus. Have you ever tasted something new and found it utterly delicious? So delectable that you wondered how dull your life would have been had you not tried it?"

Yes, your mouth. "Cheesecake with cherries on top from the Cheesecake Factory." It was the next best thing.

"Try the sushi, Abigail. Take a chance."

"You're really good at that."

"At what?"

"Persuasion."

His lips twitched up to a smile. "I suppose that's the demon in me."

I popped one of the rolls in mouth, chewed quickly, swallowed and sipped down some wine, which didn't help much because I wasn't much of a drinker.

"Did you like it?"

"It wasn't too awful."

He chuckled. "I like your honesty. It's refreshing." He slid a small dish filled with brown liquid toward me. "Try it with some soy sauce."

I did as he suggested but my curiosity emerged and I suddenly found myself prying. "You're very domesticated for a demon," I said. "You cook, you own a business. Do you own this home?"

"I do. I've lived here for five years. I was in the middle of moving from my condo when I met you for the first time. That might explain why I was distracted and failed to remember to report my change of address."

"Oh." I wasn't sure how to respond. *I'd* distracted *him*? He was beautiful and glorious. I was sure he had women lined up for his attention.

No. Don't be naïve, Abby. The man in front of me existed on this earth to seduce the weak, steal from the innocent and betray the naïve. And to make everyone around him think it was okay to do the same. If women were lined up, it was out of pure ignorance. I'd been policing demons long enough to know that.

"Isn't it funny how fate keeps luring us together?" He reached across the table and set his hand on top of mine.

I pulled away, wringing my fingers together in my lap. "I run into the same demons all the time. It's my job. Nothing to do with fate. In fact, I think people who believe in fate are chumps who wait around to see what life is going to give them rather than being proactive and getting it themselves." My cheeks felt flushed as I finished my senseless rant and I realized I had no idea what I'd just said. My only goal had been to disagree thoroughly. I was fairly certain I'd accomplished that. I could tell from the way he was narrowing his silvery eyes at me.

"Such a cynic, Abigail. I'll have to do something about that."

"No disrespect intended." I concentrated on my words this time. "But all I want from you is what's in your computer."

"All right then." He stood, dropped his napkin on his plate and extended his hand to me. "Let's be proactive and make our way over to the den."

I stared up at him briefly before accepting his assistance. The man bewildered me to say the least. I wished I could read his mind and know his thoughts. What sort of game was he playing, if any at all? Why was he agreeing to help me? And what did he think he was going to get from me in return?

"But you'd insisted we finish eating first," I reminded him.

Siméon led me across the room with his fingers lingering on the small of my back. "I believe I lost that battle." He pushed open the door to his office. "My computer awaits."

He flicked the light switch on and wheeled an extra chair up next to his large oak desk. I sat beside him as he booted up, waiting impatiently for him to say something else. I hoped I hadn't hurt his feelings but what did he expect from an Angel? He knew how we were.

The large, flat screen monitor revealed his desktop, a picture of about a dozen people grouped together, posing with a smile on the steps of a large porch. Siméon was kneeling down in the middle in between a girl who looked like his receptionist and a teenage boy who had two rabbit ear fingers above Siméon's head.

My curiosity piqued and I pointed toward the screen. "Is that Harley, your receptionist?"

"Good eye." He winked at me. "She's also my great-niece."

"Really?" I took a closer look at the picture. The only resemblance was the black hair. She didn't have her great uncle's silvery eyes.

"She refused to allow me to pay for her college tuition so I suggested she work at my office to pay me back. She's a Keller, all right. Stubborn, proud and hard-working."

Sometimes it took a while for my mind to catch up. "So this is your human family?"

"Most of them, yes. The rest live out of state or would rather not admit I exist."

Before I could ask any of the gazillion questions that were swarming around in my head, he clicked on one of the icons and another screen covered the picture.

"Tell me about your attackers." Clearly, his family was not a subject he wanted to discuss. "Give me a description of one of them."

Blondie's image was still vivid in my mind. "One of them had longish blond hair and blue eyes."

Siméon moved the cursor around the screen. "So he was Caucasian." There was a section that read "Ethnicity". He clicked the box next to "Caucasian" and went to the next section that allowed him to choose the hair color. He clicked the box next to "blond" and then went on to the eye color.

"How tall was he?" he asked.

"I don't know. I was looking up at him from the ground the whole time. What exactly are you doing?"

"Narrowing down the search. My company's database has the description and picture of every employee and associate and associate's associate I've ever come into contact with."

"Cool," I said, surprised by his thoroughness. And questioning why the Demon Control database didn't have the same capability. We were really behind the times.

Siméon gave me a cute grin. "Yes but don't think you won't be paying me back."

There it was. I knew his help would come with a price. Damn half-breed. "I will *not* have sex with you," I informed him.

He cocked his head at me, seemingly amused by my response. "Abigail," he said. "If I pleasure you again it'll be a mutual decision just like before. And, believe me, it won't be a quickie on my desk." He leaned toward me and whispered in my ear, "Next time I plan to take my time…and savor you."

I gulped and looked away. "There won't be a next time," I mumbled and felt his knuckles brush against my cheek.

"If you say so." He returned to his computer search, giving me my personal space back.

I let out a sigh of relief.

"Tonight, all I ask is for you to answer my questions. I want to know all about Abigail Angel before you leave here."

Wonderful, I thought. Maybe I should just strip and let him have his way with me.

Seconds later, he exchanged seats with me and gave me full access to search through all two hundred fifty-six blond-haired, blue-eyed demons in his database, including demons from out of Denver Demon Control boundaries. I was impressed.

"Why do you have so many?" I asked. "Where did you find them all? And with pictures?"

"Hmm... I'm afraid it's my turn to ask questions, sweetheart." He edged his chair to face me, propped his elbow on his desk and rested his gorgeous head on his fisted hand.

Before he could see the effect his undivided attention had on me, I turned to the monitor and clicked through various demon faces. None of which matched my attacker.

"You know my human age," he said. "What's yours?"

"It's rude to ask a lady that question." In truth, my human age was twenty-eight. But why not keep him guessing?

He chuckled. "My apologies. What about your family? Where are they?"

I didn't see the harm in answering that question but I continued my search, hoping I'd spot Blondie before Siméon's interview became too personal. I wasn't accustomed to sharing the private details of my life with anyone, especially someone I barely knew. Besides, why did he care? We weren't friends, quite the opposite, actually.

I humored him anyway. If answering a few questions was all it took to find who I was looking for then I'd play along. "I'm not sure where my parents are right now. They're missionaries and they travel around the world a lot."

"Do you miss them?"

I shrugged. "Yeah but I'm used to not seeing them often. My dad has been on this mission to save the world since I was a baby and my mom joined him when my sister and I headed off to Angel Academy."

"Your sister. Where is she?"

Ugh. Why did he care? "She married right after she graduated, so she's living a human life with her family in Phoenix. I haven't seen her in a long time." And I wasn't sure I wanted to. I was still angry with her for deserting me.

"Is that what you want as well? A human life with a family?"

Way too personal. "I'm happy where I am." There was a tart edge to my voice to warn him off. Then I turned the tables. "What about you? Do you want a family of your own?"

"No. Where did you get the red hair and brown eyes? That's a rarity for Angels, isn't it?"

"Thanks for the reminder. I was told I resemble my paternal grandmother. No family, huh?"

I felt his hand graze my neck and slip into my hair. He had a gentle touch, sweet and intimate. Nothing evil about it. That worried me. Evil I could deal with. Evil I understood. Sweet and intimate from a demon was not normal. As far as I knew, it wasn't in any of the textbooks at Academy and it certainly wasn't evident in any of my experiences as a Demon Control officer.

"Do you have a boyfriend, Abigail?"

I clicked faster. Two hundred and five demons to go. "No."

"Do you want one?"

Was he offering? "No."

"Have a bad experience?"

I laughed despite myself. Was he writing all this down? He could file my name under "L" for Loser, so he would know where to find me whenever he wanted some amusement.

"I'm assuming that's a yes. Tell me about him...or them. They had to be morons to let you slip from their grasp." His hand drifted back down and he lightly massaged the precise area where my left wing springs. He circled the sensitive flesh with his warm fingers and I had to wonder if he knew exactly what he was doing to me.

I held in the moan forming in my throat. Why, oh, why could he not be of the dateable persuasion? "Um. Let's just say my unusual looks aren't very appealing to the men I hang around with."

His hand froze mid-circle. "You're kidding, right? I don't believe that for a second."

I dared a glance at him. He truly did look confused, bless his heart. I was half-tempted to leap into his lap and reward him for it. But I turned back to my current task instead.

Focus. Focus. Focus.

Three more blond demons passed over the screen as I pressed down on the mouse. They were all starting to look alike. I refreshed my memory of Blondie from what I could remember from the rooftop. His eyes were set close together. He had a strong chin. Sort of looked like Fabio.

I passed through a few more faces and then *Bingo*. A perfect match. "Here he is," I shrieked, elated to have made any headway in this investigation. "Detective Abigail Angel at your service." I used my best Sherlock Holmes impression.

Siméon didn't laugh or give me any emotion at all. "That's who attacked you?" he asked, focusing in on the demon in question.

"Yeah, that's him, all right. He was the leader of the group. Do you know him? What do you have on him?" I was more than eager to find this guy before he caused anymore harm.

"He doesn't look familiar. Let me check it out. Do you mind switching seats again?"

"My pleasure." I stood and let him pass behind me, disregarding the slight brush of his hand on my butt cheek. I was too thrilled with my discovery to get angry.

A new page was up on the monitor before I'd even taken a seat. He sent it to the printer and closed everything down.

"Wait. I thought you could let me look at Piper's file now." I flashed him my sweetest smile.

It didn't seem to influence Siméon. He pulled the paper from the printer tray and handed it to me, suddenly all business. "Piper's of no importance, I can tell you that much. You don't need to worry about him."

There wasn't a lot of information on the page. Only a name, Cesar Knight, his description and his last known location, which was a motel in East Denver.

"This is it? You had over a dozen pages on Piper."

"Piper used to work for me. I don't know anything about this Cesar character."

"Well, then let me have the Piper file. Maybe there's something in there."

Siméon shook his head warily. "I'm sorry, Abigail but I can't do that."

"Why not?"

He combed a hand through his hair and let out a breath. "Do you think you're the only one who will have consequences over our meeting? If the Lord of Hell discovers I'm aiding and allying with an Angel, then my next trip down will be even more agonizing than it usually is. I can't chance that. The human side of me is too weak."

Weak wasn't a word I'd use to describe any part of Siméon. How could I have known? "What happens to you...when you get deported?"

"I've only been twice in my life but each time took a couple years from me. I don't want to get into details, sweetheart." He grinned but not before I noticed a glint of pain in his eyes. "All I can say is I try to avoid that."

"I'm sorry. I didn't realize." I felt awful for putting him in this situation.

"It's my choice." He cupped his hand to my cheek. "I want to help you but there's only so much I can do and only limited information I can give you. You'll have to understand that."

I nodded and stood as he did. Without another word, he took hold of my hand and led me to the front door. I followed, absently.

Much about Siméon Keller was a mystery. And the new things I'd learned tonight only brought up more questions. What exactly happened to his human side when he was deported to Hell? How close was he to his human family? How did they feel about having a demon as a relation? Did they love Siméon? Did he love them? *Could* he love them? As far as I knew, demons didn't have that emotional capability. But humans did. Humans were driven by love. It was evident by the lyrics they sang, the novels they wrote and the movies they created. A human would live or die for love.

"What's on your mind, sweetheart?" His question brought me out of my thoughts. He was holding out my jacket for me, waiting patiently for my attention.

"Can you love?" I blurted out and his eyes widened. It was times like these I needed a filter for my mouth. "You don't have to answer that. Sorry."

He chuckled and slid my jacket onto my shoulders but didn't let go, as he held on to my collar, gathering me closer. "I do believe I can. Like I said, my human side is very weak." His smile made him appear to be in his mid-twenties rather than the early thirties I had guessed before. He was adorable and yet so charming and confident.

"Love isn't a weakness." I had no idea why I was arguing the point. I couldn't care less about love. Maybe part of me didn't want to leave, so I was stretching out my time with him. MOG help me but I was actually starting to like the half-breed.

He tugged lightly at my collar. "It can turn a man to mush. Make him do things he wouldn't normally do."

I froze as his lips came within an inch of mine. The little voice inside my head was screaming at me. *Run, Abby!* Sadly, my love-deprived body had other ideas. I stayed put.

He closed his eyes and inhaled. "I've been strong enough to stay away from you for five years. But now here you are again. Your scent, your sensual voice, your delicate body, your lips." He opened his eyes again, only lifting them enough to take in the body part in mention. "Would it be unspeakable if I were to kiss you before another five years passes?"

"Kiss?" His words were still lingering in my mind, trying to find a place to settle, when one of us moved—possibly me—closing the distance.

And he kissed me.

His lips were warm and gentle as they molded into mine. I maintained control. I had to. I couldn't make the same mistake twice. A simple kiss was one thing but... *"Mmm."*

He sighed, allowing his hypnotizing scent to sweep over my cheeks. I breathed him in and wanted more. My addiction was more powerful than my will. I couldn't deny that. Nevertheless, it was just one kiss. Then I would stop. Really, I would.

Seeking the taste of his mouth, I lifted up onto my tiptoes and parted my lips to provoke a deeper connection. Siméon didn't hesitate to grant me my wish as he slid his delicious tongue into my mouth.

A moan slipped out from deep inside me and he drew me closer. One of his arms went around my waist while the other gripped my bottom. He lifted my body to his and pressed me against the door. I felt his abundant erection in his jeans tighten against my stomach.

My hands strayed, deceiving me, sliding up under his shirt and roving over the lean muscles in his back. A part of me knew I should stop and push him away. He was a half-breed...but so human and so very good.

"Wrap your legs around me," he said, only breaking away from my lips for a second.

I did as he asked. How quickly a simple kiss could escalate, I thought. But I didn't care. Not at this moment when my body was encompassed in his warmth and aroma. I wanted more, not less.

He broke the kiss and my legs tightened when I saw the hunger in his eyes. "Can I take you to my bed, Abigail?"

I opened my mouth to answer but stopped when I felt a relentless pounding against the door behind me.

"Abby, I know you're in there." Judd's muffled yell came from the other side. "Get out here, now."

Oh, crap. What timing. Stunned, I wiggled out of Siméon's grasp. He allowed me to the floor but didn't release his embrace.

"I thought you didn't have a boyfriend." He grinned and arched an inquiring eyebrow.

"Judd's just a friend."

More pounding. This was the equivalent of a cold shower, for sure. Who the heck did Judd think he was following me here?

Reluctantly, I eased away from the warmth of Siméon's body. "I have to go," I whispered and zipped up my jacket.

"I'd like you to stay. I'll tell him to leave."

"No." *Heck no!* "I'm sorry. I'll get in trouble if I stay." Actually, I didn't know what would happen. As far as I knew, no Angel ever dared to spend the night with the enemy. No Angel ever wanted to. Not until this very moment. I shook the nonsense out of my head. "Besides, Judd's a stubborn ass. He'll never leave without me."

"But he's not your boyfriend?"

"Not even a little bit." I looked up into Siméon's questioning eyes. "And I'm seriously considering the friendship status right about now."

"Abby, I can hear your voice," Judd yelled again. "What the hell's going on in there? Open the goddamn door before I break it down."

I reached for the doorknob but Siméon's hand covered mine. Then I felt his lips brush against my ear. "Call me tomorrow," he said in his low yet commanding voice.

What could I possibly say? There was a lunatic outside, yelling at the top of his lungs, probably waking the neighbors. I felt like a teenager past curfew and I was mortified beyond words.

When I didn't answer, Siméon lifted his hand away, letting me go. I didn't look back as I stepped into the nippy air and shut the door behind me.

Judd was bundled in a black leather jacket and scarf. His nose was pink from the cold. And his expression was livid as he glared at my well-kissed lips. "You made out with him, didn't you? What are you *thinking*, Abby?"

I rolled my eyes and headed toward my car. "You're not my keeper, Judd. You didn't need to come all the way over here in the middle of the night to check on me."

"The hell I didn't." He followed at my heels. "Did you do it again? Did you screw the half-breed?"

"No and if I did, it wouldn't be any of your business." Just a few more feet to the VW, that was all I had to get away from Judd and his *big* mouth.

"None of my business, huh?" He grabbed my hand and swung me around to face him. "What am I then? The shit at the bottom of your shoe?"

"What?"

"I stuck by you through your first foul-up with this slime ball. I defended you against all the name-calling. I even punched Felix in his fat gut when he said you were easy."

"You did?" I had no idea. That jerk Felix. He was the Angel who took my virginity in the backseat of his Buick and then never asked me out again. How dare he call me easy.

Judd dropped my hand and clenched his fists in front of him. "I'd fucking do it again too, but not if you keep this shit up, Abby. I've no clue what your obsession is with this fucker. All I know is you'd better knock it off. I won't stand by and let you ruin yourself for his sick benefit."

"He's not like that." For some reason, I felt the need to defend Siméon. To tell the world he wasn't that bad. "He helped me find one of my attackers." I clutched onto the paper in my pocket and pulled it out for Judd to see. It was the only thing keeping me from bursting out in tears from shame and humiliation. That and the fact that Siméon wasn't a slimeball. I knew better now but I was pretty sure I'd never convince Judd otherwise.

He grabbed the paper from my hand and looked it over. "What did you have to do to get this?"

I snatched it away and stuffed it back into my pocket. "Nothing." Except having to answer a few personal questions but Judd didn't need to know that.

"Right." He shook his head. "Get in your car and drive straight home. I'll follow you."

"Do what you want," I snapped. "I was going home anyway."

*****

Lois' office was pitch-black except for the glow emanating from the computer monitor. Judd had insisted we look up Cesar Knight in the Demon Control database right away but the early morning crew had taken over the office. This was the only other choice.

I'd cheerfully agreed. I was just as eager to get these animals. The sooner the better.

I peered over Judd's shoulder as he typed in the name and hit enter. The computer whirred and searched through all the thousands of files. Demon Control never archived anything.

"It's not finding anything, Abby."

"It's not done yet, Judd." So impatient.

I'd tried to stay mad at him for dragging me out of Siméon's house but after hearing that he'd slugged Felix on my behalf, I softened. Judd really was the best friend a girl could have. How could I stay angry?

He tapped his foot on the ground and cracked his knuckles. "Still nothing."

Now, I began to worry. I pushed Judd over and made him share the chair with me. Together, we gaped at the screen as it finished its search.

There were zero matches for Cesar Knight. He wasn't in the system.

My heart sank.

"Huh. The half-breed gave you some bogus info, babe. Hope you didn't give up too much for this."

I ignored Judd's smirk. "Our system's outdated, you know. Maybe he has an alias."

"Or maybe Keller's screwing with you."

"He wouldn't do that."

"For the love of…" Judd shot off the chair and started pacing the small, dark room. "He's a demon, Abby. He *would* do it and he'd enjoy it. The dirtbag has an Angel lusting after him. If you don't think he'd use that to his advantage, you're more naïve than I realized. I wouldn't be surprised if the filthy half-breed was behind the attacks."

"I'm not lusting after—" I stopped before I turned pink from lying. "I'm done talking to you. There's a logical explanation for this and I'll get it from Siméon tomorrow."

"No you won't. You're staying the hell away from him."

I stood, perched my hands on my hips and glared up into the whites of Judd's eyes. "I've lived most of my life without a father. What makes you think I want one now?"

"Father? I am anything but a father figure to you—" With a look of irritation, he rubbed his temples. "Do me a favor. No wait, do yourself a favor and take Pauline or somebody with you next time you see him, okay? I don't trust him to keep his hands off you and it appears you aren't protesting." He brought his hands to cup my cheeks. "Forget about your reputation as an Angel. Forget about any rules Demon Control might have against fornicating with the enemy. Think about me instead and how I won't be able to look you in the eyes anymore if you sleep with him again. And I *really* like looking into your eyes, Abby. Do you understand that?"

"Yes," I whispered. I completely understood. The ultimatum was set. I'd lose Judd if I lost control with Siméon. As far as I was concerned, my choice was as palpable as the man before me was.

Chapter Ten

Siméon,

Avoiding me is not an option. If you believe you are above my power, you are naïvely mistaken. It is imperative that we speak.

Give my courier a time and an isolated location where we can meet or I'll find another way.

~SSS

* * * * *

The sound of the phone ringing woke me with a start. Fuzzy brained, I flung off my comforter and checked the alarm clock for the time. I blinked to clear my vision and then noticed it was only nine forty-five a.m. Since I hadn't gotten to bed until past four a.m. and then I'd tossed and turned for another hour or so, I was definitely going to bawl out whoever was daring to disturb my sleep.

I picked up the phone, which was lying on my mattress next to me. I'd fallen asleep while debating whether to call Siméon and ask him for an explanation about why Cesar Knight wasn't in the Demon Control database. He should've been there. How else could the demon have had a thumbprint on his chest? I remembered it clearly. Cesar's shirt had been unbuttoned and I'd seen it. Only an Angel had the authority to put it there. And, dang it, how else could an Angel have found him if he weren't in the database?

There had to be some logical explanation but part of me was afraid to find out for sure. What *if* Siméon had led me astray by giving me false information? I shook the thought out of my head for the hundredth time and answered the phone.

"This better not be Judd."

"Abigail?" Pauline's angelic voice made me cringe. "This is Pauline. Were you expecting Judd?" The cutsie way she said his name made me want to barf.

"No," I said with an unintended growl. I cleared my throat and started again. "What's going on? Is something wrong?"

"I'm sorry if I woke you. Um, MOG wanted me to set up an appointment for you. She'd like to see you before your shift begins."

"Are you the receptionist again?" My hopes rose. I didn't have anything against Pauline, not really but she wasn't exactly a great help out on the streets.

"No. MOG came to my room this morning to tell me." Pauline's voice dropped a notch. "I'm a little worried."

"Worried about MOG?" My interest was piqued.

She sighed into the phone. "I shouldn't say anything else. You'll see what I mean. How about two? Is that okay?"

"Sure." I hung up and dropped back onto the mattress, growing paranoid. What if MOG had viewed my little make out session with Siméon? What if Angels, Inc. finally came to their senses and realized I wasn't meant to be an Angel? Tramps didn't deserve to have Angel status and there was no way I could deny that I was one now. Sure, I hadn't slept with him but if Judd hadn't shown up and stopped me... Boy, was I pathetic.

I was going to be punished with a life of humanity, I could feel it in my bones. I'd have to leave Judd and Eli and go find refuge on my sister's couch in Phoenix. What else could I do? I had no skills. I hadn't been educated in a human school. I'd be useless as a human.

Useless!

The manila folder on my dresser yanked me out of my pity party. Siméon's extended file—I'd forgotten all about it.

Deciding not to worry about my fate as an Angel until after my meeting with MOG, I pulled the folder into my lap and opened it up. There had to be something in it to either credit or discredit the man who'd made me forget who I was with just one kiss. With all my heart, I wanted to believe he was decent and good. I had to believe he was trying to help me, to help Angels, Inc. But I knew I had to expect the worst.

He was a demon, after all.

I skimmed past all the things I already knew — his age, occupation, past strikes and deportations. He'd only had two just like he'd said. At least he hadn't lied about that.

Then I got to the good stuff. His known family. His human mother's name was Rose Keller. Siméon had lived with her up until his eighteenth birthday. I continued to read but there wasn't any more information about her or his other human relatives. Odd. I wondered if she was still alive. If Siméon had been on the earth for sixty-nine years then surely there was a possibility. And there had been an elderly woman in that picture on his desktop.

I read on. His father, a full demon—

"What's that?" Judd's voice made me jump. He was standing, arms crossed, with my apartment door wide open.

"Dang it, Judd. What the heck is wrong with you lately?" I gathered the papers and stuffed them into a dresser drawer. "You don't knock anymore?"

I turned around in time to see a glint of guilt pass over his blue eyes. "Sorry," he muttered and closed the door behind him. His hair and clothes were more wrinkled than usual and it looked like he'd gotten less sleep than I had.

He walked the small distance to my bed and sat, rubbing a hand over his unshaven face. The only other time Judd had been anywhere near my bed was when he was whacking a spider off the headboard with his shoe. I hate spiders. He had been doing me a favor. Now, I didn't know what he was doing.

I watched him from the corner of my eye as he fell back onto the mattress and groaned.

"You okay?" I swiveled to face him. He really was a nice-looking guy, I couldn't help but notice. Pauline wasn't wrong to have a crush on him. He had strong, masculine features. And his scruffy and disheveled look only added to the sex appeal. A bad boy as an Angel—who would've thought it? If ever he decided to choose one woman, instead of the many women he'd sifted through during his early twenties, I was sure he'd make her happy.

I knew it wouldn't be me though. We were friends and nothing else. He'd made that clear six years ago when he hadn't asked me out on a second date. Then again, I don't recall him ever going on more than a date or two with any one woman in particular. He'd played the dating field like a pro, only taking a hiatus in the last couple of years. I'd assumed he'd run out of prospects. His perpetual excuse was he was exhausted with hearing women talk about marriage. It wasn't in him to be tied down, he always said and a little sexual gratification wasn't worth all the nagging an Angel could churn out.

So it seemed that was why he'd never made a move on me, or I on him. Well, other than he might not find me as attractive as the other Angels. I always thought he wasn't interested, as was the case with the other men I'd dated in the past. I was too different.

Which made Judd's next move incredibly confusing. He grabbed my hand and pulled me to lie down next to him. I went along with it and rested my head on his chest. After all, we'd cuddled on the couch many times while watching a movie or a ballgame. This wasn't unlike that. Other than, well, we were on a bed.

He sighed and gently raked his fingers through my hair. "I'm sorry I've been such an ass lately." His voice was low and comforting and his touch felt amazing. "It's just that this whole deal has me so worked up. I'm worried that more Angels are going to be harmed and I'm worried you're falling into some sort of trap with this half-breed. And I can't do a damn thing about any of it."

"I'm not falling into anything—"

"I know, Abby." He kissed the top of my head. "You're smarter than that. I get it. But you can't deny you're attracted to him for whatever reason."

I kept my mouth clamped shut, not refuting or affirming the claim.

"Siméon's obviously not stupid." He pulled his hand away and stuffed it under his head. "Out of all the Angels, he picks you to mess with. He saw that you weren't the typical Angel and took advantage of it."

I rewound Judd's words in my head and played them back. I was pretty sure I was offended. "What the hell is that supposed to mean?" I perched up on my arm to glare down at him.

"I didn't mean anything by it, Abby. You know you're different."

"So you're saying he can't *possibly* be attracted to me. The fact that he likes me couldn't *possibly* be the reason why he's helping me and giving me attention." I willed any tears from forming. I was *not* a superficial person and wouldn't allow myself to get upset over one of Judd's idiotic remarks.

"Oh, hell. That's not at all what I'm saying, honey. Listen." He yanked me back down and trapped me under his arm. "You know what I think of you." His dark eyes pierced into me, begging me to come to an appropriate conclusion.

I wouldn't make it that easy for him. "No, I don't but I'm beginning to figure it out."

"*Shit*. Don't make me say it. You see how I look at you sometimes."

"How you look at me?"

"Yeah and I'm constantly flirting with you. I wouldn't do that if I didn't find you attractive."

I stared up at him for a moment. He looked pained. As if what he was saying might cause a reaction he didn't want to hear. Or deal with. I'd realized a long time ago that Judd had a commitment phobia. A huge fear of marriage and everything that entailed. Even so, I'd never mentioned it or pushed him toward conquering the phobia with me or with anyone else.

His Adam's apple moved up and down. "You understand now, right?"

"Sure." I understood nothing but I didn't like that Judd was uncomfortable around me. It wasn't normal and I really needed normal when it came to my best friend. I wiggled out from under his arm and sat at the edge of the bed, giving him his space back. "Did Pauline talk to you last night?" I asked, desperately wanting to lighten the conversation.

"Pauline?" He sat up beside me, pressing his jean-clad thigh to my gray sweats. "Not really. She came into the break room and opened the soda machine for me with a key I didn't know existed. Didn't say much, that I can remember. Why? Something happen on duty?"

"I found out she's got a crush on you." I didn't know why I was telling him. Maybe this was the wrong change of subject. All I needed was for Judd to miraculously overcome his irrational fear and send me a postcard from their honeymoon.

"She told you that?"

"Yep." I looked up to see his reaction. A broad smile covered his face and he laughed. "What?" I asked, not finding the humor in it.

"I'm trying to picture having sex with a frigid robot. It's not exactly turning me on."

"Well, apparently, you could have your pick of frigid robots. I got the impression that more than a few Angels have been checking you out. Maybe it's time you started dating again. You were so good at it the first time around." I tried not to sound bitter but failed miserably. I knew Judd wasn't my property. I knew he'd eventually fall in love with someone. I just didn't want it to be anytime soon.

He gave me a familiar look from the corner of his eye. "What about you? Do you have a crush on me?"

I grinned, glad to have a glimpse of my friend back.

He continued to badger. "I know you want me. Why even deny it?"

Playing along, I jumped up, grabbed his shoulders and placed my leg on his thigh. "Judd, darling." I attempted to make my husky voice sultry. Sad attempt. "One of these days I'm going to take you seriously and what are you going to do then? Run?"

He chuckled and gathered me against his hard chest. "You're too chickenshit to take me seriously. Plus, I thought you'd given up on men. Remember?"

Again, the idea of him being on my bed staggered me a little. I can't say I hadn't fantasized about what sex with Judd would be like. There had been some weak and lonely moments now and then, alone in the middle of the night when he'd crept into my mind. But it hadn't been until right now that I'd entertained the notion of him having the same thoughts about me. Flirting was one thing, action was another. And Judd had never once acted out anything more than a peck on the forehead. It would've been silly to think that he'd want anything else from me.

Now as he mellowed and stared into my eyes with what *appeared* to be desire, I felt something. A possibility. *Could* Judd be attracted to me? Might there be something besides friendship between us? Gathering courage, I decided to test it out. What could it hurt? The only other person interested in me was a half-breed, so why not?

I brought my hands up to caress his strong jaw and felt his fingers tighten on my waist. Encouraged, I moved on by pressing a kiss to his nose. It was innocent enough. He didn't react much. I wet my lips a little and kissed his stubbly cheek. He closed his eyes and I took another step, softly kissing the corner of his mouth. And then—

"I, uh—" He eased away from me, his face flushed. "I should go, Abby. I told Eli I'd grab breakfast with him."

He stood and I gulped down a big dose of humility. Oddly, the rejection hurt more than I thought it would've. What had I been thinking trying to make a move on Judd? He probably thought I'd lost my mind. Heck, maybe I had.

"Yeah, I have to get ready," I said, avoiding eye contact. "I've got an appointment with MOG later."

"Oh?" He jangled something in his pocket. Probably loose change. "Let me know how that goes. Okay?"

"Sure thing." I retreated to the bathroom in a hurry and listened as my front door opened and shut.

Darn it. If I hadn't known where I stood romantically with Judd before, I certainly did now.

Chapter Eleven

I had a few hours until it was time to see MOG, so I decided to grab some lunch. And maybe stop by Siméon's office. I believed an interrogation on my part was in order and I wasn't inviting anyone along, despite Judd's advice. It wasn't as though I'd be alone in a house with Siméon this time. With Harley, his great-niece, at her desk, I'd have no choice than to sustain some self-control.

Self-control? Hmm... That was something I'd been lacking lately. Making out with a demon and attempting to do the same with my best friend—within hours—were probably two of the most despicable things I could've done. I was turning into a hussy before my very eyes.

Damn. I really needed to add more cheesecake to my diet.

Shaking the depressing thought out of my head, I picked up my fully charged cell phone from my passenger seat and dialed Siméon's office number.

"Keller Temporary Employment Agency," Harley answered in a monotone voice. "How can I help you?"

"Hi, this is Abigail Angel. Could I speak with Sim—er, Mr. Keller, please?"

I heard her blow a breath into the phone. "Sure. Hold on," she said, sounding like the young college student she was.

A jazzy piano tune played into my ear until Siméon picked up. "Hello, love."

I ignored the "love" comment. "I'm coming over. Do you like hamburgers?"

"I'm more a sushi kind of guy," he mocked. "Kidding. I'll like whatever comes with you. No onions though."

"You got it." I hung up and drove through the nearest drive-thru.

Ten minutes later, I dropped a bag of food on Harley's desk, interrupting her typing. "Are you hungry?" Why not make nice with the fam?

She eyed the greasy paper bag, her brow piercing standing at attention. "I'm a vegetarian."

"Oh." I picked it back up in a hurry. "Sorry. I can take off the meat part, if you want. There's some onions and ketchup in there too. And the bread has sesame seeds." I shut up before I could make a bigger fool of myself.

Harley's lips puckered up into a scowl. "That's disgusting."

No point in furthering this conversation. I didn't have a clue how to handle humans. Demons were my specialty. "I'll just take this in to Sim—Mr. Keller then."

Siméon's door opened and a gorgeous man with dark skin and green eyes exited. A demon, of course. He inhaled my Angel scent, winked at me and then turned to Harley. "Good afternoon, ladies. Stay out of trouble."

"Bye, Mr. Adams," Harley said, rather enthusiastically. "Good luck with your new job."

He nodded and smiled before the elevator door shut and took him back to the first floor.

Harley turned to me, all civility gone from her face. "You know, you can't stop in here anytime you want. Mr. Keller's a busy man."

"I understand that and I wouldn't be bothering him if my business with him wasn't important."

"I'm not stupid," she said before I could escape from her glare. "I know what you are. And I know what you people have done to my uncle before. I don't care if he likes you. Just so you know I never will. In fact, I think I kind of hate you."

What exactly had ole Uncle Siméon said to her? It was apparent she, a human, knew about Angels and demons. But how much did she know?

"What do you mean?" I played dumb, hoping she'd elaborate.

She rolled her eyes at me. "Who do you think nurses him back to health when he returns to Earth all beaten and battered? He's not evil like the rest of them. He's human. And if you ask me, I'd say you people were the evil ones for not seeing that. I thought you were supposed to protect humans, not throw them into danger." She stood and glowered at me. The black hair and heart-shaped face resembled Siméon but her brown eyes and pale skin couldn't have been more dissimilar. "Why don't you stay the heck away from him? He deserves better than you. And if he winds up hurt again *because* of you, you better believe I'll track your ass down and show you what Hell on Earth is."

"Harley." Siméon's low voice brimmed with warning from behind me. "That's quite enough."

I turned my head to see him standing at his office door, frowning at his great-niece. In a way, I was relieved he'd stopped her but I wouldn't have minded hearing more about what this young woman had to say. It was quite an interesting perspective. One I hadn't ever thought of. One that made me lose my appetite.

Harley plopped her thin, lengthy body back down with an exaggeration only a teenager could achieve. "Fine. Whatever." She gave me one more stabbing glare and continued with her work.

Somewhat shaken, I passed by Siméon into his office and set the bags of food down. Before I could turn, I felt him behind me, wrapping the warmth of his arms around my waist.

"I apologize." His voice was soft against my ear. "She's seen much more than she ever should have. I'm afraid it couldn't be helped. The last time I'd served time in purgatory, my sister sent her to stay at my house to wait for my return. They feared for my life since the first time I'd come back with a head injury. I'd been alone for several days before someone found me."

Unwanted remorse ate at me for being a part of anything that caused him pain. "I'd never known that to happen to a demon."

"Well, full demons have a much safer journey, albeit just as mentally agonizing, I'm sure." He gripped my shoulders and turned me around to look at him. "I'd rather not talk about it, if you don't mind. I'll speak to Harley about her behavior. I want you to feel comfortable coming here and to my home. More importantly, I want you to feel comfortable with me." He leaned in and tenderly pressed his lips to mine.

For a moment, I submitted, enjoying the sweet, enticing kiss. But the little voice—my exasperating conscience—reminded me of Judd's ultimatum. And I broke away.

"I need to speak to you about Cesar Knight." I bit my mouth shut and gingerly patted his chest before maneuvering around him and sitting on one of his leather chairs. Distance was necessary when it came to Siméon.

He didn't respond as he sat in the chair beside me, watching me carefully.

"He wasn't in the Demon Control database." Guilt and anger battled inside me as I spoke. I didn't want him to be punished for helping me but I also felt deceived he'd given me false information when Angels' lives were at stake. "Is that his real name? Or did you send me on a wild goose chase?"

He shook his head and focused in on a paper he'd pulled off his desk. "Have any more Angels been hurt?"

"Not that I know of." It irked me that he wasn't giving me his full attention. I grabbed the paper from him and set it back on his desk, forcing him to take notice. "Am I wasting my time seeking help from you, Siméon? I understand if you *can't* help me and if that's the case, then I won't bother you anymore. Either way, I don't want to be made to look like an idiot."

"An idiot?" He relaxed back in the chair, spreading his leather-clad legs and eyeing me suspiciously. "Did that Judd character make you feel like that? When you couldn't find Knight?"

"No." I waved a hand to dismiss the irrelevant subject. "Judd doesn't have anything to do with this."

"I doubt that's true. It seemed he was very much in your business outside my home this morning."

"You were listening with your superpower hearing, I assume," I said scathingly.

"I'm sure all of Denver heard your argument, Abigail. And I can't say I liked it very much. Who is he to tell you whom you can and can't see? Does he have some sort of control over you?"

"Of course not." I hated to think of it that way. "He's worried about the backlash I'd get if I were to…you know…do it again." I gestured shyly toward his large desk. "Sex with you hasn't exactly made me the most popular person at Angels, Inc."

"And that matters to you? To be popular?"

"Popular? No. Respected? Maybe."

In a lithe move, Siméon slunk out of his seat and kneeled before me, wedging his body between my legs. He settled his hands on my outer thighs and drew me close. "I've lived my life neither human nor demon," he said. "Only some creature in between, fitting in nowhere. If I spent every waking moment worrying about what someone thought of me I'd be one clinically depressed bastard." He smiled and pushed a lock of hair behind my ear. "Abigail, you've got a heart, a soul and a beautiful head on your shoulders. Trust yourself to know what's best for you."

If it were only that easy, I thought. "I understand what you're saying but I've made some really bad decisions in the past."

"According to whom? You?"

I shrugged. "Sometimes it's easier not to overanalyze."

He chuckled, showing his youthful side. I couldn't help but tilt my head and stare into his beautiful eyes. They made me forget my worries, if only for a moment, soothing me, allowing me to overlook that his lips were drawing closer to mine. A content sigh escaped me as we met and molded together. His arms wrapped around me while his mouth made quick work of making me forget everything and anyone else that existed.

This was heaven on earth. *This* was why my self-control was nearly nonexistent.

MOG help me.

"Mr. Keller," a voice called off in the distance. I ignored it but it grew more insistent. "Mr. Keller. Siméon!" Harley yelled through a speaker on the desk.

Siméon pulled away, not looking pleased and made his way to his phone. He spoke in short answers to Harley while I gained my composure, straightening my clothes—a simple t-shirt and jeans today—and applying fresh lip gloss.

I was getting tired of damning my actions, battling what felt right or wrong versus what truly was right and wrong. If I were the judge and jury, I'd have myself locked up in a padded cell and the key thrown to the depths of the Bermuda Triangle weighed down by a ton of bricks. Thankfully, I didn't have that power as an Angel.

"It appears my next appointment is here," Siméon said, setting down the phone. "Sorry we didn't get a chance to eat. Or…talk." He smiled and my dim brain finally lit up. He'd successfully avoided answering *any* questions about Cesar Knight and had achieved another make out session in the process.

Damn half-breed. How did he do it? How did he turn my mind into mushy pulp in a matter of minutes?

I stood and clenched my hands together. "You are the most conniving, scheming, son of a bi—"

"Wait a minute, sweetheart." He put his hands up and moved quickly to stand in front of me.

"Stay away, Keller. I swear if you touch me again I'll deport your ass without thinking twice."

His grin grew larger, as if holding back a laugh. "Your cheeks and lips get extra rosy when you're mad. It's very sexy."

"Take a picture then. You won't be seeing this face *ever* again." I swung around and stomped to the door. "I'll find those assholes on my own. Who needs your help anyway? Certainly not me."

I grabbed the doorknob. Blood pumped through my body, heading straight up to my face. I was furious and humiliated and…and…let down. I couldn't pinpoint what my expectations for Siméon had been but he certainly hadn't met them. The jerk.

"Abigail?" His voice was close to my ear and it wasn't until then that I realized I'd frozen. My body wouldn't move. Not until I'd given him a piece of my mind. For whatever reason, he'd become too significant in my life to let him go this easily.

I turned around and glared up at him. I intended to yell at him. I intended to make it so he'd sorely regret messing with Abigail Angel. However, the look on his face gave me pause and all I could say was, "What?"

"You might find Peter Piper somewhere around the Lawrence Street Shelter." His voice was so low I could barely hear him. "He hangs out there sometimes when he's unemployed."

"*What* took you so long to tell me this?" I tried to sound snippy but it came out all wrong as relief flooded through me.

"Do I still need to take a picture?"

"We'll see." If what he said was true, he'd get so much more than a picture.

* * * * *

Before heading back to Demon Control I swung by the homeless shelter Siméon had mentioned. I knew exactly where it was. Considering I'd been policing Denver for ten years, I knew exactly where *everything* was. Up until recently, it had started to become monotonous—up one street and down the other, chasing demons who repeated the same malevolent acts on the same idiotic humans over and over again.

Now, as I drove past the shelter searching for Piper, my heartbeat hiked up a notch from the adrenaline coursing through me. If I found him, it wouldn't be the same old thumbprint to the chest deportation. No. I'd have to take him in for interrogation. I'd have to take him down, cuff him and drag him kicking and screaming to the Demon Control Interrogation cell. The thought of it thrilled me.

It also made me come to my senses. I didn't have a pair of demon cuffs with me. Moreover, I wasn't confident I'd be able to detain him by myself. I needed a partner. Somebody. Pauline, bless her heart, would have to do. I'd drive through here when we were out on duty tonight. If I spotted Piper then, I'd let her in on the situation and we'd take him down.

But I had to keep it hush-hush until then. If the Angels knew my little bit of information, they'd swarm the area and scare away every demon in the proximity. Then I'd have no chance of finding Piper.

Besides, if Siméon was sending me on another wild-goose chase, I didn't want anyone to witness my mortification firsthand. No way. The sting would be bad enough as it was, not to mention my rage. Yep, if Siméon was pulling my chain he might as well consider himself deported. And I wouldn't feel an ounce of guilt for doing it.

I did a u-turn and headed back to Demon Control. There was no sign of Piper anyway. I'd simply have to wait.

At five after two, I was standing in the reception area in front of MOG's apartment. I couldn't really call it an office considering she never left the place. How she didn't go cuckoo for Cocoa Puffs was beyond me.

Then again—I sniffed the air and the strong scent of marijuana filled my nose—maybe this was MOG's way of beating insanity. I knocked on the door since Pauline wasn't there to let me in. Nobody answered, so I knocked again.

"Who izzzz it?" I heard MOG singsong from the other side of the door.

"It's Abby."

The door slid open and I walked in. It shut behind me quickly, nearly hitting me in the ass. I ignored that and scanned the room looking for MOG through the swirls of smoke in the air. The room was a mess with empty Doritos bags and pizza boxes scattered about.

"MOG?" I called out, concerned.

A tiny hand rested on my shoulder and I jumped. "Here I am, dear." She walked around and stood in front of me. Her eyes were bloodshot, her hair was ratted and her rumpled clothes had stripes of Doritos residue.

"You okay?" I felt silly asking the holy messenger of God if she was all right but, dang, she looked *awful*.

"Oh, I'm absolutely wonderful, dear. Absolutely wonderful." She grabbed my hand and tugged me onto a beanbag, settling herself next to me. "And how are you?" She was so close her raunchy breath blew directly into my nose.

I tried not to inhale as I talked. "Uh... I'm fine. Actually, I've been doing a little investigating and I might know where to find Peter Piper, one of my attackers. If I find him I'll bring him in for interrogation." What was the point of giving her my source? She'd probably envision it sooner or later on her own.

"That's nice dear." She stared blankly around the room almost as if she hadn't heard a word I'd said.

"You sure you're okay? You don't look so hot."

Her smile instantly transformed into a deep frown. "Oh, Abigail," she said and slumped into my arms. "I'm no good. No good." Tears started to run off her cheeks and onto my arms. I had no idea how to react. I'd never comforted anyone in my life. I'd never had to. So I just sat there and listened.

"I only want peace for my Angels." She waved her hands dramatically as she spoke. "But that…that *butthead* has taken it all away. All the tranquility is gone and all that's left is fear and anguish and…and pain. My poor, poor Angels. How will I ever make it up to them?" Her shoulders shook as she sobbed.

Oh, boy.

"Um, MOG, what happened to the Angels? Did more get hurt?"

She shuddered and sat up. Her pupils widened as she stared at me. "You haven't heard? Four more have lost their thumbs. One has perished and one has escaped to bring us the news."

Perished? Oh, no. The attacks were getting worse. "Who died?"

"Christina Angel." More tears dripped off her chin. "She was so beautiful and vibrant. And that *butthead* took it all from her."

"Oh. Wow." Sure, I was saddened by the death of an Angel. How could I not be? She was my sister in the war against demons. We Angels were a family. Although Christina was one of the many Angels who'd scorned me, I'd never wish harm to her. And I promised myself just then that I'd avenge her death. "What do you know, MOG? I want to do everything I can to stop this."

MOG's face brightened and she yanked a handkerchief from her pocket to wipe her face. "I'm so glad to hear you say that, Abigail. I need your help."

"Okay. Just tell me what to do and I'll do it." I was more than ready to kick some demon ass.

A slight pinkness colored her cheeks. "I've noticed you've been spending time with the half-breed."

Crap. I knew she'd find out. "I didn't...we didn't... It was just a kiss, really."

MOG waved my response away. "Not to worry, dear. Not now, anyway. In fact, you've done Angels, Inc. a great favor."

"Really? How so?" Boy, this was embarrassing.

"You've befriended Malakai's son. You've given us hope to end this."

"Malakai? I don't know who that is."

"Oh but you do know his son, Siméon Keller. You know him quite well."

"This keeps getting better and better. Is Malakai *the butthead* you've been talking about? He's Siméon's father?" I really should've found time to read more of Siméon's extended file, so that none of this would've been as shocking as it was to hear.

MOG smiled coyly. "Yes. Malakai's the leader of this revolution. Now, I don't know this for a fact but I've been thinking and he's the only demon in this area powerful enough to escape my visions. He's the only one evil enough to spit on the Powers That Be Pact by harming Angels. Believe me, back in my demon policing days I remember coming toe-to-toe with this fiend more than once. He's not to be taken lightly. And I'm sure he's acquired even more strength over the years."

"But how is he so powerful? What makes him so special?" It was times like these I wished I'd paid more attention in school.

MOG thought about it for a moment. She didn't seem to mind I was completely clueless. What a sweetheart. "I suppose he's the equivalent of a MOG for the demons. The Lord of Hell, Lucifer, has entrusted him with certain abilities just as God has entrusted me. He's what we call a Satan's Senior Servant or a Triple S threat. However, instead of having visions, as I do, his abilities lie more in his need to deceive and persuade. Does that make sense?"

I nodded, feeling like an ignoramus. How had I not known a demon like this existed? More important, how had I not realized I'd had sex with his son? Ergh. "Are you sure it's him? This Malakai character might be innocent, you never know."

"Oh, Abigail. He has to be the one behind this revolution and I should've realized sooner. It wasn't until I viewed Mikey Tyson's deportation that it all came together. He told you the answer was right in front of you. And Siméon has been there right in front of you. I should have warned you of his father's existence five years ago. I guess I underestimated Malakai's power."

I gulped as my next question came to mind. "And Siméon? Do you think he's a part of it?"

MOG tapped her finger on her chin. "I'm not sure about that. It's hard to tell if he's been in contact with his father since finding out about him, seeing as I can't view Malakai. You see, Siméon's an unusual case. He wasn't aware he had demon in him until adulthood. Before then he thought he was simply human, as did Angels, Inc. In fact, no one knew except his mother and, well, Malakai, who swept into the boy's life after he turned eighteen. Ever since then Siméon's been on our radar."

I let it all sink in, unsure whether to feel sorry for Siméon or to be angry with him. It seemed that was becoming a familiar dilemma for me. Dang it. I hated feeling uncertain about my feelings. "So what would you like me to do?" I asked warily.

Another dose of color painted MOG's cheeks. "I'd like you to become Siméon's friend."

"His *friend*?" I thought about how I couldn't stand in the same room with him without wanting to rip his clothes off. "I'm not sure I can do that."

"Or more than a friend, if that's what you'd like."

Now my cheeks were burning.

"I know you're attracted to him, Abigail and I don't blame you. He's a striking creature. Actually, if I thought he'd indulge me I'd take your place."

"*Really?*"

She waved her hand, showing me the messy room. "It would sure the heck beat being cooped up here, don't you think?"

"I guess, but...what about the consequences? What if I were to slip up like before? Not that I want that to happen. Because I really rather it wouldn't. But..." How could I say this without sounding like a masochistic nymphomaniac? "I can't lie, MOG." I forced the next words out. "He *tempts* me."

"Good." She clapped her hands together and I nearly fell off the beanbag in shock. "So this won't be an imposition on you. I want you to get as close to Siméon Keller as possible. Do whatever it takes to get him to lead you to Malakai. After he's found and deported, not only will your actions be reprieved, you'll be rewarded."

Holy cow. "Uh, I don't know about all this. What'll happen to Siméon?" I couldn't help but care.

"If we conclude he's involved in any part of the revolution, he'll be deported as well. If not, then he'll be free to go."

"I see."

"Whatever it takes, Abigail. I want Malakai found. I want the anarchy stopped, or more Angels will suffer. I know this isn't exactly standard orders for an Angel and I wouldn't ask it of you if this wasn't a dire situation. But I've been consulting with all the other MOGs in the area and they agree that this is our best chance. Do you understand?"

I nodded, unable to speak, unable to breathe. My mind was buzzing with the new information. Or maybe it was the new round of smoke circling my head coming from the doobie MOG had just lit up. She was smiling, apparently happy with her plans for me.

Me? I was scared out of my mind. I may not be the most virtuous Angel but I certainly wasn't a seductress or...or a *spy*. Spies have to lie, right? Siméon was going to see right through me.

I pushed off the beanbag and stood to my feet, preparing to leave before MOG gave me any more orders.

"Oh and Abigail?"

Gulp. "Yeah?"

"If you do find Peter tonight, if Siméon isn't lying to you again, then be careful, okay?"

Dang. "You saw all of that too, huh? I don't know why I even bother telling you things. You already know everything I do."

"You tell me because you're an Angel, dear and Angels are honorable."

"Maybe... Although not altogether innocent at times," I had to admit. "But you already knew that about me."

"Don't be so hard on yourself, Abigail. Your wayward behavior just might save us this time around."

Chapter Twelve

ಐ

Siméon,

Do you honestly believe you can ignore me? After all I have done for you I'm disappointed you would treat me so poorly. Now, my son, I must use other measures.

I'm well aware of your relations with that redheaded Angel. Abigail, is it? My servants have informed me of your interesting relationship and I have to say I'm quite impressed. I don't believe in all my years I've ever been able to seduce one of those little sprites. Not that I've wanted to. They're most disgusting. But, it seems, you've found yourself a winner. A pet, possibly?

Tell me, Siméon, is she dear to you? Does she entice your inner demon? Is she like no Angel you've met before?

Well, since you refuse to answer me I suppose I'll have to find out for myself.

~SSS

* * * * *

Now that I had a direct order from MOG to sin my ass off in order to find Malakai—who I still wasn't fully convinced was behind the attacks—I was even more ramped to find and capture Peter Piper. With him in our possession it might not be necessary for me to navigate my one-way trip to Hell via seducing Siméon.

What was MOG thinking? Heck, what was I thinking even considering taking orders from my pothead boss? Whom I adore, of course.

Don't get me wrong. If MOG ordered me to strip naked and do the tango with Satan himself to protect my fellow

Angels I'd start unbuttoning pronto. I had that much faith in her and in her position as MOG. Nevertheless, I couldn't help having some doubt in her — our — strategy.

More importantly, if Siméon's father truly was our evil leader *de jour*, how was I, a mere Angel, going to stop him? My brain hurt just thinking about it.

First things first, I needed to find Piper. I had to believe Siméon wasn't leading me astray. I *needed* to believe he wasn't part of the revolution leading me down a dead-end path. Sure, he was half-demon. You bet he'd been more interested in corrupting me than helping me but the annoying voice inside my head was once again telling me that he was more good than evil. More human than demon.

I took the elevator all the way down to the basement, which held the Demon Control Interrogation Cell as well as the equipment supply room. The doors opened and I swung a left, heading down the fluorescent-lit hallway toward the steel door that read "DANGER. DO NOT ENTER". I pressed my thumb to the scanner located right where the doorknob should have been. Three small lights blinked red, yellow and then green before the door slid open.

I stepped inside and immediately noticed Felix gaining his balance as he stood behind a steel-plated counter that fit the width of the otherwise white room. A television was blaring ESPN from a corner in the wall. He grabbed the remote control in front of him and switched it off.

"Hi, Felix." Being civil to the jerk who had taken my virginity and then called me easy behind my back to my best friend wasn't effortless. Actually, it was taking an awful lot of tongue biting. Wasn't it just lovely that this was the guy I needed to schmooze with to get the equipment I needed to detain Piper? Ergh.

"Hey there, Abby." He leaned over the counter and waggled his eyebrows at me. "Haven't seen you around for a while."

Yeah, there's a reason for that, big boy. I'd been avoiding him, attempting to forget how naïve I'd been at nineteen years old. Trust me, that was a difficult undertaking when we both lived in the same seven-story building.

I quickly did a once-over of his body. He didn't look so hot. Some of the Ex-Angels really had let themselves go. Mind you, Felix wasn't exactly svelte when we were dating but now he had to be pushing four hundred with the way his belly was overlapping that counter.

"We should catch up sometime," I forced myself to say. Dang it. Can I just say how difficult it is to talk through gritted teeth?

He didn't seem to notice with his attention veered toward my chest.

I cleared my throat and attempted a smile. "Right now what I really need is a pair of demon cuffs and shackles. And a roll of duct tape wouldn't hurt."

He snorted and a pea-sized something flew out of his nose, landing on the sleeve of my jacket. I shuddered but held my smile, casually flicking the slimy wad onto the floor. What did I ever see in this guy? Eww.

"What're you going to do with those, Abby? Plan to catch a demon, do you?"

I'd forgotten Felix's dialogue sometimes mimicked Yoda from *Star Wars*. It was all starting to come back to me like a roundhouse kick to my cranium. Thank God I'd come to my senses and had stopped looking for a husband. Look what I could've ended up with, for crying out loud.

"Possibly," I said, distracted.

"Oh, yeah?" His chubby cheeks squeezed into his eyes when he smiled. "A part of the revolution, is he?"

"Uh, maybe. Can't really talk about it. It's sort of top secret."

"I get it." He winked at me. "Discuss it later, we will. After you bring him in, right?"

"Sure. Sounds great. Could I get that stuff now? I'm running late."

"For the big takedown?" His eyes lit up and the small bulge in his too-tight pants expanded. I guess if you work in a ten by ten room by yourself all day long, little things will get you excited. But *gross*.

"Yep. You got it." I waved my finger toward the door behind him, reminding him to get a move on.

He finally got the hint, wiped the drool pooling at the side of his mouth and buzzed his way through the door behind him. Another steel door that I was pretty sure only Felix, MOG and Lois were able to enter with their thumbprints. That was what we'd been told, anyway. I'd never actually attempted it.

Five minutes later he came back with a standard blue and yellow Angels, Inc. duffle bag.

"Found you a few goodies, I did." Felix plunked the bag onto the counter and unzipped it. He pulled out a pair of demon cuffs and leg shackles. "Do not, I repeat, do not lose these. They're made of a special metal humans have yet to discover. Way stronger than carbon steel, they are. And even more lightweight than titanium. Break out of these babies, your captive never will."

I picked them up and dangled them from my fingers. They looked exactly like the regular handcuffs we used for practice at Angel Academy but lighter and maybe a little bit shinier.

"Same goes for the leg irons." He dropped those down next. "Know how to use these, do you?"

"Of course." I may not have been able to memorize the Bible verse by verse but I knew how to be physical and work with my hands.

"Good. And remember Demon Control rule number four, do you?" He pulled out a leather blindfold and the duct tape I requested.

"Uh, never reveal an Angels, Inc. facility to the enemy."

"Intentionally or unintentionally. Got it, Abby?"

"You bet." I stuffed everything back in the bag. A jolt of excitement surged to my belly at the thought of the new toys I'd get to try out. With any luck.

Felix burst my bubble when he set down a portable scanner in front of me. "Press your thumb here to sign this stuff out. Lose anything and be suspended from Angel status until further notice, you will. And I'll hold the cuff keys until you bring the captive back to the interrogation cell, understand?"

"Really?"

His lips curled up to a grin. "Or figure out another deal, we could." He winked his itsy bitsy eye at me.

I pressed my thumb onto the scanner without further ado. "Thanks, Felix. See you around."

Easy, I am *not*.

* * * * *

I waved to Pauline from across the office but she pretended not to see me and continued her conversation with Tiffany Angel from first shift. It appeared I wasn't making any headway in the friendship department there. Oh well. What did I really want from her anyway? Angel's night out with pink fruity drinks, slurred conversation and men hitting on us all night? Hmm… Well, the last part didn't sound too bad.

Judd's hand around my wrist yanked me from my thoughts and into his cubicle. Eli was sitting down at his chair, frowning up at us.

"Hi," Judd said, not giving me full eye contact.

Geez, was he still upset about this morning? I'd take it all back if I could. Trust me.

"Hi," I said right back at him. "What's up?"

He stepped closer and lowered his voice. "I, uh, wanted to apologize for this morning. You know, with the way I responded."

"Oh, that." I shrugged but, of course, my blazing cheeks gave me away. "No big deal." I forced my attention to Eli who was glaring up at me. "What's wrong with you?"

"Nothing. I'm friggin' wonderful." He swiveled in the chair and pulled up his Angel-mail account, dismissing me.

I mouthed, "What's his problem," to Judd.

He rolled his eyes and sighed. "Don't take it personally. He's pissed because they demoted him to desk clerk at the AOD center."

"Oh, Eli, I'm so sorry." I bypassed Judd to pat Eli on the back. "How did it happen? I thought you were one of the best over there."

"Like it matters." He brushed my hand away and stood. For the first time ever I noticed little whiskers growing outside the distinct lines of his meticulous goatee. Wow. He really must be upset.

"It does matter, Eli," I said. "Angels, Inc. has no right to demote you. It's wrong and it certainly doesn't make any sense."

"You think I don't know that?"

"Well—"

"It's fucked up and the sad part is I've seen it coming for a long time now. I worked my ass off to avoid it but it happened anyway." Eli's dark glare stunned me. I'd never seen him this angry. And if I didn't know better I'd think it was targeted toward me.

I took a step back. "I'm really sorry this happened. I know it sucks—"

"I don't want your fucking pity."

"If it were up to me—"

"It's not. It's up to some other dumbass woman who thinks she's superior to me and every other male Angel out there."

Judd's hand rested on my shoulder protectively. "Knock it off, Eli. Abby's not your problem and you know that."

Eli rolled his eyes, which were reddening and growing teary. "You're right, Judd. I'm wasting my time here talking to you two. See you around." He pushed past me and stomped away.

I sniffed back my own tears. Poor Eli. He didn't deserve to lose his Angel status. None of the men did. But there wasn't anything I could do about it, so why was Eli gearing his frustration toward me?

"Don't worry about him, Abb. You remember how I was when it happened to me, right? I was bent out of shape for several months before I pulled it together."

"You pulled it together?" I joked.

He smiled, finally giving me full eye contact. "What's the duffle bag about?"

"What this?" I dropped it on the ground. "Um, I might detain Peter Piper tonight." I couldn't lie.

"You know where he is?"

"Possibly."

He shoved his hands in his pockets. "You went to see Keller again. Alone?"

"Nothing happened. Well, almost nothing."

Judd shook his head. "God, Abby. You can't do this to me."

To him? "What exactly am I doing to you? As far as I can see, you and I are nothing more than friends. You made that clear this morning, so why would you care what I did with Siméon?"

I knew it wasn't fair to him to dredge up this morning's event but, darn it, my ego had suffered a blow and I was still upset about it. I hadn't expected Judd to drop down to his knee and propose marriage. I hadn't even expected him to *like* the kiss. But he could have humored me. He could've pretended I *didn't* repulse him.

He was supposed to be my best friend, after all. He ought to know my quirks and my needs and this morning I needed him to make me feel like my enemy wasn't the only person in the world who thought I was desirable.

And he'd failed me miserably.

I noticed Judd's jaw clench tight and then twitch like it always did when he was upset. He murmured something that sounded like, "fuck it, fuck it, fuck it," before he grabbed my hand and led me down the hall.

Oh, crap. He'd finally lost his mind and it was all my fault. "Where are we going, Judd? I'm already late for my shift. You don't want me to be late, do you?"

He pushed open the custodian's closet, dragged me inside with him and shut us into darkness. I could hear him rustling around until the dangling light bulb above our heads clicked on, giving the small room a dim glow.

"Don't tell me Lois gave you the janitor's job. What did you *do*, Judd? I always told you to cut down on the cursing but you never listen to me, do you?"

"Shut up, Abby." He stepped toward me, forcing me to back up against the wall right next to where the damp mop was hanging.

I stared up into his eyes, which appeared black rather than the usual soft blue. "Okay, buddy, you're scaring me. You want to back up a few and let me out of here, please. I'm getting a little claustrophobic."

He braced a hand on each side of my head and pressed up against me. His chest was hard against my breasts and his lips were lowering...lowering.

Holy cow. Was he planning to kiss me? "Uh, Judd? What are you doing? Listen, I was just kidding around about this morning—"

"Shut. Up. Abby."

"Don't tell me to shut—"

Then he kissed me.

Hard.

Commanding lips pressed against mine. Hungry. Wanting. Urging me to respond.

And I did. I parted my mouth and let him in. His tongue invaded me as if it belonged there. Staking its territory. Making me forget where I was and what I was doing.

In a closet, I reminded myself. *With Judd. And he's kissing you. Hello!*

It was all soaking in right as he drew away. His lungs expanded against me as he breathed and I watched, speechless, as a smug grin formed on his face.

"Think about that," he said in a low husky voice. Then he gave me a small peck, pulled the string to the light bulb and left me in the dark. Alone.

I took in a deep breath and ran my fingertips over my lips. I was trembling and I wasn't sure why. I'd enjoyed the kiss, as I'd predicted I would. And it was exactly what I'd expected from him. Matching his personality, it was rough, to the point and it warmed me from my heart straight down to my quivering thighs.

What I hadn't anticipated was that my first kiss from him would be in the custodian's closet next to a damp mop that smelled like a mixture of mildew and Mr. Clean. Not to mention my complete and utter bafflement as to why he'd decided to kiss me in the first place. Literally, leaving me in the dark.

Was this the start of something between us? Did he finally realize that he's infatuated with me and wants to fulfill my fantasies? Yeah, right. Common sense should tell me he kissed me to put an end to my obsession with Siméon. Judd didn't want me, he just didn't want me to desire the hottie half-breed.

Ergh. The more I thought about it, the angrier I became. I seriously needed to get out of this closet and get on with my day. I reached blindly toward the door and tripped on what sounded like a pail of water. Before I could figure out which way was up, I crashed through the door and landed facedown in the hallway with about a gallon of soapy water beneath me, clinging to my t-shirt and jeans.

Double ergh. One or two Angels giggled and whispered "tramp" as they stepped over me, not bothering to lend a hand.

Why, again, was I concerned about their safety?

Oh, because I had a conscience. That was right. Stupid me.

I tossed the pail back in the closet and kicked the door shut with my foot. About a dozen or so desk clerks and Angels peeked over their cubicle walls to see what was causing the racket. As soon as they saw me glaring back at them, they either grunted or rolled their eyes before sitting back down again.

"No, I don't need any help," I mumbled to myself. "Sit back down and relax. Really. I'm okay."

Chapter Thirteen

My cell phone vibrated in my jacket pocket for the gazillionth time since leaving Demon Control, so I decided to turn the power off before the thing overheated, or whatever it was cell phones did when exhausted by the new popularity of its owner.

Half of the calls were from Judd and he probably just wanted to make up an excuse for the kiss in the closet before I freaked and proposed marriage to him. Ha! Or he wanted in on some of the action tonight.

Well too bad. He'd had his chance to talk to me between the time it took me to change my clothes up until I'd left the garage. But, no, he'd disappeared like a coward. So forget him. If he couldn't face me like a man then I'd ignore him like a woman.

The other calls were from Siméon but I wasn't about to answer his phone call with Pauline in the car with me. How he'd gotten my number was a mystery, like most everything else about the half-breed.

I couldn't help wonder what he wanted though. Especially since I'd passed Lawrence Street Shelter twice already and hadn't seen anyone who looked like Peter Piper.

What were the odds anyway?

"Um, Abigail." Pauline shifted in her seat next to me. "I think we're going in circles. Didn't we pass this street already?"

I shrugged. "What does the file say again?" We were supposed to be hunting down a demon who called himself Garth Vayder, if you can believe that. I'd picked his file out

Angel Vindicated

because he was a drug dealer who usually sold on the streets, which meant Pauline and I would have to drive around to find him. Which meant I could pass by the shelter as much as I wanted.

Or not. Pauline cleared her throat. "It says he usually sells over by Sixteenth Street Mall and isn't that, I don't know, on Sixteenth Street?"

Smartass. I liked her better when she was shy and quiet but apparently she was warming up to me. "All right," I said. "I'll do a u-turn and head back that way."

I slowed down as the shelter came into view again. A long line of grungy looking men stood at the doorway probably waiting to either get their dinner or find a bed for the night. It was another crisp evening so I silently prayed they'd all get in. What a horrible way to have to live.

I swerved into a parking spot right in front of the building and switched on my turning signal, pretending to prepare for a u-turn. Narrowing my vision, I took a good look at every man to see if Piper had showed up in that line since the last time I'd driven past but he was nowhere in sight.

"Do you know something about this demon that I don't?" Pauline asked. "Does he come here?" She waved her hand toward the men. "To this homeless shelter?"

"Good question. Why don't I go find out?" I snatched Piper's file from my glove compartment and slipped out of the car before Pauline could question me.

The first three guys in line didn't look like the talkative type, the fourth guy had a guardian Angel hovering above him and was glaring at me, daring me to try something. Demon Control Angels tried to keep out of the Guardian Angels' way as much as possible. They weren't the friendliest. A bit too protective of their humans, maybe. And I wasn't in the mood for a bitch slap tonight, so I skipped down to lucky number five. He had on about seven layers of clothing and he was smiling at me as if he'd known me his entire life.

"Hi there." I pulled out a photograph of Piper.

"Savannah?" He asked with a lilt of hope in his voice.

"No, sorry, dude. My name's Abigail. Have you seen this guy around?" I lifted the photograph to his face.

"Savannah," he repeated, so I moved on to man number six.

"Hi there. Have you seen this guy around?"

Number six's face was severely sun damaged with dark blotchy spots here and there and deep-set wrinkles on his forehead and around his eyes. "What are you? A cop?" he asked, warily.

"No. Not me. I'm an Angel." I winked at him. "My wings are at the cleaners'." Usually that got a chuckle or two out of the humans I ran into but this guy wasn't impressed with my sense of humor.

"Jesus saves," he mumbled in an exhausted tone.

"Amen," I said.

He rolled his eyes at me and pointed to something behind me. "He's under the cross sign over there."

I jerked around and lo and behold, Peter Piper was lighting up a cigarette underneath the "Jesus Saves" cross-shaped sign hanging out from the corner of the building.

Hmm. I loved irony.

Casually, I thanked man number six and walked back to the car. I sat in the driver's side and reached for the duffle bag in the backseat. "See the guy under the 'Jesus Saves' sign?" I asked Pauline.

"Uh, yeah."

"His name is Peter Piper and I have reason to believe he's one of the demons who's been attacking Angels."

She gasped. "Are you sure? What should we do? Who should we call?"

"We're going to have to detain him. I have everything we need in here." I jingled the metal around in my duffle bag.

Pauline gave me a "where did you get that?" look but didn't say anything.

"Once he sees us he's probably going to bolt, so we're going to have to think on our feet."

She shook her head and I noticed her eyelids begin to blink rapidly as if they wanted to up and fly away. Nervous habit, maybe. "I don't know how to do that. How do I do that? I'm just the receptionist and he's a killer. What if he takes my thumbs? I *need* my thumbs. No one will ever marry me if I don't have thumbs. Certainly, not Judd. No. Not anybody. Who wants a mutant wife? I can't think of anyone."

"It's okay." I patted her hand. "Take a deep breath and try to relax."

Her eyelids continued to flutter as she drew in a ragged breath and blew it out. *What a time to have a nervous breakdown. Sheesh.*

Piper was still smoking his cigarette, leaning up against the brick wall. He was right there. Right in front of me. My heart was pounding out of my chest. It was almost too good to be true.

"Listen," I said. "I'm going after him. I'm pretty sure I can take him on my own. All I need you to do is drive the car around the block and open the door for me when I kick his ass into the backseat. So can you do that for me?"

She gulped. "Yes. I think so."

"You're strong, Pauline. You're an Angel. You can do anything. Okay?"

"Okay," she said weakly.

Great. I should've brought Judd instead. He would've helped no matter what the consequences. He'd been a warrior when he'd had his Angel status.

I took a breath, shoved off my jacket and stuffed the cuffs in my back jean pocket. I'd just have to shackle Piper's legs and duct tape his mouth when I had him in the car.

"He's probably going to run down Lawrence Street after he spots me, so drive around to the next block as fast as you can and wait in that parking lot, okay?"

"Sure."

"Please, Pauline. This is important."

All I got was a nod. It had to do. I couldn't waste any more time.

As soon as Pauline had driven off I headed toward Piper in a full-on run. I figured he was going to notice me whether I skipped, walked or did cartwheels, so why not get a running start. I was about three yards from him before he yelled, "Oh, fuck!" and took off down Lawrence Street.

Good. Hopefully Pauline would come through for me. Hopefully she wouldn't leave me stranded.

I continued to run after Piper. My shoulders twitched as my wings begged to break free. But they would only slow me down so I willed them to stay.

Piper threw his cigarette back at me but it fell short. Next the paper bag crashed at my feet. I leaped over the shattered glass and continued after him. Cars zoomed past us as we ran in the opposite direction. One car honked and the passenger yelled something crude in my direction. Low-life human.

I tried to focus. Piper was nearing the end of the building and I was a mere two feet from grabbing him and throwing him to the ground.

He took a sharp turn when he reached the parking lot where I'd told Pauline to wait and ran along the backside of the building. There were about a half a dozen cars in the lot and my VW wasn't one of them.

Probably not here yet. Just focus on the jerk kicking stones up at me.

He hurdled over the hood of a car, slowing me down a bit. He was making more of an effort to get away from me this time around—a good sign that this wasn't another trap.

A chain link fence stood in his path next and I was gaining on him again. This was my chance. He leaped up, grabbed the top and attempted to fling himself over but I got a grip on his calf and jerked him back down...too hard. He fell back down on top of me. His side rammed into my chest, knocking the air from me and jabbing the cuffs into my poor butt.

"Stupid bitch. You didn't learn the first time?" He brought his fist around and made contact with my jaw.

I grabbed for him as his body lifted from mine but I only caught air.

He stood at my feet, staring down at me with those gorgeous brown eyes and that nasty smile. "Stay down, bitch. Good girl."

"I don't think so." I kicked my leg out and swept him off his feet.

He stopped his fall with his hands and launched forward into another run out toward Twenty-Second Street.

Damn, I was going to lose him. I hopped to my feet and followed, maybe too far behind to be able to catch up this time. I was a fast runner but not that fast.

He was almost to the sidewalk when I saw a motorcycle stop short in front of him, blocking his path. Siméon. It was Siméon! Oh, he was so going to be rewarded for this.

Piper stumbled and turned back to see me seizing his wrist and twisting it around toward his back.

He fought me until I kicked out his feet again and pushed him face down into the concrete. Siméon hurried over and helped confine him while I put the cuffs on.

"Siméon Keller?" Piper said with his cheek smashed into the ground. "You're helping the Angels?"

Siméon didn't respond. He looked at me. "Where's your car?"

I scanned the parking lot and saw my VW sitting in the corner. "It's not far. I can handle it now." I nodded toward my prisoner. "Thanks for this."

"I didn't have a choice," he said in a gruff tone. "Answer your phone from now on. I don't want to worry about you."

Piper let out a wicked laugh. "Worried about a fucking Angel? Are you kidding? The Lord of Hell is going to punish you, Keller. Once he finds out you're helping this bitch, you're going to experience pain you've never felt before. And I'm going to enjoy your suffering."

Siméon gripped a handful of Piper's hair and leaned over him. "You'll keep your mouth shut, you subservient piece of shit," he threatened. "Do you think anyone will believe you? You're nothing. Worthless."

"And who are you? The bastard—"

Siméon lifted Piper's head and slammed it into the ground. The brutal act shocked me and I fought to keep a tight hold on Piper as he curled up in pain.

Angels were all about protocol and control. We followed the rules and maintained our anger. If we didn't, well, we'd end up with a desk job. So, needless to say, watching Siméon use excessive violence took me back.

On the other hand, I couldn't help but appreciate the fact that he was on my side…this time.

"You know who I am, Peter," Siméon whispered angrily into his ear. "And you know what I can do to you. Consider this a warning." He grabbed Piper by his coat and dragged him to his feet. I held on to his wrists, feeling annoyingly petite next to the two large demons. "Abigail is going to take you for a little road trip now and you're going to be good."

"Fuck you." Peter spat at Siméon's face. "You've fucked with the wrong guy and you'll go down with the Angels now.

I hope this bitch's pussy was worth it." His laugh stopped short when Siméon threw a swift cross hook to Piper's already bloody jaw. The demon's body jerked to the side but I held him upright.

Enough already. "You can stop roughing him up now, Sim. Geez. I need him to be able to talk."

"I won't allow him to disrespect you, Abigail."

"I'll be fine. Sticks and stones, you know?" I began to push my grumpy prisoner toward the car.

Siméon followed but then stopped short. "Call me if you need my help."

"Don't worry," I shouted over my shoulder. "I'll be super."

And, hopefully, now that I have Peter Piper in custody I won't have to seduce and betray you.

Chapter Fourteen

Now that we had Piper blindfolded and almost fully swathed in duct tape, Pauline settled into her seat and stopped fluttering her eyes. Piper had thrashed, kicked and spat at us when we'd loaded him into the car. He'd left us no choice other than to bind him from head to toe. That tape was going to hurt like a mother when and if we decided to pull it off. Funny, I didn't feel the least bit guilty.

"Who was that man who helped you?" Pauline asked with a shaky voice.

"Hmm?" I was surprised she'd noticed anything at all. I'd found her curled up in the passenger's seat all nice and cozy when I'd finally made it to the car with Piper.

"The man with the motorcycle. Who was that? He resembled the demon we thumbed last night. What was his name? Simon Keller?"

Peter mumbled through his taped mouth from the backseat so I pressed on the brake, jerking him forward. "Siméon. Yeah, that was him," I admitted. She'd find out eventually anyway.

"Oh..." Her finger tapped on her chin. "Is that the demon you, uh, had, uh, you know. It's been a few years now."

"Yep, he's the one." What was the point in denying it? "He's part human though."

"I see. It was all true then. I never knew whether to believe the rumors."

Rumors? Lois had practically announced it over the loudspeakers. She'd been determined to make every Angel aware of my "traitorous lechery" as a way to punish me seeing how MOG had excused me without even a warning. I guess MOG thought the backlash I received from the other Angels would be enough. And it had been. Believe me.

I glanced in the rearview mirror. Piper had settled down and was listening to every word we said. "Maybe we should save this talk for later. Why don't you call in and let them know we're coming."

I drove up and down a few wrong streets before heading to Demon Control just in case Piper had an entourage. Leading the wolves to the sheep was the worst thing that could happen at this point.

Pauline snapped her phone shut and looked at me. "Lois said she'd send out two Ex-Angels to help us bring him in. Where do we take him? I've never done anything like this before."

"We'll play it by ear." I drove into the garage, pressed my thumb to the scanner and waited while the metal gate rolled up.

My breath caught when I noticed Judd standing beside Felix by the basement door. His arms were crossed across his chest as he watched me with those intense blue eyes. A vivid image of him kissing me in the closet flashed into my head and I had to shake it off. I couldn't get all nervous and gooey around him now. No way. I wasn't *that* type of woman. Especially when I had serious work to do.

Focus, Abby.

Pauline perked up beside me when Judd opened her door. "Hi, Judd. How are you?"

"Great. Why don't you step out so Felix and I can retrieve our little prisoner?"

"Oh, he's hardly little." I yanked the passenger seat up after Pauline got out. Certain parts of my car were temperamental and required the "Abby touch".

Piper started in on the tantrum again while Judd and Felix lugged him out. He jerked back and forth until he whacked his noggin on the door panel, knocking himself unconscious.

"What a fucking idiot." Judd dragged Piper to the ground and then held up his upper half while Felix lifted his lower half.

"Nice binding job, Abigail," Felix said with a chuckle. "Enjoy that, I bet you did."

"Shut the hell up, Felix," Judd said before I could respond.

"I can speak for myself, *Judd*." I locked up my car and followed them.

Pauline scanned her thumb on the door and propped it open so the two men could carry Piper inside the hallway.

"Fine," Judd said to me over his shoulder. "You want to do everything your damn self. You don't even answer your phone when I call you. I don't know why you insist on being so goddamned stubborn."

"I didn't need you."

"No? Your beat-up face tells me different."

I swept my fingers across my bruised jaw where Piper had gotten in a lucky shot. It wasn't that bad.

Pauline cleared her throat. "Abigail had help from a half-breed," she announced, smiling at Judd as if he held the only key to the house behind the white picket fence. "It was very interesting."

Judd wrenched his head back to glare at me. "Unfuckingbelievable, Abby."

We walked the rest of the long hallway in silence. I had nothing to say to Judd. Or the other two, for that matter. Where was the gratitude for bringing in one of the bad guys? Where was the love? Sure, I'd had help from Siméon. So what?

Without him, Piper might've gotten away and we'd be back at square one.

Heck, if we didn't have Piper I'd be shopping for lingerie and spy gear. *Chew on that, Judd.*

Felix directed Pauline to open the next door on the left and we all clambered inside the room. I watched curiously while Judd and Felix carried Piper into the holding cell and set him on what looked like an electrocution chair. Yikes. I'd never seen *that* before.

Pauline let out a small gasp. "Well, I'll just be in my apartment if you all need me." She turned on her shaky heel and left.

Judd looked up at me, emotionless. "Why don't you go with her?"

"I'm not going anywhere. We've got work to do."

Without further ado, the two men cut and ripped off the duct tape along with the demon's clothes. Piper woke up with a jolt and started murmuring against the tape on his mouth. He thrashed about but Judd and Felix fought to secure his wrists, ankles and forehead with leather straps, bounding him tightly to the chair. Naked.

I turned my head, unable to watch. "What are you going to do to him?"

"Nothing if we don't have to. But we have permission to do whatever the hell we want." Judd tore off the tape on Piper's mouth. "Start talking, demon."

"Suck my cock, fairy boy." Piper spat toward Felix. "Or suck his if that's the way you do things around here." He smiled up at me wickedly and I couldn't help notice an erection growing between his legs. "You can set the elfin bitch on my lap. I'll show her what a real man feels like." He lips twitched. "Or did Keller already beat me there? Huh, Angel cunt?"

"Get out the whip, Felix." Judd grabbed me by the arm and walked me out the door and halfway down the hall. "Go up to your apartment and stay there."

I jerked away from his grasp. "No. He's *my* prisoner. *I* found him, *I* detained him and *I* brought him in. Not you. Not Felix. And are you kidding about the whip?"

"Please," he whispered through clenched teeth. "If I have to hear another word about you and that half-breed I'm going to explode."

"Explode then. See if I care. But I highly suggest getting a grip. You're going to give yourself an aneurism."

"No, you're going to give me… Never mind." He shook his head and backed me up against the cold brick wall. "Abby," he whispered. "Didn't that kiss today mean anything to you?"

"I don't know," I said stubbornly. "Was it supposed to?"

"Abigail." Lois' stern voice sent unpleasant shivers up my spine. Judd backed up, allowing me to face her.

"Hi, Lois." I gritted my teeth. It wasn't easy stifling my irritation. "We have Peter Piper in the interrogation cell. What would you like us to do with him?"

Her eyebrows rose above her thick black glasses. "Judd and Felix already have orders, Abigail. Didn't they tell you? You're free to go play or whatever it is that you do on your time off."

I sensed a whole heck load of condescending in her voice. "But he's my prisoner."

"Not anymore. I'm employing the Ex-Angels for this particular job." She brushed past me and headed to the interrogation room. "Come, Judd. There's no time to waste."

"I'm sorry, Abby." Judd pressed a kiss to my cheek. "I have to do this. I'll tell you what happened when it's all over."

Chapter Fifteen

෨

I pounded on Siméon's door and rang his doorbell but he didn't answer. Darn. He wasn't home. I'd wanted to be anywhere but Demon Control after being dismissed by Lois. I'd pushed myself to the limit to bring Peter Piper in and what did I get for it? Certainly not the respect I deserved.

Nope. Lois and the other Angels' poor opinion of me would never change. What was the point of trying? Well, other than being an Angel was my identity and demon law enforcement was my job. Who or what would I be without it?

That didn't change the fact that I was furious. And disappointed. And all I craved right at the moment was to be touched like I mattered. I wanted to talk to someone who held me in high regard, who didn't look down on me.

Usually, that was Judd but damn it, he'd betrayed me tonight. He hadn't thought twice about taking that job right out from under me. And, oh, I bet he felt good about it too.

Men!

The faint roar of a motorcycle drew closer and I watched gleefully as Siméon pulled up in his driveway next to my VW. His shoulder length ink-black hair was windswept and his silvery eyes took me in with curiosity.

I walked to him as he got off the bike, clad in black leather. I pursed my lips to keep from drooling.

"Are you okay? What happened?" He drew me close. He smelled of sweet autumn breeze mixed with his sensual musky scent.

I breathed him in and suddenly felt calmer. "I'm fine. Nothing's happened yet. That I know of, anyway."

"I thought you'd be heavily probing Peter by now."

"The case was taken away from me. I don't really want to talk about it." Talking was the last thing I had on my mind.

He nodded thoughtfully. "You want to come in?"

"Yes, please."

"Why don't I park your car in the garage as a precaution? I don't want your friend banging at my door again tonight."

I'd agree to just about anything right now. I handed over the keys and went to wait for him inside.

The interior of his house was colder than it was outside and I wondered if he ran the air conditioner all year. Or maybe, as an Angel, I was too sensitive to wintry temperatures. Either way, I sank down into the couch, grabbed the chenille blanket that hung over the couch and wrapped it around me.

The sound of my keys hitting the dining room table brought my attention to Siméon. He laughed when he saw me cuddled up in the blanket.

"It's not funny."

"It's adorable, my little iron-deficient Angel." His sexy smile didn't fade as he draped his leather coat over a chair and walked into the living room. "This might help." He flicked a switch on the wall to start the fireplace.

"Instant gratification. Impressive."

"You like that?" He sat down beside me and gathered me into his lap, enveloping me in a warm embrace. "What about this?"

"This is okay too." I wasn't quite up at the seductress level. Even though MOG had given me the green light.

Become Siméon's friend. Or more than a friend, if that's what you'd like.

But I didn't want to think about betraying and seducing a man I was starting to respect. Possibly, starting to fall for. Whether I wanted to or not, it was happening. So what if his father *might* be behind the attacks? Siméon hadn't done anything wrong. In fact, he'd proven to me tonight that he was on my side. He hadn't let me down.

He was good. He had a soul. I could feel it deep down in my belly as I sat so close to the beating of his heart.

Two fingers tilted my chin up to meet his eyes. "You want to talk about why you decided to visit me? Not that I'm complaining. Just curious."

I shook my head.

"No? You want to discuss anything else?"

"Not really." I slid my hand up and down the ridges on his stomach to give him a better idea about what was really on my mind.

He grinned knowingly. "Hmm… Let me think. You want to look for bad guys on my computer? You want to question my integrity? Wait. You're here to give me another strike. Am I warm?"

"Don't tease me. I'm not in the mood for teasing."

"What are you in the mood for, love?" He slipped his hands around my neck and into my hair. "You don't have to be shy with me. I'll give you whatever you ask for. I think I've proven that tonight."

"You did. Thank you." My body trembled as I readjusted to straddle his lap. I wanted to be closer to him. I wanted him to ease my anxiety. Make me forget about Peter Piper. Forget about the attacks. Forget about my guilt. Forget everything and everyone.

Leisurely, he swept off my jacket and the blanket covering me. "I don't think we need these anymore. I'll keep you warm." He wrapped his powerful arms around my waist and crushed me to his lean, taut body.

The inside of my thighs quivered from just listening to the sound of his honey-smooth voice. It occurred to me that I wasn't the seductress. I was the prey. Frankly, I didn't care one teensy bit now that his mouth was on my neck, licking and lightly nipping at the sensitive area just below my ear.

Mesmerized, I ran my hands up and down his biceps, over his wide shoulders and across his chest. Every inch was solid perfection. I wanted to explore more of him...with much less clothing between us.

As if reading my mind, he reached and tugged off his t-shirt. "I love the feel of your hands on me," he murmured and pressed a kiss to my lips. "Be careful of your thumb though, love." He grinned playfully. "I don't want to be deported from heaven to Hell without a good reason."

"Don't give me a reason then," I joked along but casually tucked my thumbs into my palms. He wasn't going anywhere.

"Mmm." He gripped my bottom and pressed my heat to the abundant erection in his pants. "You're going to be the death of me, aren't you?"

"Never." I wrapped my arms around his neck and boldly molded my lips to his mouth, sensually flicking my tongue against his. I rocked my hips toward him, feeling him grow even larger.

"We're going to the bedroom." His voice rumbled in my ear as he lifted me.

I wrapped my legs tightly around his waist, happy to go wherever he wanted to take me. Thankfully it was to a place where I could get rid of the rest of his clothes. I wanted to see and touch every inch of him. Five years of fantasizing was too long. I couldn't hold back anymore.

He kicked open his bedroom door and dropped me on his California king. Just as I'd expected. His bed took up more than half of his room. I ran my hands over the black silk comforter. It was everything I'd imagined from the four-poster bed down to the... Was that a mirror on the ceiling?

"Sim?" I caught his attention as his pants plunked to the floor. I had the urge to ask how many women he'd had in this bed but thought otherwise. Did I really want to know? He was gorgeous with the power to persuade any human. And apparently one Angel.

"Just a few, love," he answered my unasked question. "None quite as beautiful and tempting as you though." Completely naked, he crawled onto the bed, slipped both my tennis shoes off then threw them over his shoulder.

"A few?" I curled my feet up. "Like the woman you seduced on her wedding night?" The reason I'd had to give him his first strike. I'd always wondered about her. Had he brought her here? Had she regretted giving her body to him? Or had one night with Siméon been worth breaking the vows she had made just hours before?

"The only woman I want to think about right now is the sassy redhead lying on my bed." He slipped my socks off and tossed them as well. "You'll never guess how often I've dreamed about getting you here." He climbed up my body and kissed my lips.

"You've dreamed of me?"

"Almost every night since the first time I laid eyes on you."

Boy, was he good at this seducing business. I forgot about the other women and reached down to unzip my jeans. He helped by tugging them off and then ran his hands back up my legs, stopping at the edge of my panties.

I thanked my lucky stars that I'd shaved this morning. I peeked down at my panties as he stripped them down. They were the cute pink ones with the little baby blue bow at the front. Not too bad. They could've been much worse, believe me. I released a breath.

On the way back up, he stopped to kiss my mound before working my t-shirt off me. I'd have helped if I hadn't been utterly paralyzed from my eyebrows down. It was happening. And I was allowing it. Damn it if I wasn't thrilled out of my mind. Even the little voice in my head was quivering in anticipation.

"You're trembling, sweetheart." He released the front clamp to my bra and succeeded to toss that into the ever-growing pile of clothes. Then he sat back and stared, inching his attention down my body. His gaze lingered at my breasts and gradually lowered to where my legs spread open for him.

I'd never felt more nude, more exposed. As nonchalantly as possible I covered my nipples with my hands and clenched my knees shut. He'd seen me naked before but it seemed it was happening in slow motion this time.

"Why are you timid all of a sudden?"

"Not used to being examined under the microscope. So sorry."

He chuckled and brought his hands up to my knees. "I'm only enjoying the view, sweetheart. You have a beautiful body and I want to remember it lest I never get the chance to see it again." He eased my legs apart and sank down on top of me.

"Oh." I moved my hands to his shoulders and allowed the full contact of his heated body. It felt wonderful. "I guess there's always that. Oh—" I gasped as he nudged his cock against my opening. "There's always that chance. We're not exactly…mmm—" I felt his hand caress my breast. "We're not on the same team."

"Don't worry, love." He lowered his head and licked my pebbled, love-starved nipple. "You'll be cheering for me in no time."

His silly grin made me burst out in giggles but I quickly quieted as he went back to work. His warm tongue swirled around my tight areola. Then he took me into his mouth, mercilessly sucking until I arched up toward him in surrender.

Taking the hint, he released and pressed a kiss to my nipple. "Are you very sensitive here?"

I nodded. "It's been a long time since someone's even touched me. But I like it."

"How long?"

"Hmm. About five years."

He smiled. "Did I ruin you for all other men then?"

"Sure." I lifted my hips, pressing myself against his cock. "Can we quit talking now?"

He locked up his lips and threw away the key before giving the other breast the same treatment as the first, although ruthlessly ignoring my pleas for surrender this time.

I felt myself growing wet for him. Sopping and quivering with want. Though sensitive, my body yearned for more.

"I need you inside me," I whispered, knowing full well he could hear me.

"Patience," he said as he kissed his way down my belly. "While I savor you." Gently, he slid a finger inside me.

"Okay," I said breathlessly. Who was I to argue? I closed my eyes and relaxed, willing myself not to scream in delight as his tongue flicked across my clit.

He licked, sucked, nibbled and delved until I moaned and shuddered against him. Limp with pleasure, I could only watch as he kissed his way back up.

A desperate hunger hid behind his hooded eyes as he lowered his head and pressed his mouth to mine. It was hard to believe I could make a man look that way. As if I was the only woman he'd ever wanted. In this moment, I felt close to him. Nothing mattered but the connection between our bodies, between our souls.

Except Judd. He mattered. *No, don't think about him. Not now.*

I wrapped my legs around Siméon's hips and stared up into his heavy eyes. "Please," I said. "I need you." Before I changed my mind. Before the guilt came over me.

He sank into me then, filling me completely with one push. "Oh, Abigail. I've wanted this for so long." He withdrew halfway and eased back in. "You're so wet for me."

Heat surged through my thighs and belly. I clung to him, pressing my fingers into his back. I attempted to meet his thrusts, lifting my pelvis up. It was so much better than I'd remembered. The room spun around me until I caught sight of the mirror above us.

The image staring back at me was glorious. My pale legs wrapped around his tan body. My hands clamping into his broad, muscled back. His tight buttocks clenching as he drove into me.

It was sinful and oh, so good.

"Siméon," I moaned as a burning wave rolled through me.

"Yes, love, come for me."

"Yes, yes. Oh, God, yes!" The wave intensified, boggling me senseless as I released.

Siméon thrust twice more before groaning and collapsing his full weight onto my body.

We both panted and I ran my hands over his back and down his buttocks, getting my fill before it all ended. He was perfection. Every inch of him. And I wasn't sure this intimacy between us would ever happen again. Or if I could ever let it happen again.

"Sweetheart?" His breath was warm against my ear.

"Yes?" I turned my head to kiss his cheek and push a damp strand of hair from his face.

"I do believe I've fallen in love with you."

"But you're a demon." I searched the floor again for my panties but didn't see them. My heart was pounding and my mind wasn't working properly. "Demons don't love. They lust. Maybe it's just lust."

"Does this mean you're not going to admit you love me too?" Siméon leaned back on his pillowed headboard still completely naked and gave me a devilishly playful grin. "You're hurting my feelings."

"Demons don't have feelings," I reminded him and tugged my t-shirt over my head. "I don't see my panties anywhere. Do you see them?"

"I'm part human, you're forgetting. I can love you if I want to. And I do want to whether you cooperate or not. I'm insanely in love with you. I want to share this bed with you every night for the rest of my life, which is a big commitment considering."

"See? You want to have sex. Sex has nothing to do with love, well, much." I dropped to the floor and looked under his vast bed.

"Fine. I want to make you sushi and let you buy me hamburgers. I want to argue with you and let you win."

"Let me win? Excuse me?" I stood up and perched my hands on my hips.

"I want to wake up in the morning and reach over to kiss your cute freckled nose. I want to sink my hands into your fiery hair and pull you to my lips. I want to eat your delicious pussy for dessert every night."

"Whoa! That's enough, big boy." Wait until MOG gets a load of this.

"I want you to get mad at me for reasons beyond my control and then do everything I can to make it up to you because I hate seeing you upset."

"Wait." I put my hand up to stop him from continuing. "Please, let's think this through rationally. You've known me, what, three or four days?" Oh, heck. Did demons lose all rationality after sex?

"Over five years, actually."

"But we haven't spent that much time together. You barely know me."

"I have an entire file on you."

"You what?"

"And I plan to add your intriguing interest in music. I noticed you have quite a collection of Aerosmith CDs in your car, particularly from the seventies and eighties. Aren't they a bit before your time?"

"You don't know my age and Aerosmith is classic. See? We don't even share the same taste in music. How could you possibly love me?"

"You're twenty-eight human years old and I went to my first Aerosmith concert when you were just learning how to use those lethal thumbs of yours. I was invited backstage once, in fact. I could share my story sometime, if you like." He stood and walked toward me in all his naked glory. Broad shoulders leading down to a tan rippled stomach leading down to... Wow.

Damn, why did he have to be so tempting? So persuasive? So...so wicked?

"Do you want this?" He opened his hand and my panties unwrinkled in his palm.

I grabbed for them but he tossed them to the floor. "Now, that's not very nice—"

My heartbeat pattered sharply as he pulled me to his chest. His lips covered mine and I couldn't help but ingest his scent and his taste. I kissed him back because, well, because it made me feel more alive than I'd ever felt. In his arms, I was more than a defective Angel with a bad rep. My flaws disappeared. My confidence rose. My mind calmed.

"Mmm..." I took in a breath as he broke the kiss.

He lifted my chin and forced me to look into his bewitching eyes. "Stay with me tonight, Abigail. Who cares what anyone thinks?"

The phone rang from somewhere in the bedroom, breaking the magical spell Siméon had me under. I cleared my throat and pulled away from his grasp to finish getting dressed.

Siméon growled under his breath. "Who the hell would call at this hour?" He picked up the phone from his nightstand and put it to his ear. "*What?*"

His alarm clock told me it was just past one a.m. It was probably one of his girlfriends craving a booty call. Whom was he kidding? He couldn't possibly be in love with me. Even if there was only a small percentage of demon in him, I was sure it would be enough to give him a substantial libido.

It must be lust. And the fact that I was forbidden territory must tempt his evil side.

"It's for you." His gruff voice grabbed my attention and I turned to see he'd lost the smile he'd had all evening. Actually, he looked pretty dang irate.

"Who is it?" I whispered, suddenly feeling like a teenager past curfew again.

"Take a good guess."

Judd. Wonderful. Why was he calling here?

Siméon handed me the phone and then dropped back onto the bed, resting his hands behind his head to watch the show.

My cheeks flamed from the obvious scrutiny. Was he taking more notes to put into my "file"?

I took a calming breath and answered. "Hello?"

"Abby, thank God I found you." Judd's deep voice filtered into her ear. "You weren't answering your phone again. What are you doing over there? *Fuck*. Never mind. Don't answer that."

"Judd, why are you calling me? I'm an adult. I don't need your constant supervision."

That evoked a smile from Siméon. I swiveled on my heel to avoid seeing his face.

"Listen, Abigail," Judd practically yelled into the phone. He never called me Abigail. "Go in another room so *half-breed* can't hear me talk."

"No. Just say what you have to say." I wasn't playing.

"Please. This is extremely important. You'll understand once I explain."

Curiosity got the best of me and I put a finger up at Siméon to tell him I'd just be a moment.

He quickly got to his feet. "Stay. I'll leave." He grabbed his pants, planted an audible kiss on my lips and left me alone in the room.

"Goddamnit, did he just *kiss* you?" Judd bellowed. He let out a few expletives and then I heard something crash in the background.

I waited for his outburst to pass, only allowing a speck of guilt to eat at me. Judd had no claim on me, I reminded myself. A single kiss in the janitor's closet didn't make me his. "Just tell me what's going on, okay? He's gone."

"You're lucky I don't have time to drive over there and kick his *fucking* ass."

"Oh, boy. Save the macho act for later, will you? And tell me what's wrong."

"We found a bug on Piper," he said. "Felix thinks it might be a tracking device so we're evacuating Demon Control and closing down the public part of the garage. Most of the Angels are cooperating but MOG and Lois refuse to leave."

"So what does this mean? You think the demons know where we're located?"

"We can't take any chances. They could eat us alive if they find our location. You know as well as I do we're not equipped to handle a full-on attack, especially since we're not allowed to carry firearms. Fucking pact."

"This isn't good, Judd. What are we going to do?" A new round of guilt hit me. How could I have been so stupid to allow this? I'd never even thought to check for a bug.

"I want you to go to the AOD center and hang with Eli. Get the hell away from that half-breed. He's not safe."

"Don't be ridiculous."

"Abby, don't you think it's awfully suspicious that he told you where to find Piper and then helped you detain him just so Piper could bring a bug back to Demon Control? It was all a goddamned setup, I know it."

I didn't think he knew a damn thing but I wasn't going to waste time arguing. "I'll be right there to help with MOG."

"No. I don't want you anywhere near here. Go to Eli's."

Like hell. I hung up and collected the rest of my clothes, yanking them on as fast as I could. This was my error and I was going to make it right.

Chapter Sixteen

The parking garage was eerily empty when I drove in. Most of the Angels had already evacuated as ordered. I knew they'd be assigned to room with another Angel at the Angel of Death or Guardian Angel center until this all cleared up. It was mandated in the Angels, Inc. Emergency Handbook. I remembered this detail only because I'd ingrained in my mind how awful it would be to share a room with a Guardian Angel. They were very protective of their property and did *not* like sharing.

Rooming with an Angel of Death wasn't all that appealing either since they worked varying hours and they loved to talk about their morbid tales of human fatalities. Eli had nauseated me on more than one occasion.

I parked in the spot closest to the elevators. Judd's black Chevy Silverado and Lois' Oldsmobile sat by themselves in the distance as well as one other car I didn't recognize.

On the way up the elevator, I powered on my phone and called Judd.

"This is how you answer the phone," he said instead of the polite hello. "It's so simple an Ex-Angel can figure it out. Why can't you?"

"Don't start. Where are you?"

"I'm in my apartment packing the essentials so they don't get pilfered by demonic assholes."

"Good idea. I'll do the same. How are MOG and Lois?"

"MOG's high again therefore not too concerned about Demon Control being attacked or anything else for that matter but Lois is working on her. They should be packing up right now."

The elevator doors opened to the office, which was dark except for a few computers that were undoubtedly left on in the mad dash to vacate. I let the doors shut again and pressed the button for my apartment floor. A horrible feeling sank to the bottom of my belly.

I took a calming breath. "Peter Piper? Where is he?"

"You're not going to like this."

"What? Where is he?"

"My guess would be he's in Hell. Felix freaked when he saw the bug and deported him before I could stop him."

I pinched the bridge of my nose. I never should've let Piper out of my sight. "Great. Did you happen to squeeze any info out of him before that happened?"

"The good news is I confiscated the bug before Piper was sucked back to Hell. I'll send it to the Angel lab at the AOD center to see exactly what it is. If it's not a tracking device, then Demon Control isn't under any immediate danger and we can all move back in."

"And the bad news?"

"The bad news is Piper is either very loyal to his leader or very frightened of him. He wouldn't tell us anything."

"Shit," was all I could say.

"I know."

The elevator doors opened and I jumped a little when I saw Judd standing on the other side. He had a duffle bag slung over his shoulder and a look of despair on his face.

We both snapped our phones shut and stuffed them in our pockets as I stepped out to meet him.

"Hey," he said, taking in my disheveled appearance.

"Hey." I sincerely hoped I didn't look like a woman who'd just had amazing sex with the enemy. I casually brushed my fingers through my tangled hair and straightened my shirt.

Judd sighed in clear frustration. "Hurry and pack up what you need. We need to get out of here."

"You shouldn't be mad at me," I said. "Go ahead and gripe about MOG or Lois or anybody else who pisses you off. I can deal with that." The ascending numbers on top of the elevator distracted me for a moment. Good. MOG and Lois were leaving, I thought and turned back to Judd.

He opened his mouth to say something but I put my hand up and continued. "But you're supposed to like me unconditionally. We're partners in this crazy world. You're the only Angel I can talk to."

Judd reached around me to push the elevator button for the garage floor and then gave me his attention. "It's complicated." He growled under his breath and rubbed a hand over his five o'clock shadow. "Jesus, Abby. I can't be mad at you. You drive me nuts and most days I'd like nothing more than to lock you up somewhere so I won't have to worry about you. But the truth is you're the only one I've got too. And I kind of like it that way."

Not being able to help myself, I wrapped my arms around his waist. I missed our normalcy. I missed *him*. And at the same time I yearned to be back with Siméon. What was wrong with me?

Judd enclosed me in his arms and squeezed. "It's going to be all right," he whispered into my ear. "We both made mistakes but we can start over new. I'll wait for you in the garage and then we'll head over to Eli's and find somewhere for us to sleep." He pulled back and looked at me with those warm, comforting eyes. "And then we'll talk tomorrow, okay?"

I wasn't sure how to answer, knowing MOG wanted me to put on my spy hat. I'd have no other choice than to go straight back to Siméon's house. Especially since we were no closer to ending the attacks. Quite the opposite now that Piper was gone. And if Malakai was behind this fucking rebellion, Siméon was the only route I could think of to finding him.

"See you in a sec," I finally said when the elevator doors closed with Judd behind them.

I gathered myself together and went to pack up a few things. If the demons hadn't located the building already then maybe Felix had been wrong about the tracking device. A girl could hope.

I grabbed a backpack out of my minuscule closet and started stuffing it with clothes. A couple of pairs of jeans, my two favorite sweaters, my pajamas. None of which were made for a temptress who needed to betray a man who'd professed his love to her.

My heart lurched forward just at the memory of his voice saying those words.

Stop it, Abby. He's a demon. He was only toying with you.

But, dang, it felt so good to hear.

I was so stopping to get some cheesecake on my way to Siméon's house. Maybe having a little piece of heaven in my belly would keep me focused on the task of finding Malakai rather than how great it felt to be lying underneath Malakai's son.

I needed a plan. Everything Siméon knew about everyone was on his computer. He'd admitted to that more than once, so he had to have data on Malakai. The hard part would be bypassing any passwords Siméon had set up.

No. The *hard* part would be getting away from Siméon and alone with the computer. And what if Siméon didn't want me in his home? I'd left him without even saying goodbye this last time. There was only so much a guy would take. Right? I guess that was where the seduction would come into play.

A loud bang interrupted my thoughts and scared me off my feet and onto my bed, which was shaking from the explosion. It had been an explosion, hadn't it?

Oh, God.

I scrambled to my feet and went to the window. It was difficult to see out the tinted glass, especially since it was dark out. The only things I could make out were the streetlights and a lone car's headlights driving along the street below.

Another bang shook the floor beneath me and the light in my room flickered briefly. What the hell was going on? I didn't want to stick around to find out.

I flung my backpack over my shoulder, made a mad dash to the door...and stopped short when I smelled smoke. Fire. The building was on fire.

"Shit. Heck. Heck. Heck. What should I do?"

I'd never trained for this type of emergency. Or at least I didn't recall training for escaping a burning building. No, I probably would've remembered that.

Relax, Abby. Just get out.

I touched the door to see if it was hot. No, it was okay. I pushed it open and stepped out into the hallway. The fluorescent lights above me were dim and making a buzzing noise. Above the elevator, the floor numbers were blinking frantically and tendrils of smoke were licking up from under the doors.

Definitely a fire somewhere.

"Help!" I heard a muffled cry coming from behind the elevator doors. "Dear God, get me out of here!"

MOG. Holy cow. "I'm coming," I yelled. "Hold tight."

With all my Angel strength, I wrenched the doors open. A dark cloud of smoke whipped into me and invaded my lungs. I coughed the gaseous vapor out and waved it away from my face. It spread into the hallway and all around me, so I pulled my t-shirt over my mouth and nose.

"Abigail," MOG screamed from above my head. I looked up and saw that the elevator had jammed right below the ceiling but I could see MOG kneeling down on the floor of the elevator with only about a foot and a half of space showing.

"We have to get you out of there. Is Lois with you?"

"No, she left a little before me. Said she was going back to the office to get her Bible. Said she'd meet me in the garage."

So had Judd. I prayed to God they got out okay. "Can you squeeze through?" I asked. "Slide out on your tummy and I'll help you down."

"I'll try but with the Doritos and pizza diet I've been on…" She disappeared for a second and then her bare feet shot out of the small space. "Catch me, Abigail. I trust you."

"I'm here for you, MOG."

Her tiny body slid through with ease. I gripped onto her waist and helped her to the floor. She staggered a little, gave me a weak smile and started coughing at the new emergence of the menacing smoke.

I grabbed her hand and guided her into my apartment, closing the door behind us.

"What should we do next?" the Holy Messenger of God asked me. Me?

"Um, I think we should put in fire escapes and a sprinkler system when we rebuild. What do you think?"

"Excellent idea. And for now?"

An abrupt pounding on the window caught our attention. I swiveled on my heel to see Siméon on the other side, gripping onto the outer wall. He pounded again, unable to see us through the mirrored tint.

"Abigail," he shouted but came to us in a muffled murmur through the thick glass. "Are you in there?"

I ran to the window. "Yes, I'm here," I shouted in return. "I'll try to break the glass! Get back!"

He nodded and scaled to the side. This was the first time I'd ever appreciated the wall climbing abilities of a demon. And probably the last. But, boy, was I grateful for it now.

I lifted my leg to kick the window out but MOG stopped me. "You'll cut your leg, dear. Here…" She ran across the apartment, picked up my television, ripped the cords from the wall and my precious TiVo and hauled it over to me. "Use this."

"My TV? I'm not throwing my TV out the window. Do you know how long it took me to save up for—"

MOG maneuvered around me, lifted the television over her head and heaved it toward the window, shattering it into pieces.

"No!" I watched helplessly as my favorite form of mindless entertainment crashed to its death. "Oh, hell."

"There." MOG swiped her hands together. "Now we get to live."

Siméon punched out the remaining sections of glass with his fist, still holding on to the side of the building. "Let's go, Abigail," he said.

I leaned out the window and looked down. Fire was flickering out the first floor windows. "You have to take MOG first."

His eyes shifted to MOG and then back to me. "Don't be ridiculous. I'm not leaving you."

"Can you carry us both?"

"No."

I shoved MOG in front of me. "Then come back for me."

"Damn it, Abigail." He gritted his teeth. "We don't have time to waste."

"You're right. So take her and hurry back for me. I'm not leaving this building before she does. Got it?"

MOG wobbled beside me. She'd been under too much stress lately and now her building was crackling up in flames.

And it was all my fault. I shushed her before she could argue for me to go first and helped her onto Siméon's back. "Hold on tight, okay?"

MOG nodded and then with haste he was scaling back down the building, avoiding the busted-out first floor windows. The second story's windows were blocked up to completely hide the Demon Control office, which was probably ablaze at that very moment. The acrid smell from the floors beneath me stung my nose, burned my lungs and irritated my eyes. I held my head out the window trying desperately to catch some fresh air but the rising smoke from below wouldn't allow me.

I gasped for a decent breath of air and didn't dare look behind me. I felt the scorching heat on my back and saw the smoke streaming out on each side of me, reaching up for the heavens and I derived a sickening conclusion. The fire was close. Too close.

"Abigail." Siméon grasped my arm and I flung my eyes open, not realizing I'd shut them. "Don't faint, love. You'll have to hold on to me."

With the little strength I had left, I sat on the windowsill and scooted down onto him, wrapping my legs around his waist and my arms around his neck. I continued to cough and my eyes continued to water as he fluidly scaled down the building.

I don't know how he'd found the Demon Control building or how he'd known which window to go to and I didn't care. He'd saved both MOG's life and mine.

He leaped to the sidewalk, holding me tight to his body and darted across the street to where MOG and Judd stood.

Judd? I took a second glance to make sure I wasn't hallucinating. Thank heavens. Judd was okay. He'd made it out in time. His clothes were shredded, barely covering his body and he had bloody nicks and cuts here and there, probably from the explosions but he was alive and standing. And he looked so damn good.

I sobbed and coughed against Siméon's shoulder until he set me down on my unstable feet. Before I could catch my balance, Judd whirled me around and pulled me into a bear hug, lifting me off the ground.

"God, Abby, I'd thought you'd died."

His tight grip led me into another coughing frenzy.

"Put her down, you fool," Siméon said. "She needs air and I need to get her to a doctor."

Judd eased me down so I could sit in the grass by MOG, whose eyes were glazed over, dazed as she watched Demon Control burn.

"You?" Judd folded his arms in front of him and stood eye-to-eye with Siméon. "You're not taking her anywhere. You're the one who caused this."

Siméon took a similar macho stance. "You think I did this? Why would I try to kill the woman I love?"

"Ha! Love? Is that the bull you've been feeding her? Demons *can't* love. Abby knows that. Every Angel knows that. But nice try, dickhead."

Siméon scowled and gave me a quick glance before glowering at Judd again. "I wouldn't have risked my life just now saving her if I didn't love her."

"Don't play the hero card. You saved her because I told you to crawl your diabolical ass up the building and get her. How did you find us anyway? Explain that one, chump."

"I followed Abigail after she left my home. She'd left upset and I didn't have a good feeling."

"Nice one, half-breed. Very perceptive of you, considering you planned this shit to happen."

Sirens wailed in the distance, growing louder by the second.

"I don't want to be here when the human authorities show up," I said to deaf ears. "I want to leave."

They continued to argue but I was too exhausted to keep up. And we were missing someone, I suddenly remembered. *Lois.* My heart jolted to a stop.

"MOG, where's Lois?" I asked.

She shook her head. "She left right before I did... She went to the office... Abigail, she—I don't think she would've had enough time to get out." A tear rolled down her black-smeared cheek. "She's gone."

"Oh, no. I'm so sorry, MOG."

"Don't be sorry." She clasped my hands in hers. "It's not over yet, is it? You know what to do, dear." She looked up at Siméon who was now only inches from Judd's face as they hollered back and forth.

I gulped and nodded my head. I knew exactly what I needed to do.

"I may as well deport your ass right now." Judd's face grew red as he shouted.

"Try it." Siméon narrowed his eyes and tapped his finger on his chest. "Make the first move. I dare you, *Ex-Angel.*"

"No one's doing anything." I quickly stood and squeezed in between the two, coughing up a storm for effect, even though my lungs had cleared. "Siméon's right. I need a doctor." Hack. Hack.

Hack. Hack. Hack.

Judd pulled me to him and away from Siméon. "Then I'll take you to one." He glanced toward the burning building and warily rolled his eyes. "I'll call a cab."

"A cab?" I said, confused. Until it finally dawned on me. "Oh, geez. My VW and your Silverado are toast, aren't they?" Could my life get any worse? Yes, I thought, humbled by Lois' absence. I could've been killed today. I could've lost my best friend. And MOG, who I respected and was slowly bonding a friendship with.

"I have a car." Siméon stepped in and took my hand. "And I have a human family member who is a doctor who works at a nearby hospital. He owes me a huge favor."

"Hallelujah." MOG stood to her feet. "Abigail, go with the half-breed to get checked out. You're obviously suffering from smoke inhalation. Judd and I will stay here to deal with the human authorities."

"No way in Hell," Judd said. "The AOD center has an Angel doctor. We'll go there."

A police car came screaming down the street with a fire truck not far behind.

"Go with him, Abigail," MOG ordered, grasping Judd's arm. "Call as soon as you're done and I'll have Judd pick you up." She turned to Judd and gripped his shoulder. "Besides, you'll need your Angel status reinstated straight away, as well as all the other Ex-Angels. We're going to need every Angel we can get to devise and execute a counterattack."

Judd's jaw dropped open, apparently shocked and speechless. I wanted to stick around to congratulate him. He'd finally gotten his Angel status back. But I decided this was my best chance to escape with Siméon. I just hoped neither of the men would hate me for it after everything was said and done.

"Let's go," I whispered to Siméon.

He wasted no time leading me to a sleek silver Jaguar coupe parked haphazardly on the side of the road. Wow. Where did this guy get his money?

I jumped into the passenger seat as he slid in on the driver's side. He looked even more delicious behind the wheel of this baby, if that was possible. And I wanted to shoot straight into questions about the engine's horsepower. Was it a V8? Zero to sixty in how many seconds? How many miles per gallon?

Angel Vindicated

I opened my mouth to speak but I couldn't. Tears welled up in my eyes. *My* car was gone. All the work I'd put into it was pointless, a mere memory with nothing tangible to reward me for my efforts.

Everything was gone. My CD collection, my clothes, my TiVo, my favorite pillow, the new hair products I'd purchased the other day.

Pictures of my parents and my sister and her family.

Everything.

I had nothing but the tattered clothes on my body, my jacket and my stupid cell phone.

The other Angels—Judd, MOG, Pauline, Felix and the rest—they'd lost everything as well.

Including Lois. She may have been snide and self-righteous but she was an Angel. And Angels stuck together. Her imperfections were her own as mine were my own. Who would I be if I didn't mourn for her?

It all whirled around in my head, making me sick to my stomach.

And it could've so easily been prevented if I'd looked for a bug before bringing Peter Piper in.

It was my fault. I was the one to blame. Could I ever be vindicated for this mistake? I doubted it but I could try.

Siméon intertwined his fingers with mine and brought my hand up to kiss. "It's going to be okay, love. I promise."

"I can't go back to them," I said through sobs that were anything but an act. "It's my fault they lost everything and I don't know if I can ever face them again."

Maybe this spy thing wouldn't be all that bad since I was believing every blubbering word that shot out of my mouth.

Siméon was silent as he pulled into the hospital emergency entrance. I'd planned to seduce him to convince him to let me move in with him but what the heck, a pity party might work too.

"Can I stay with you for a while?" I whispered.

His car jerked to a stop as he parked. "You want to live with me? What would your boyfriend think?"

"Judd? I told you he's not my boyfriend."

"Will he be calling and banging at my door at all hours?"

I heaved out a sigh. "How do you want me to answer that, Siméon? I have no control over Judd just as I have no control over my life right now. I've lost everything and as soon as the Angels find out I was the reason they're home and office is burned to the ground then I'm sure I'll lose my job as well." I rested my hand on his thigh. "I'm asking for a favor that I have no right to ask. I'm aware of that and I completely understand if you don't want me in your home."

He stared at me for a moment before replying. "On three conditions."

I gulped. "And they are?"

"I ask that you respect my privacy. My home office is off limits. If I see you in there, I'll ask you to leave, no exceptions."

"Okay. That's no problem." *If he doesn't find out*. His home office was the first place I planned to investigate when given the chance. "Condition number two?"

"If you're living with me in my home then you're mine."

"What?" I didn't like the sound of that. I was nobody's property.

"My woman. My lover. Whatever you want to call it. You're *mine*." A feral intensity glimmered in his eyes as he stared down at me. "Which means no leaving in the middle of the night when he does come for you and I know he will. No meeting up with him. No physical contact with him whatsoever. Is that going to be a problem?"

I shook my head no. Judd wasn't going to want to speak to me ever again, anyway.

Siméon caught my chin and held my head still. "Are you ready for number three?"

"Of course." *Not at all.*

"I want you to believe me when I say I love you and that I'd never do anything to hurt you. And I want you to promise me you'll never intentionally hurt me."

"I, uh, I promise." I was so pathetic. The heat rising up my chest and into my cheeks was undeniable. I didn't want to hurt Siméon. I really didn't but it was inevitable. I needed to find Malakai. And unless Siméon was going to point me in the right direction, I'd lie, cheat and steal to do it on my own.

Siméon's grave expression let me know he thought I was full of it. "The death of me," he murmured and leaned in to press his warm lips to mine. "I'll settle for two out of three for now. Let's go find my nephew."

Chapter Seventeen

Siméon's nephew was a middle-aged physician with bright blue eyes, a kind smile and salt and pepper hair. I returned his smile as he sat on the edge of my hospital bed. At least he didn't seem to loathe me like Harley did. Instead, he stared at me as if I was his own personal science experiment. Wonderful. I foresaw multiple poking and prodding.

"I'm Dr. Keller," he said. "But you can call me Thomas." He pulled out a little light and flashed it in my eyes. "Siméon tells me you were caught in a fire. That must have been frightening. How are you feeling?"

"Super," I said. "Really. I don't think this is necessary at all."

Thomas ignored me and looked up at Siméon who stubbornly had his arms crossed in front of him. "I don't know the rules." The doc chuckled. "Do I listen to the Angel or the demon?"

"You listen to your uncle," Siméon said. "Continue, please. She inhaled a lot of smoke and nearly passed out."

"I'm a fast healer," I argued. "All Angels are."

Thomas put the stethoscope to my chest and listened. "Your lungs are clear but I'm afraid your temperature is a bit low, as well as your pulse."

"That's normal," I said. "Another Angel thing."

"I see." Thomas' eyes widened with intrigue. "You see, I've never actually met one of your kind before. This is all very new to me."

Siméon leaned forward and clasped Thomas on the shoulder. "What about a chest x-ray? An MRI or some blood tests?"

"Sim!" I sat up and threatened him with a glare. "Why don't you just order me an enema while you're at it? I'm *fine*. You've already taken him away from patients who truly need him. I think it's time to go."

Siméon's cell phone rang in his pocket and he put up a finger for us to wait as he took it to the other side of the room.

I rolled my tired eyes and turned to Thomas. "I'm sorry. I wouldn't have bothered you but Siméon insisted."

"He can be quite persuasive at times, can't he?" He winked at me. "Are you two friends then?"

"You could say that." I had no idea what to call my relationship with the half-breed. Time to change the subject. "Are you Harley's father?"

"Harley? Oh, no. She's my brother's child. My niece. Say, Siméon should bring you to the birthday party tonight, if you're feeling up to it. Most of the family will be there. And I know Mother would love to meet an Angel. She's always spoken so highly of your people."

"So you all know about us?"

"We've all caught on, yes. And believe me, Harley's the only one of us who has harsh feelings for the Angels. Quite the opposite, in fact. The rest of us appreciate what you do for humanity." He patted my hand.

I couldn't help but smile. I liked the way this human thought.

"Whose birthday is it?" I asked.

"Birthday?" Siméon shoved his phone back in his pocket and ambled over. If I looked as exhausted as he did, I was in trouble. Not to mention my pale skin was covered with a thin layer of soot. Thank MOG there wasn't a mirror in sight. I did *not* want to see how bad I knew my hair was, or if I had any left.

"My mother, *your* sister," Thomas said. "You didn't forget, did you?"

Siméon sank down onto the bed and sighed. "That's tonight, isn't it?"

"Yes and you should be there. She hasn't been well lately and she's expecting you."

"Of course I'll be there." He shot me a hesitant look. "I'll bring Abigail with me since you're obviously giving her a clean bill of health."

"Whoa there." I put my hands up. "Don't you need to ask me if I want to go? Or have you forgotten that little thing called free will?" *Or did I give that up when I'd agreed to be his? Damn.*

"Consider it another condition, sweetheart." He gave me a weary grin. "I have a strange feeling I shouldn't let you out of my sight for a while."

* * * * *

I was too tired to think about sex as I looked down at Siméon's big, comfy bed. If heaven could exist in a two hundred fifty square foot bedroom then this was where it would be. The sheets were silky soft and the mattress had just the right amount of cushion. And the pillows…oh, they were calling my name. *Abby, come lie your aching head on me. Forget about being a spy or a seductress or a loose, lying tramp of an Angel who single-handedly helped the demons burn the only hope for humanity.*

"You betcha," I murmured and started to fall onto the mattress but Siméon grabbed me by the waist before I reached heaven.

"Don't you want to take a nice hot bath first, love?" he whispered into my ear.

"A bath?" That didn't sound too awful either. I couldn't remember the last time I'd taken a bath, not with the miniscule showers Demon Control provided.

"Yes. We don't want to get the sheets all dirty, do we?"

"No way. I would never do anything bad to those sheets." I leaned into him for support. If I had to stand another moment, I was going to collapse.

I don't know where he got the strength to scoop me up in his arms and carry me to the bathroom but I wasn't about to protest. I relaxed and nuzzled up next to his warm body as he walked into the master bath attached to the bedroom.

He sat on the side of the large tub and held me in his lap, which was almost as comfortable a feeling as the bed. I didn't see him turn the water on but I could hear it running behind me.

"Let's get these clothes off you," he said in a low, rumbling voice. He shimmied my t-shirt over my head, one of his hands grazing the sensitive base of my wings.

Okay, so maybe I was thinking about sex just a teeny bit. How could I not when the sexiest being I'd ever encountered was undressing me?

He reached for the hook to my bra next. But the doorbell ringing stopped him before he could release the clasp.

He exhaled a breath and stood, setting me down in the same spot where he'd sat. "I'll be right back." He pointed to me. "Stay here."

Right. Last time I checked I wasn't an Angel who liked taking orders. And even though my body wanted to sink into the steaming water filling up the tub, my mind thought differently. Someone was at Siméon's door and I wanted to know who it was.

I waited until he was out of sight and then I slipped out into the hallway, tiptoeing across the thick carpeting. Deep murmuring voices gave me an idea that the guest was male. Demon? Human? I couldn't tell.

I edged along the wall until I got to the end, hoping any super-hearing beings present couldn't hear me.

"Is she here?" the unknown male asked. "There's a faint smell."

My shoulders twitched, begging for my wings to form. A demon. Oh, boy.

"Back up," Siméon growled. "You try to come in my home again and I'll kill you. Understand?"

The demon chuckled. "Somehow, Keller, your threats aren't as intimidating as they used to be. Why do you suppose that is?"

His voice sounded familiar. I searched my memory for a match but came up with nothing.

"Give me the note and get out of here," Siméon said.

"My my, you're in a hurry, aren't you? Are you sure you don't want to invite me in? I've never tasted Angel pussy before."

A commotion that sounded a lot like a fist hitting flesh had me too intrigued not to peek. With one eye, I looked around the corner and saw him. The green-eyed, dark-skinned demon who I'd seen leaving Siméon's office the other day. No, it was just yesterday but it seemed like a lifetime ago.

Blood dripped from his nose and Siméon had a tight grip on his shirt.

"Leave," Siméon said. "And the next time Malakai wants to send me a message, tell the coward to do it himself instead of sending one of his minions. I'm right here and I'm not going anywhere."

I backed up when I heard the name. Malakai. So Siméon was in contact with him. But it clearly wasn't a friendly relationship. I didn't know what to think of the information I'd just heard. I was exhausted and I had to admit my feelings for Siméon clouded my judgment.

As quietly as possible, I made my way back to the bathroom, finished undressing and slipped into the tub. The water hit the top of my breasts so I shut it off.

I needed to look busy, like I hadn't just spied on Siméon. I grabbed the bar of soap, lathered it in my hands and washed the ashy soot off my body. My neck, arms, breasts, stomach…

"Do you need some help with that?"

The soap slipped from my hands when I heard his voice. "Oh, uh, well." *Snap out of it, Abby!* "Who was at the door?" I squeaked. I actually squeaked.

He sat on the edge of the tub and pressed two fingers under my chin, forcing me to look into his eyes. "His name is Victor Adams. He works for my father. Mostly courier work."

"Oh?" I hadn't expected honesty. "What did he want?" Might as well go for the gold.

Siméon brushed his thumb across my lips. "It's not important."

"Really? Well, who's your father? Maybe I've met—"

"Abigail." He stopped me. "Let's not pretend you don't know everything about me. I'm sure your database mentioned my father, did it not?"

My cheeks burned. "Yes, it did," I admitted. "Although I only know his name. Nothing more." Partly true.

"That's all you need to know." He stood and tugged off his shirt. "You'll never meet him, I can promise you that. He'd eat you for breakfast. Hell, his courier wanted to eat you for breakfast. Malakai isn't like any demon you've come across."

"Is he behind the demon revolution?" The words slipped out of my mouth before I could stop them. Some spy I was.

Siméon silently fumbled with his belt buckle, not giving me eye contact. "Is that what you think?"

"I don't know."

"Do you suspect I'm involved? That Judd character seems to have a strong opinion on the matter."

"No," I answered without a smidge of doubt in my voice. "You don't have anything to gain from destroying Demon Control. But maybe Malakai does. What do you think?" *Please say you consider it a possibility and want to help me stop him.*

His pants fell to the floor and he stepped into the tub then wedged his body behind mine, straddling me between his powerful legs. "I think," he began, gathering my hair into a ponytail, "that you should leave the investigation to the other Angels. You're with me now and I plan to keep you safe from any harm."

Hmm... *That* definitely wasn't one of the conditions I'd agreed to. I nestled my shoulder blades against his chest and closed my weary eyes.

For now, I'd humor him.

Chapter Eighteen

I pressed my knees together and adjusted the hem of the peach and cream print sundress Siméon had bought for me. How he'd ordered it and had it delivered to his front door before I'd woken was beyond me. But here it was. A dress. On me.

I couldn't remember the last time I'd worn one, or I'd simply blocked it out of my memory. Probably I'd worn one on a date with Felix once…or twice.

Blah. *Don't go there.*

"You look beautiful, love." Siméon saved me from rehashing the ugly memories. His silvery eyes burned into me from the driver's seat, dropping slowly down to my bare legs.

I clenched my knees tighter but the heat the man produced burrowed deep inside me. Dang it. How could he make me want him with a simple look?

We pulled to a stop in front of a two-story brick and frame house with a large wraparound porch located on a large lot in the small town of Erie, about thirty minutes north of Denver. The background of the photo on Siméon's desktop immediately came to mind.

The sun had set an hour ago but the house was brightly lit from the inside out. Every window on the first floor framed humans laughing and talking. Children swung with glee on the porch swing and ran in and out of the open front door. Their mothers sat in wicker chairs and gossiped nearby.

And they all knew I was an Angel.

I couldn't try to pretend to be one of them like I did with every other human I'd ever met. Blending in to the crowd would be impossible. Even worse, they knew Angels were the reason Siméon had been deported to Hell twice before.

I let out a nervous sigh. "I might feel a little more comfortable meeting your family if I had underwear on underneath this thing. I'm not exactly great with humans in the first place."

Siméon had ordered a dress, sweater, matching bag and sandals but conveniently had forgotten the rest of the outfit. Everything I had on was lovely, and more than I could afford with a year's savings, I was sure, but a pair of panties would have been nice.

He leaned over and ran his warm hand up the inside of my thigh. "Sorry, sweetheart. It'll be our little secret, okay?" He kissed me as his fingers wedged up further, pressing up against my clit.

I half gasped, half moaned and thought maybe the no-panties dilemma wasn't such an awful thing.

Until I heard a rapping sound on Siméon's window.

"Hello? Siméon! Are you coming in anytime soon?" Harley's muffled yell startled me and I pushed him away.

Siméon chuckled and kissed my cheek.

"It's so not funny," I muttered and tugged my hem back down again.

He rolled down his window an inch. "Give us a moment, Harley. Go tell your Nana Naomi we'll be right in."

I swear I could hear her eyes roll followed by hands planted firmly on hip as she swerved and stomped back to the house. Great.

"I think she really likes you," Siméon said with a devilish grin.

"Oh, ha ha. She hates me and I'm sure she'll have the rest of your family doing the same once they hear about where your hand was a moment ago."

"They'll love you and even if they don't it doesn't matter what anyone thinks of us. Remember?" He didn't wait for a response as he pulled me closer and pressed his warm lips to mine.

My cell phone buzzed and vibrated inside my new peach clasp purse sitting on my lap. I gulped down the dread. It was probably Judd again. He'd called five separate times today without leaving a message. Mostly while I'd been asleep in Siméon's bed. It hurt like crazy that I wouldn't see him for who knows how long. If he ever agreed to see me again, that was.

"He's relentless, isn't he?" Siméon shook his head and sat back in his seat. "Why don't you answer it?"

"You don't mind?" I gestured toward the crowd slowly forming on the porch, waiting to meet the Angel.

"He'll just keep calling if you ignore him. I'll meet you inside." He kissed my cheek and left me to answer Judd's call.

"Hello?" I said more meekly than I'd intended. *Sure, Abby, own up to the guilt with the very first word out of your mouth.*

"Hey, Abby." He sounded relieved. Not at all angry. "Are you alone?"

"Alone as can be. What's up?"

"MOG told me why you went with the half-breed." He said half-breed as if it were acid in his mouth. "I just want you to know I don't think you should proceed with this mission if you don't want to. I'm sure MOG would understand. You're not safe with him. And MOG says his father is even more of a threat."

I held my tongue. I could argue the fact that neither Siméon or Malakai had been proven to be a part of the revolution but I knew Judd wouldn't listen to reason. That was why I was here. To find the truth. I glanced over to where Siméon was being greeted. Handshakes and pats on the back.

A couple of children grabbed onto his legs and he leaned over to ruffle their hair.

"I'm not in any danger at the moment," I said. "But you'll be the first person I call if I need backup. Okay?"

He sighed into the phone. "I don't like this one bit. I swear, Abby, if I find out he's hurt you or persuaded you to do something you don't want to, forget about deportation, I'll kill the motherfucker."

"Aw, that's sweet," I teased. "You really do care about me."

"I'm not kidding, Abby."

"I know. Relax, macho man. I'll be fine. And I want you to trust that I'm here to get a job done. I owe you and all the other Angels at least that." My error had altered their lives significantly, after all.

"Bullshit. You don't owe anybody anything and if you even think about blaming yourself for the building burning down then I'll drive over to that half-breed's house and bring you back with me kicking and screaming. I know you, honey. Don't let guilt be the reason why you're doing this. It'll only get you into trouble."

I closed my eyes and imagined him smiling that cute half-grin. "I miss you," I said.

He cleared his throat. "Miss you too… I, uh… Hey, are you going to make it for Lois' memorial? It's noon tomorrow at the GA center."

Hot tears welled up in my eyes. "She's really gone then?" I hadn't wanted to fully believe it.

"Yeah, the human authorities didn't find any bodies but her car was still in the garage close to where a car bomb had gone off."

"Damn. They're fighting dirty, aren't they?"

"They're evil, Abby. They'll do whatever it takes. So can you come tomorrow?"

"I'd better not. I don't want to lead any bad guys to the GA center. But I'll be thinking about you."

He chuckled. "Honey, I'm always thinking about you. Be safe, okay? I'll do my best to investigate from this end. I already sent the bug into the lab and Felix, Pauline and I are going out to question demons who have worked with Siméon in the past. It would be helpful if we knew more about Malakai."

I ignored the Pauline bit. "Look up Victor Adams. I found out this morning he's Malakai's courier." Thankfully, they could access the Demon Control files from any Angel facility.

"Victor Adams. Got it. Good job, Abb. I'll talk to you soon. And don't forget you promised to call me if you feel the least bit threatened."

"No problem. Oh and Judd?"

"Yeah."

"Congrats on getting your Angel status back. You should've had it all along."

"Thanks. And no shit. Talk to you soon."

I snapped my phone shut and stuffed it back into my purse, feeling like a heavy weight had been lifted from my shoulders.

Not only was Judd talking to me, he was helping me.

* * * * *

Siméon held my hand as he introduced me to his family members. I'd counted three nephews, one niece, a multitude of greats and even one great-great. But his sister was who I was most curious about. She'd grown up with Siméon. They shared the same mother.

She'd possibly know something about Malakai.

I scanned the crowd who'd stopped laughing and talking to stare at me. Maybe waiting for me to do something angelic or miraculous, like cure a disease or part a body of water. Or maybe even glow with innocence and purity under a golden halo. Huh. Like that was going to happen.

"So where's the birthday girl?" I asked, breaking the silence.

"Right behind you, Angel." I heard a woman's soft voice.

Siméon whirled me around and led me to the corner of the room. Sitting in a wheelchair was a tiny elderly woman. I wondered how much older than her brother she was. She couldn't have been younger than eighty years.

"What are you doing hiding in the corner, Naomi?" Siméon asked. "That's so unlike you."

"Yeah, well, some of us aren't as pushy as others," she said. "I was simply waiting my turn to be introduced."

"Of course. Naomi, this is Abigail." He peered down at me with a slight grin. "Abigail, this is the birthday girl, Naomi."

"Nice to meet you," I reached out to shake her hand.

"Nonsense," she said. "I'll have a hug, if you don't mind."

"Oh, why not." I leaned down and awkwardly patted her back, afraid I'd hurt her delicate frame. Before I could stand, she grabbed my cheeks and squeezed.

"My, you are a beauty." She squinted her eyes at me as if trying to get a better look although she was only inches from my face. "Are all the Angels this gorgeous?"

"Well," I said through squished lips. I liked this human but I was sure she was only being nice. "I'm afraid I'm at the lower end of the beauty chain. Quite different from the rest of them. But thank you for your kind words."

She released me from the surprisingly tight grip and I edged back to the security of Siméon's body.

"Abigail's very modest," he said and took my hand again. "All the other Angels I've ever met nauseate me. She's by far the most beautiful." He brushed his fingers across my heated cheek. "Absolutely lovely."

"Ha!" Harley's voice boomed across the room as she strode toward us, looking more like a demon than any I'd seen before. Nose flaring. Pierced eyebrow arched in fury. Lips pursed. She stopped short in front of Siméon and gave him a shove.

He didn't budge. "Don't start, Harley. She's my guest."

"She's your enemy, you...you dork." She searched for a name to call her great uncle. I had a feeling she rarely disrespected him, if ever.

Her eyes met mine and I matched her glare. I'd had a sister growing up. I knew when to give and when to fight back. When to throw punches and when to duck.

I wasn't ducking this time. "Why don't you back off, Harley? I'm not going to hurt—"

Naomi interrupted. "Harley, honey, I understand your worry over your Uncle Siméon, however this Angel is our guest and you will treat her as such. Understood?"

Silent tension filled the air as Harley seemed to mull it over, still keeping one eye on me.

"Oh for God's sake, Harley," Siméon muttered beside me.

"Fine," she finally said, turning to Naomi. "But only because I don't want to spoil your birthday party."

Siméon pressed his hand to my lower back. "Shall we eat dinner then? I'm starving."

* * * * *

Dinner was amusing. Naomi told me vivid stories of Siméon's childhood. Apparently, he'd been a little demon from the start. All through school, he'd goofed off, Naomi explained. Somehow he'd convinced his teachers to allow him to not only pass but to give him a high grade.

"It used to anger me so," Naomi admitted. "And he was the same with Mother and Father. Siméon would break a vase after playing ball in the house and he'd come out of the punishment with a cookie in his hand."

Siméon cut in. "I believe you've given me a share of cookies yourself, Naomi."

Everyone laughed and I played along. Did they not realize the power a demon had over a human? How easy it was for them to persuade? When the laughter died, I turned to Siméon.

"Who was your father?" I asked.

"He was my stepfather, actually," he said. "We called him my father because he raised me. I knew no other until later."

"Yes." Naomi smiled and reached for my hand on the table. "Siméon wasn't aware of his actual parentage until he was an adult. And then, well…" Her face soured into a frown.

Siméon gripped my knee under the table. "How about a lighter subject?" He turned to a teenaged boy who was sitting to his left. "T.J., have you decided on which university you'll attend?"

I attempted to follow the conversation, especially since the boy seemed to glow when he talked to Siméon. He was obviously a fan. But my mind was elsewhere. Just what had made Naomi so grim? Malakai coming into the picture? Had something awful happened?

Well, duh, Abby. She'd found out her beloved brother was not fully human. But there was something else. Something more painful. Hmm…I'd have to investigate that a little further. Later.

After everyone had finished their desserts and Naomi had opened her presents the party began to die down. By the way, Siméon had bought her diamond earrings and said it was from both of us. Like I could afford costume jewelry let alone diamonds. But I got another big hug out of Naomi so I didn't protest. Humans were so weird.

Anyway, the families with small children said their goodbyes and left while the adults sans children made their way to the basement, which seemed to serve as a game room/bar. One of Siméon's nephews—darn, I'd forgotten his name already—pulled out two bottles of wine and began to pour the wine into glasses.

"Want to shoot some pool?" T.J. asked Siméon. He'd included himself with the adults but I guessed his age to be sixteen or seventeen. He was adorable, I noticed. His black hair—a strong family trait, it seemed—swept down his forehead and over his ears and he had dimples on each side of his cheeks.

Siméon shrugged and grinned playfully. "I'd feel awful if I beat you. Again."

"Ain't gonna happen, Princess of Darkness. You're going down this time."

I couldn't help but laugh. "Princess. That's a good one."

Siméon peered down at me, not amused. "You thought that was funny?"

"Hilarious, actually," I said. "You should go defend your honor before I lose all respect for you."

He dipped down and whispered in my ear, "I'd planned on doing that tonight when I bring you to the edge of insanity, thrusting my cock inside you until you scream my name." He winked at me and headed to the pool table. Speaking over his shoulder, he said, "But a game of pool might work just as well."

My inner thighs trembled from the rumble of his deep voice in my ear. MOG help me, I wanted the half-breed and couldn't deny I looked forward to going home with him after this party ended.

Damn. Was it almost over?

Naomi wheeled her chair up to me then. She was quite good at sneaking up on people. Or maybe it was just me.

My cheeks warmed under her scrutiny. "Hi, Naomi," I said. "Are you enjoying your party?"

"Eh." She shrugged. "I'm ready for a warm bed and a soft pillow."

I smiled. "I can relate." Boy, could I relate.

"Mmm-hmm. I bet." She nodded and the silver curls on her head bounced up and down.

"Pardon?" I examined her expression. Surely, she hadn't heard what Siméon had whispered to me. Had she?

"Do you mind if I steal you away for a moment?" she asked, dismissing my confused state. "I'd like to have a little chat before you leave."

I agreed and followed her to an elevator door I hadn't noticed before. So this was how she'd snuck up on me. Once upstairs, we sat in the cozy living room. A grand fireplace took up a large part of the wall. Above it, numerous family photos hung in a collage of wooden frames. One, I noticed, was of a teenage Siméon in a cap and gown, holding his diploma. He looked innocent and entirely human.

I sat on the loveseat where she could easily roll up next to me in her wheelchair, as she did without help. I liked that she was independent.

"Siméon seems quite fond of you," she started. "It's wonderful to see him so happy."

"Ah." I didn't know what to say.

She patted my hand and continued. "Is this odd for you? Dating a human?"

"Well..." How could I explain this to her? "Uh, it's more the demon part that gets to me, really."

She met my eyes square on. "I don't like to think of Siméon as demon. He's too good for that. And if you ask me, he's denied himself happiness for far too long because of it."

"Because of what?" I wasn't following.

"Because he doesn't have the full benefit of being human even though he's more pure than most people I know. If a human makes a mistake, we can be forgiven. If Siméon makes a mistake, he's sent to Hell."

"It's a little more complicated than that, Naomi." I hated to be the bearer of bad news. A demon was deported to Hell if they went out of their way to corrupt a human. It had nothing to do with what a human would consider a "mistake". Mistakes were never planned out and executed.

Demons didn't make mistakes. They made deliberate attempts to bring evil into the world. Siméon obviously hadn't explained this to his family. No wonder Harley hated me so much. She thought I sent innocent people to be tortured.

Naomi shrugged my response away. "Even so, I'm glad he's finally found someone he can relate to. Someone who knows all about Siméon and can accept him anyway."

I opened my mouth to respond but she put up her hand to stop me.

"He's watched patiently as I lived my life with my family," she said. "He's watched me get married and have children and watched as those children had children. You get the picture."

"Not really."

She continued, undaunted. "I'd love nothing more than to see Siméon get married and have a family of his own." She looked at me expectantly. "Do you understand what I'm saying?"

Boy, I hoped not. "Um, we should get back to the party, don't you think? They're probably wondering where we're at."

"Abigail, you could give my brother such happiness. How wonderful would it be if he were to marry an Angel?"

I stood and steadied my legs. "I'm sorry. I'm just going to go get some fresh air." *And get away from you.*

Marriage? Kids? A family?

Not with a demon. I don't think so. Heck, not with anyone with the way my life was going.

Naomi started to say something but I was out the door before she could finish. It was all too much. Siméon had said he'd loved me and now his sister wanted me to marry the guy. I'd never felt so wanted in my life. Yet I was sick with guilt over it.

I was here as a spy, for crying out loud. Not to fall in love.

How easy it could be.

I kept walking down the stone path lit by a series of solar lights. It led down to a winding creek, I could see from atop of the hill where the house sat.

I reached the edge of the creek, leaving behind the echo of laughter coming from the basement of the house. Taking its place was the trickling sound of cold water running through the creek. And...and another sound. Something familiar that brought a smile to my face.

Aerosmith.

My eyes followed the pleasant noise down the path to where it forked from the creek and wound up to a wooden building, smaller than a barn. Maybe a garage. It was barely visible from behind the trees that surrounded it. I could make out light filtering out of small curtained windows.

I grew curious. Was it yet another family member? A friend? Who would be out here missing the party?

Well, besides me, the coward.

Chapter Nineteen
ಐ

I followed the path up and listened as the music grew louder. A man was singing along with the song, *Sweet Emotion*. Nice. He was killing the lyrics but at least he was giving it his all. I gave him credit for that.

Gravel from the driveway crunched under my feet as I turned the corner and peered through the opened garage door. A man with a long black ponytail was hunched under the hood of a car. A convertible Citroën DS to be exact. Damn.

"No way," I said before I could stop myself.

The man dropped the wrench in his hand and jerked his head up, hitting it on the hood of the car. "Fuck!"

"I'm so sorry. Are you okay?" I sprinted over and patted his back—as if that could help his head. *Great job, Abby.*

He was wearing a black t-shirt that stretched taut over his broad back and shoulders. And as he turned around to meet my eyes, I noticed he had a striking resemblance to Siméon. Definitely a relative. Besides the fact that this guy had dark brown eyes instead of silver and, of course, much longer hair, he could've been Siméon's twin.

But there was only one thing on my mind. "Is that a Citroën DS?"

His dark eyes narrowed in on me. "1966 DS21. Who the hell are you?" he asked in a voice similar to Siméon's deep tenor. Before I could respond, he spun around and stormed toward the radio, flipping the switch off.

My enthusiasm didn't falter. "Do you have any idea how rare that car is? Tell me more," I said. "Did you restore it? Is it yours?"

"Who are you? The car police?" He looked me up and down as he wiped the grease off his hands with a towel. "Wait a minute. Aren't you supposed to be inside right now with the other partygoers, drinking and having a grand ole time?"

"I escaped." I took a step closer and ran my hand over the smooth cherry-red paint and the aerodynamic body design created years before its time. "Beautiful. If this is yours you are one lucky S.O.B."

He chuckled and brushed past me to open the car door. "You can get in if you tell me your name."

"Sorry. I guess I forgot to introduce myself." I blushed. "My name's Abigail. What's yours?"

"Abigail?" His lip curled up to a half-grin. "Siméon's Angel, right?"

"I came here with Siméon, if that's what you mean. Are you going to tell me your name?"

"Kaleb." He motioned toward the car. "Get in if you like. It has some of its original interior."

Ooh. Could one have an orgasm from sitting in a car? I was about to find out.

I took him up on his offer and slid behind the wheel. My hands traveled eagerly over the leather upholstery and then went to the wheel. "I had a refurbished 1972 Volkswagen Super Beetle until early this morning," I said. It was still so hard to believe I'd lost everything and I didn't look forward to when it all sunk in. What a mess I was going to be.

He slid into the passenger seat next to me but I kept my sight on the car. Mainly because this man's presence was just as air-consuming as Siméon's was. And here I'd thought demons were gorgeous. This human put most of them to shame.

"What happened to your car?" he asked.

I shrugged and gave him a quick glance. "Sore subject. Don't really want to talk about it."

"Ah. I can imagine." He slunk down into the seat and rested his hands behind his head. "I've been working night and day on this car. And that's only after I'd spent years tracking down all the parts I needed. I'd go insane if something happened to it."

I dared to meet his eyes and smiled. He sung out of key to Aerosmith. He looked like Siméon. He was a car enthusiast. *And* he wasn't a demon. "What do you think about cheesecake?"

"Too many calories."

"Eh, four out of five isn't bad."

"Excuse me?"

"Never mind." What was I thinking? I had enough heartache with Judd and Siméon. I turned toward him. "So, Kaleb, why are you out here and not at the party?"

He examined me for a moment before he leaned in closer. "Siméon and I don't get along," he said. "We try to stay out of each other's way. I knew he'd be here tonight and I knew he was bringing someone my grandmother wanted to meet, so I stepped aside. I needed to work on this car anyway. Unfortunately this is the only place I have to store it at the moment."

This was interesting. Everyone at the party seemed to adore Siméon. "Is it because he's part demon?" I asked.

"Sure. If that has anything to do with why he broke up my marriage."

My mouth dropped open. "How did he break up your marriage?"

"He seduced my wife on our wedding night. She'd always had a crush on him so it didn't take much, but still, my ring was on her finger. We were supposed to spend our lives together."

Oh, geez. What was Siméon thinking? I wouldn't have believed a word of it if I hadn't been the Angel to give Siméon a strike for this very same reason. Although, I had no idea he'd seduced his *nephew's* wife. How awful.

"Did this happen about five years ago?" I asked.

"How did you know?"

"I just know," I said. "I'm sorry that happened to you."

He waved my concern away. "I should've expected it. He'd warned me not to marry her and I did it anyway." He chuckled. "Mostly out of spite. I've been butting heads with Sim since before I could walk. I never understood why everyone took his advice and listened to every word he said. It always pissed him off when he couldn't control me like he could the others."

So Kaleb was immune to Siméon's persuasion. Fascinating. I wondered if he was impervious to all demons' influences.

He reached out and brushed his rough hand across my cheek. "Does he have you under his spell too?"

"Of course not." Not really, anyway. My vulnerability to Siméon was under a completely different category. Namely lust.

"Then why are you here with him? I didn't realize Angels and demons dated each other."

"We don't usually." I seriously needed to change the subject. "What do you know about Siméon's father? I heard he's pretty fierce."

Kaleb blinked at me and then a realization came over his face. "You're not here as Sim's friend, are you?"

"Yes, I am," I answered too forcefully. "I happen to enjoy his company. A little too much, in fact."

"It's okay. I won't give you away. Are you deep undercover, or what? Are the Angels trying to take down the demons?"

My cheeks were warm. Damn it. "What are you talking about? Angels aren't aggressive." Just avenging.

"Sure. Sure. So what are you up to? Are you going after Malakai?"

The name alone sent shivers down my spine. "What do you know about Malakai?"

"You *are* after him. I knew it." He cracked his knuckles and grinned at me.

"You don't know anything. You're a simple human."

"I know enough to figure you out, sugar. What I don't understand is why Sim hasn't figured you out. Unless…" His eyes drifted down my body and back up again. "Unless he's got it bad for you. He's in love with you, isn't he?"

"Demons don't have it bad for anyone but themselves."

"Which proves my point even more. You don't even like him, do you? He's just a pawn in your little demon takedown game."

This was getting out of control. "I do like Siméon. I might even be falling for him. We've even had sex…twice." Why was I explaining this to a mere mortal?

"But?"

"No buts."

"Come on. You can tell me. We're on the same team."

I pursed my lips shut.

"Fine. You want to know about Malakai. I'll tell you about Malakai. I heard he's been out of the country for the past few years, setting up a prostitution ring in Tijuana or something like that. My grandmother keeps a close eye on the guy. She's been trying to shield Sim from him forever now. It's a futile task, if you ask me."

"Why does she?" I couldn't help but ask. "Is he a big threat to Siméon?"

"At one time, I guess. I don't know the whole story but I heard that when Sim was just out of high school, he disappeared with Malakai. He was gone for about ten years before my grandmother saw him again. She'd worried about him but she never asked him what happened during that time and Sim never talked about it. I'm willing to bet he'd crossed over to the dark side while he was with his daddy. I bet he did a lot of bad things."

"And why do you think that?"

"Well, he came back a whole lot richer, for one. He set Naomi up in this nice house. He bought a business. He set up a college fund for everyone in our family then and for years to come. Where do you suppose he got all his money? Probably not from working nine to five."

"You're just assuming." I hated to believe Siméon had been truly evil. He'd only been deported twice for minor crimes against humanity. But...I guessed MOG wouldn't have known Siméon's actions if he'd been with Malakai, who was able to divert her visions.

"Believe what you want." Kaleb reached over and gently tugged on a lock of my hair. "Don't let him fool you, sugar. I'd hate to see an innocent Angel get hurt."

His eyes veered to something behind my shoulder and then back to me. And before I could protest, he leaned in and kissed me.

"Get the hell away from her," Siméon said from behind me.

I shot up to my knees and pushed Kaleb away. He easily fell back against the passenger door.

"What?" Kaleb gained back his composure. "I didn't see a ring on her finger. Not that that matters to you. Right, Sim?"

Tension and testosterone thickened the air and I wanted nothing more than to get out of the building. I hopped from the car and ambled past Siméon but he gripped my arm.

"What are you doing in here with him?" he asked me.

"I needed some fresh air and I saw lights on so I got curious." I gulped down the anxiety rising in my throat. "We were just talking."

"Go get in my car." He looked down at me with a hurt expression. No, maybe it was anger. "I need to have a discussion with my nephew."

I glanced back at Kaleb who was now leaning up against the Citroën with his arms stubbornly crossed in front of his chest.

"Don't do anything stupid," I whispered to Siméon. "He's weaker than you."

"Go, now."

I left without another word. I had a lot to think about and breaking up a family dispute wasn't one of them.

As I made my way back to the Jaguar, I forced myself to concentrate on why I was here. Malakai. If I believed Kaleb then the demon wasn't even in the country, let alone coordinating a revolution against the Denver Demon Control Angels. But I'd seen Malakai's courier that morning with my very own eyes, so I knew that couldn't be true.

Or could it? I was confused.

I scooted into the passenger seat and pulled out my phone to call MOG.

"Yes, dear," she answered right away.

"Expecting me?"

"Of course. Any news?"

"I just got unofficial word that Malakai has been in Tijuana for the past few years."

"Ridiculous. I can feel his presence, or more so the lack of presence. I know he's close."

I sighed into the phone. I really didn't want to ask if she'd been smoking again.

"Relax, Abigail. Just continue with your task. You're doing wonderfully."

"Gotcha." I hung up and sunk into the butter-soft leather, more confused than ever. If Malakai was in Mexico then how could he be behind the demon revolution? But why did MOG feel his presence? Ugh. Kaleb must be mistaken.

Before I could fully comprehend what I'd just learned, the driver's door popped open. Siméon got in and cranked the engine.

"Kaleb still breathing?" I asked, only slightly kidding.

Siméon shot me a glare but didn't answer. I guess he wasn't in the mood. Fine. Neither was I. We pulled out of the driveway and onto the main road when my phone, which was still clenched in my hand, buzzed.

I glanced at the screen. It was MOG's number so I decided to answer. "Hello?"

"Abigail, I forgot to mention something and I thought you'd want to know."

"Yeah? What is it?"

"Apparently, your friend Eli has gone missing. He didn't come home from his shift this afternoon and Judd's been trying to reach his cell phone but to no avail."

A horrible thought came to mind. "Do you think he's been attacked? He's not a demon control agent. He's harmless."

"There's no telling until I have a vision or he shows up. I'll have Judd call you if we find out anything. I must get back to work now. Take care." And she hung up.

Angel Vindicated

Chapter Twenty

I woke up when Siméon opened my car door. We were in his garage and I'd slept through the entire drive home. Home? Well, the entire drive to *Siméon's* home.

"Hi," I said to gauge his response, since all he was doing now was staring down at me with an emotionless expression. Was he still upset with me for leaving the party and striking up a conversation with Kaleb? Or was he upset because he'd actually heard the conversation? Oh, what did it matter? I had too many other things to worry about, including Eli's disappearance. Where could he have gone?

Siméon helped me to my feet and guided me up two steps and into his kitchen. A Nordstrom's shopping bag sat on the counter. Where had that come from? I hadn't seen it before we'd left and, believe me, a Nordstrom's bag was something I would've noticed. It was a rare species as far as I was concerned.

"This is for you." He handed me the bag. "I had my assistant pick up some items while we were gone."

"Your assistant?" I looked around the room. "Another family member I don't know about?"

"No relation," he said before bypassing me and heading toward his office. "Should be a nightgown in there. I'll be out in a moment."

"All righty then." I wanted some alone time anyway.

I slipped into the master bath since the bathroom in the hall didn't have any shampoo or body soap. A shower would do wonders for my mood.

Twenty minutes later I was wrapped up in a gigantic fluffy towel and was digging through the Nordstrom bag. There were a couple of pairs of jeans—how he knew my size was a mystery—a couple of nice tops and a silky black chemise. Still no underwear. Great. Well, beggars couldn't be choosers.

I towel-dried my hair for the third time and tugged the chemise over my head. It had thin spaghetti straps holding it up and the hem hit right above my knees. Not exactly cold weather pajamas but at least it was something.

Siméon hadn't made it back to the bedroom yet, I noticed when I walked out. It occurred to me that he might not want me to sleep in his bed with him. Especially after he'd seen his nephew trying to lip lock with me. Which wasn't my fault at all. I might've been lacking in the virtue department but I had my standards. Besides, after what Kaleb had told me about Siméon, I wasn't exactly comfortable being in close quarters with the half-breed. Maybe Judd was right about Siméon after all and I didn't want to see it. Blah. My belly turned over at the thought of Siméon being one of the bad guys.

"He can't be," I said to myself. "Nope, not going to believe it."

I found the linen closet and pulled out a pillow and a big silky comforter. It was sofa city for me tonight. The leather couch wouldn't be as comfy as Siméon's bed but it would do.

The fireplace was going when I stumbled, arms full, into the living room. Siméon was still in his office. I could hear his deep, murmuring voice through the closed door, probably talking on the phone to his mysterious assistant. Or maybe his maniacal demon father. Who knew?

I could always attempt to find out later. Sleeping on the couch meant that I might have a better chance of sneaking into his office after he went to sleep. See, there was always an upside to any given situation. Right?

Yeah, yeah.

I made up the couch and then sat on the carpet by the fire to brush and dry my hair as much as possible. Going to sleep with damp hair left a huge disaster in the morning. And without my usual hair products, it would be even worse.

The office door creaked open but I kept my eyes diverted, hoping he'd continue on to his bedroom and not pay me any attention because at the moment I felt more awkward and nervous around him than I'd ever felt.

No such luck. He kneeled down behind me and took the brush from my hand.

"What are you doing?" Gooseflesh rose on my skin from his sudden looming presence.

"Helping you." His voice was whisper against my ear as he put the brush through my hair, slowly and gently. "Or actually helping myself, if you don't mind. I love your hair."

I eased my tense shoulders and decided to surrender to his touch. No man had ever brushed my hair. There was something very sweet and sensual about it.

"I understand if you don't want to sleep with me tonight," he said. "But you should understand that Kaleb's stories always have at least two sides."

"You heard what he said to me?" I should've guessed.

"Sweetheart, my ears never give me a moment's rest. I heard every word you both said." He swept my hair over my shoulder and pressed his lips to my bare skin.

I shivered as an odd mixture of anxiety and yearning rippled through me.

"I heard," his lips gingerly grazed my neck, "you tell Kaleb that you were falling for me." Another soft peck just below my earlobe. "I heard you ask about my father. And I heard Kaleb tell you things to make you doubt me. I heard it all."

"And?" I swiveled on my bottom to face him. He was stunning in the light of the fire. Resplendent eyes against golden skin. Satin inky hair that dipped to his broad shoulders. I had to take a breath at the mere sight of him.

Get it together, Abby.

"Should I doubt you?" I asked, hoping he'd say no. I was eager to hear a valid explanation for everything. Why he'd seduced his nephew's wife. Why he'd disappeared with Malakai for years and had reappeared with an inexplicable amount of money.

"Please don't." He leaned in and kissed me lightly, feather soft against my lips.

I inhaled his mesmerizing scent but managed to pull back. "You said Kaleb's stories always have two sides. Tell me your side. Tell me everything."

He exhaled a breath and stood, holding out a hand to me. I took it and allowed him to pull me to the couch where he positioned me on his lap. Tenderly, he slid his hands up and down my thigh, pushing the short chemise up with each pass.

"Kaleb shouldn't have married that woman," he said, keeping his eyes on his wandering hand. "I don't know why he'd insisted upon it." His frown deepened. "She wasn't worthy enough to be a Keller. She slept around on Kaleb with humans and demons alike and she'd treated him as if he were nothing but a pet."

"Why did you sleep with her then?"

"I was at the end of my rope, Abigail." He finally met my eyes. "One of my few pleasures is knowing that my family is happy and well. And I was not going to let her ruin Kaleb's life. He was only twenty years old. He was naïve. I had to save him."

"Why on the wedding night? You could've seduced her before that and saved Kaleb the humiliation."

"I allowed the wedding to happen because it's what Kaleb wanted. He thought she'd settle down once he had a ring on her finger and I wanted to believe that as well. But it quickly became apparent the wedding was a huge mistake. The devious little woman approached me at the reception and I'd agreed to have one dance with her. It was innocent at first. She looked like a blushing bride, happy to be married…until she rubbed her hand against my cock and whispered she still wanted to fuck me."

"You're kidding."

"I wish I were. I'd known demon women who were less shocking. So that's when I decided it was time to end it for good. I took her into the bathroom, bent her over the sink and had my way with her until she screamed loud enough for everyone to hear. Kaleb rushed to see what had happened and saw us."

My mouth gaped open. "Way to prove a point, Sim. Geez. Couldn't you have done something else?"

"Like what? Kaleb's a stubborn man. He always had been. There was no other way."

The story was so horrifying it was almost comical. I suppressed a giggle. I could *not* let myself laugh at this…this sinfulness. This disaster of a story.

"Why are you smiling?" he asked in such a serious, solemn expression.

"Sorry. Didn't realize I was." I clamped my lips together. A sacred bond of marriage had been decimated, I reminded myself. It wasn't a laughing matter.

"You think it's funny?"

"No, not at all. I'm just not used to hearing the story behind the sin. I can't help but picture it." And how sad was it that the sight of Siméon having sex with another woman made me jealous? What was wrong with me? I really needed to check into that Angel therapy. There was something seriously screwy with my mind.

"Really?" Siméon's hand stilled on my thigh. "Does it make you think less of me?"

"Oh, well, no, I don't think so. I mean, I already knew you did it. I just didn't know why."

He tightened his arm around my waist and sighed. "It probably wasn't the best course of action, I can see that now. I have to admit it's been very difficult to fight the evil tendencies that come with having demon in my soul. But I try, Abigail. My entire life, I've struggled. I know that must be hard for an Angel to understand."

Boy, was he wrong about that. Struggling with evil tendencies? Me? Nah. "I think I understand," I said. "Sort of."

"Good."

"So tell me more about that." I lifted my head to meet his gaze. "Were you struggling when you were with your father all those years?"

His Adam's apple bobbed up and down. "I think I need a drink. Would you like one? Some wine, maybe?" He gently scooted me off his lap and onto the couch and stood to look down at me.

I wasn't sure I'd ever seen him nervous. Horny, angry and satisfied at times but never nervous. "Shirley Temple with extra cherries and a wedge of lime is my favorite," I said.

"How about something stronger, sweetheart?"

"I don't drink."

"Never?"

"Well, I get buzzed on half a light beer occasionally when watching a game with Judd but nothing more than that." Why couldn't I lie to this man?

His jaw twitched when I said Judd's name. "I'll get you a beer then."

"Super."

He disappeared into the kitchen and seconds later came back with a bottle of light beer and a glass of some sort of dark caramel-colored liquor. It must've been potent because I could smell it when he handed me the beer.

I scooted over, making room for him as he sat beside me and took a deep sip from his glass.

"So?" I asked, unable to help myself. "Where were you all that time when you were with Malakai? What did you do?" The longer he waited to tell me the more curious I grew. No, I hadn't done very well on the Patience Exam at Angels' Academy. What can I say? I knew my weaknesses.

He cut his eyes to me. The silvery color glistened chillingly against the firelight.

I gulped. "I don't mean to push…but…"

"It's okay." He shrugged and took another deep swallow. "I don't mind, Abigail. Of course I won't tell you everything. You'll never be able to look me in the eyes again if you knew some of the things I've done in my past. And I can't have that."

"You did these things when you were with Malakai?" I asked. "Our records show you've only been deported twice."

"Yes. Malakai's very clever to be able to escape all of your MOG's visions." A small peculiar smile came and left quickly before he turned to me. "You have to understand that I was very young when I first met him. I was fresh out of high school and I'd thought I had a normal human life in front of me."

"Your mother never told you who your real father was?"

"Never even a hint. So when Malakai showed up and forced my mother to explain, you could imagine how shocked I was." He downed the rest of the liquor in his glass. "And angry—no, furious—with my mother and stepfather for keeping it from me. How is an eighteen-year-old boy supposed to fully grasp that not only do demons exist but I was one of them?"

I patted his leg in an attempt to comfort since I had no idea how to answer his question.

He grabbed my hand and held it. "I left with him. I didn't even ask where we were going. All I knew was Malakai had taken an interest in me and I was equally curious. He took me under his wing and showed me things that made my head spin."

"Like what?" Did I want to know?

"He showed me how powerful I was, for one. He showed me how I could persuade humans to do things for me and with me."

"Sex?"

"No, love, I never raped anyone. I swear on my sullied soul that I never forced another being to have sex with me. It has always been mutual, just like with you." He paused. "I need a refill. Would you like another?"

I glanced down at the bottle in my hand and realized I'd somehow sucked down half and my lips were beginning to numb. "No thanks. One is enough."

I continued to sip on my beer in his absence. I had a feeling I was going to need a nice buzz to get through the rest of this conversation. My mind swirled with all the evil I'd known in the past—all the demons I'd punished—and I couldn't imagine Siméon, the half-human I was beginning to care for doing any of it.

He sank down on the couch beside me again with his glass full of the same potent liquor. Without bothering to look at me, he began again. "It was more about money and power with me." He stared into his glass. "I became drunk on it, addicted to it and that pleased Malakai. It wasn't long before he made me his second-in-command."

"His second-in-command. Huh." I let that sink in. "Did you enjoy that?" *Please say no.*

He swallowed down half his glass and finally met my eyes. Lord, he looked so sad. "At first," he admitted. "My whole life I'd wondered where these wicked urges came from and for once I was able to give in to them. Malakai *praised* me when I gave in to them. He'd made me think it was my destiny, why I was put on this earth." He shook his head. "I believed him, Abigail. I was young and incredibly naïve. I used those humans to steal for us, to lie and deceive for us."

"Us?" I asked. Already, the beer lightened the load Siméon was heaving onto my lap. *Such a lightweight, Abby.*

"Yes, us. It was supposed to be for us. Malakai and his crew, me second-in-command. What a joke. I'd realized soon enough it was all for Malakai. He'd exploited all of his people, including me and took everything as his own, only sharing when we'd obey his commands."

"What did you do?" My body swayed inadvertently toward Siméon. I tried to control myself but it was fruitless.

Siméon must've caught on. He set his drink down, lifted me back onto his lap again and held me still. "You really don't drink, do you?"

I shook my head no. "Tell me the rest of the story. I need to know what you did."

"I found out where Malakai kept his money and I took it. I left him a little to survive and seized the rest. I figured I had to do something good with it for all the wrong I'd done to obtain it. So I went back home to buy my parents a nice home and…" He looked back into the fire.

"And what?" I gripped his chin and forced him to give me his full attention.

"I found out they'd passed away while I was gone. Naomi said it was a car wreck. They died instantly."

"I'm so sorry, Siméon."

"It was a long time ago. Anyway, I saw that my sister had started her own family so I gave her money for a home and set up a college fund for her children. Then I opened up my employment agency. I figured it was the best way to give demons a chance to make their own living rather than manipulate and use humans."

"Has it worked?"

"For some. Not all."

I took a deep breath. His story wasn't as awful as it could've been. And, honestly, I really didn't want to hear any more. Some things were better left unsaid, right? Well, I thought so.

"Are you okay?" His hands rested on my waist, pulling me close. "You look lost."

"I'm fine." I faked a smile and maneuvered my body to straddle his lap. But suddenly remembered I had no panties on under this slinky piece of material he'd called a nightgown.

He enclosed me in an embrace before I could move and then said something that left me stunned speechless. "I know you're here in my home right now because you think my father or I have something to do with the Angels' attacks."

Like I said, I was speechless. How did he know?

He continued. "Is that the only reason you're here? I've let myself believe it isn't. I let myself believe that you care for me. Tell me, am I completely wrong?"

"No, you're not wrong. I do care a great deal for you." Probably too much.

He gave me a skeptical look but said nothing.

"How did you know about—"

"I may only have half a soul but my mind is fully intact, Abigail. Why else would the other Angels allow you to live in my home? Especially the protective one. Why hasn't he come to your rescue? Unless they all understand why you're here."

What was the point in denying it? He had me there.

"Are you angry with me?" I asked. I thought maybe I should've been scared out of my wits that my secret spy game was blown out of the water but I wasn't. I felt safe in his arms.

A frown pulled at his lips. "It's difficult to be angry when I'm so utterly in love with you."

I didn't think I could ever get used to hearing that, particularly from the mouth of a demon. "But you can't love," I said, mostly to remind myself.

"Tell that to my heart." He gripped my shoulders. "Trust me, Abigail, I never thought I'd love anyone and definitely not an Angel who thinks I'm foolish enough to embark on a demon revolution against the only thing that's regulating the evil in the world. Hell, if I could cease loving you, I would. Regretfully, I have no choice."

I paused, my hands pressed firmly against his chest. So he loved me...but regretted it. The thought fluttered in my belly and then rose to clog my throat. I swallowed it down and forced out my next words. "I don't think *you* are behind the attacks." I truly didn't.

"My father, on the other hand?" He actually had the nerve to sound offended. "You think he's the culprit and you think I'll lead you to him. Even now after Kaleb told you he's not anywhere near here."

"I heard what the courier said to you this morning, Sim," I admitted. "Why would Malakai want to see you if he weren't in town?"

"Ah. You were spying on me? How sneaky of you."

I ignored that. "Anyway, my sources believe Malakai is behind the attacks and I happen to think they have a good reason to accuse him." My beer buzz was officially gone and I was growing increasingly uncomfortable sitting on his lap while having this conversation.

"Your sources?" He chuckled and moved his hands to grip my waist, pulling me close so I was nose to nose with him. His next words were low and ominous. "Did they also tell you to give me your body so I'd dumbly point you in the right direction? Is that why you so willingly tempt me?" One of his fingers lazily curved the crease of my buttocks.

I felt my cheeks flame up. How dare he?

"Sure. If that's what you want to think, *half-breed*," I said with a bite but damn it if my eyes weren't welling with tears. I blinked them away. "Why wouldn't I believe you'd lead me straight to him? You used to work for him. His courier was at your door this morning." I attempted to stand, to get away from him but he held me down.

"No need to explain, Abigail. An Angel has to do what an Angel has to do. I just wish you hadn't taken the rest of my soul with you in the process."

Frustration burned inside me. I struggled to get away from him but it was in vain. His grip was too tight. "You infuriate me, Siméon." I swatted at his arm. "I would never sleep with you for any other reason than I desire you." I swiped away the blasted tears that had leaked down my cheeks. "Yes, I was told to do whatever it took to find Malakai but that has nothing to do with how my pulse speeds when I'm near you. Or how my heart bursts just thinking about you. And—"

"Enough of this," he said and then he kissed me.

I half-assed pushed against his chest, not really wanting to break away. Not when his kiss tasted so damn good and his touch felt so right. Boy, I was a sad excuse for an Angel, especially an Angel on a mission.

Oh, heck. Screw the mission. I wrapped my arms around his neck and practically ingested his tongue, wanting nothing more than to forget everything and be lost in this desperate moment of passion.

His arms encompassed me, holding me tight to his body and I couldn't protest. I wanted this. I wanted him. Damn it, why couldn't I resist him?

He broke the kiss and wiped my damp cheek with his thumb. "I didn't mean to make you cry, love. I'm so sorry. You can understand my concern though, can't you? I've never been in love before. Hell, I'd almost believed I wasn't able just as you said. And now it kills me to wonder if you're only here in my arms as a duty to the Angels."

"I told you that's not true."

"Prove it to me. Please."

I slid my hands up and down his chest to buy time. I did care for him. Of course my desire wasn't the only reason I was in his home but it *was* the only reason I'd given my body to him and why I would do it again without hesitation.

Did I love him? Maybe... But I couldn't allow myself to admit to anything like that when it would only lead to heartbreak. Imagine, an Angel falling in love with a demon? Marrying a demon? Having children with a demon? No, that wasn't possible. Having an affair and a friendship was one thing, anything else was asking for trouble.

"What..." My voice broke so I cleared my throat. "What would you like me to do to prove it to you?"

"Tell me you'll stop looking for Malakai."

I let out a nervous giggle. "I'm sorry Siméon but whether you like it or not, I have to do everything I can to find and detain him."

"*If* you find him, sweetheart, you won't be able to do anything. He's too powerful."

"Then help me." I could barely believe what I was asking of him. *Help me find and deport your father, Siméon. You'll never see him again but what the hell, he's a bad guy anyway.* Well, I had to do something. Not only had Angels lost their home and their possessions, some had lost their lives. Maybe even Eli.

"Do you know what you're asking of me?" Siméon said. "I can't turn on a fellow demon, especially my father who happens to be a Senior Servant. My next trip to Hell would be fatal. It's bad enough I helped you find Piper. If I do any more..." He let his words drift off.

I'd forgotten about that. "Then I should leave and find another way. I don't want you to risk your life having me here now that you know what my goal is." It was my only other choice. I wouldn't let Siméon die. Not because of my actions. Not ever.

I quickly stood to my feet and hurried to his room to dress. MOG would be disappointed in me for not staying and furthering this part of the investigation but she'd have to deal with it.

We could find Malakai on our own.

I grabbed the Nordstrom bag off the bedroom floor and reached in to pull out some clothes.

"Wait." Siméon came up behind me and threw everything in my hands to the floor.

I turned to look up at him, confused with his actions.

"I don't want you to leave, Abigail. You can't go."

"You know I'm after Malakai. If I stay, you'll be helping me. I won't risk being the reason you die."

"And I won't let you go out on an impossible mission. I don't know if Malakai is behind the attacks but whoever is won't think twice about going after the other Angels. You're safe here and as far as I'm concerned, you're staying here."

"No, I'm not." I reached down to grab a pair of jeans.

Without warning, Siméon lifted me and tossed me onto the bed. I landed on my back, bounced up an inch or so and fell back down. *Whoa*. How was it that he was so much more powerful than the other demons I'd encountered? I could at least match their strength. Did he possess some of his father's powers? It had to be. He was only human otherwise.

Before I could gain back my composure, he straddled me and pressed my arms to the mattress.

"Stop bullying me." I wiggled underneath him. "Do you think I'm going to let you demon-handle me?" He might have a smidge more strength but I could still take him.

He rolled his eyes at me as his hair fell, nearly touching my cheeks. "I'm not hurting you."

"But you're trying to control me. I don't like being controlled."

"I'm trying to stop you from running out of here and into danger. You're safe with me, Abigail. I want you to stay."

"And I want to go. I have a duty to my people and since you can't help me then I'm leaving. You can't hold me here forever, buddy. As soon as I get the chance, I'm gone."

"Jesus, Abigail. Why are so you goddamn difficult?"

I managed to squirm out from under him when he loosened his grip. I made it to the door but he was right behind me and was able to slam it shut before I could escape.

He leaned up against it and let out a sharp breath. "Fine," he said. "If you stay, I'll help you find Malakai."

I was confused. "But I thought you said your next deportation would be fatal? I'm not going to ask you to risk your life."

He shoved his hands in his pockets and shrugged. "I lied."

"*What?*"

"It probably won't be fatal. I'll *probably* get off with a warning. Hell, the Demon Council might even reward me for seducing an Angel. I don't think it's ever been done before."

"You're kidding me. You lied? You'll be rewarded?" Was he lying now? I couldn't read him.

"I don't really know, Abigail. I just don't want you to leave. I'll do anything." He closed the small distance between us and braced my face with his warm hands. "Stay the night, at least. We can work the details out in the morning. I promise you won't be disappointed."

* * * * *

Siméon's arm held me tight to his chest as he breathed evenly in slumber. I'd been watching the green digits on the alarm clock change for what seemed like hours. The sun was rising and I hadn't slept a wink. My stomach grumbled. I needed some sustenance.

And maybe it wouldn't hurt to visit the infamous home office before Siméon woke. He'd left me confused the night before. I hadn't known if or when he'd been lying and about what. All he could really tell me was he hadn't wanted me to leave.

So I stayed. MOG help me. After all was said and done, I'd still wanted him.

I gently lifted his arm, set it down on the mattress behind me and turned to see if he'd woken. His eyes were closed. Long, dark lashes shadowed his cheeks. His full red lips were parted, breathing in shallow breaths.

My mind marveled at where those lips had been just a few of hours ago, kissing every inch of my body, satisfying me to the core with his mouth, tongue and his…well, you know.

Ignoring my aching inner thighs, I climbed from the bed and slipped the chemise back over my head. Goose bumps rose on my flesh as the chilly air in the room attacked me. It had been nice and cozy in Siméon's arms and I was tempted to crawl back into bed.

My stomach grumbled again so I grabbed Siméon's dress shirt off the floor and wrapped it around me. His intoxicating aroma wafted up and tickled my nose. I covered my face with the lapel and inhaled.

If only things were different. Then I could love him back, give him everything I had to give. Instead, here I was taking everything I could take. He deserved more than that. But my fellow Angels deserved to have their lives back, as well. And as far as Siméon saying he'd help me find Malakai, well, I'd believe it when I saw it. I wished I could trust him. There was just too much at stake.

I shook the thought out of my head and tiptoed out to the kitchen. My priorities were set—food first, snooping later. My stomach wouldn't have it any other way.

I opened the fridge and my eyes veered to a Cheesecake Factory takeout box. *No way.* On top there was a note that said, "Enjoy, Abigail. Love, Siméon."

So maybe I could trust him a little. He definitely knew the direct route to my heart/taste buds. How could someone who buys me cheesecake be anything but praiseworthy?

I finished off a thick slice along with a large glass of milk, fat-free, of course and headed to the office. The house was silent except for the sound of the door creaking open as I turned the handle and pushed.

I stopped short and listened closely to the silence that filled the house. Could the man hear everything in his sleep too?

Nah. I stepped inside and let the moonlight guide me to the computer, where I sat down and hit the power button. The hard drive whirred and came to life. So far, so good.

The desktop picture of his family came up and I took a second to study it. Everyone I'd met at the birthday party was there except Kaleb. Poor guy. At least he wasn't stuck with the whore wife. Siméon had made sure of that. And he was a good-looking human. I was certain he'd find someone else in no time. More importantly, he had a sweet convertible 1966 Citroën DS21. Who could say that? Not many. I'd say he was in pretty good shape, if you ask me. *Really* good shape.

Okay, focus, Abby!

I readjusted my vision and clicked on the icon that simply read *Database*. Like I'd imagined, it was password protected. Hmm... I typed in a few guesses but nothing worked. Darn. Too bad I wasn't a hacker. My computer skills were intermediate, at best.

Frustrated, I sprang from the chair and paced the room. I stopped in front of the black metal wastebasket. A single piece of paper crumpled on the bottom caught my eye. I scooped in, picked it up and straightened out the edges.

The handwriting reminded me of the calligraphy from the eighteenth century, decorative and beautifully penned across the paper. Weird. I brought it over to the computer screen to get a better look. And read,

Siméon,

It pains me to realize my own son doesn't want to have anything to do with me. Ignoring me whilst allying with a bloody Angel. What kind of fool have you become in the years past? I was willing to forgive your precious employment agency as it's given me something to chuckle at over the years. Really, to think you could tame demons into living the sad, pathetic human existence. Oh, you are so naïve, my son.

I cannot forgive how you've turned your back on me. I'm your father, your leader, your maker. You know firsthand what power I can give you. And you've seen the devastation my band of demon brothers has done to these bitch Angels. We no longer need to be controlled by them. Imagine what the world would be like without their intrusions.

Power. Money. Sex. Everything we've ever dreamed. There will be no one to stop us once the Angels are out of the way.

This is your last chance, Siméon. Be rid of your little pet project and join me in this earth-changing venture.

~SSS

"Holy shit," I whispered. My hands trembled and I felt like I might throw up.

"Abigail. What are you doing in here?"

Chapter Twenty-One

I turned on my shaky heel to see Siméon standing at the door with his arms crossed, wearing only a pair of denim jeans.

Instead of lust filling my mind, it was anger. Wait. Make that full-on rage. "You knew and you lied." I slammed the letter into his bare chest and pushed past him. I didn't ask how long he'd known. I didn't care. All I could think about was getting out of his house and away from him.

What was I thinking trusting him? Making love with him? I was such a fool.

He followed me to the bedroom. "If you read this," he shook the paper in the air, "then you'll realize I didn't want anything to do with Malakai and his plan. I've completely washed my hands of him and all his evil. Don't you see that? Doesn't it mean anything to you?"

Siméon could've been singing a show tune for all I cared. His words meant nothing to me now. He knew his father was guilty and he didn't tell me. How could he not tell me? I'd lost my home because of Malakai. Angels have died at the hands of his "band of demon brothers".

I tugged on my jeans, stuffed my chemise into the waistband and tied his dress shirt in a knot at my waist. I scanned the floor and spotted my tennies. "I'm getting out of here," I said and jammed them on my feet.

"For God's sake, Abigail. Listen to me." He grabbed my arm and pulled me to him.

I yanked away from his strong grip and asked him the question that was on the tip of my tongue. "Did you know he was going to destroy Demon Control? Did you?" Heck, why didn't I just leave? I couldn't believe a word from his mouth anyway.

"No, that was a complete surprise." He reached for my cheek but seemed to think better of it and slid his hands into his pockets instead. "I would've warned you if I'd known. And I sure as hell wouldn't have allowed you to leave my house to run straight into danger."

Fine. I sort of believed that. "Did you know Peter Piper had a bug on him when you helped me detain him?"

"Of course not, Abigail."

The little voice inside my head said he was telling the truth. Okay. Good. "How long have you known your father was behind the rebellion?"

He dropped his head for a moment and then met my eyes again. "It's not important."

My heart sank. "It's important to me. How long?"

"I didn't think it would go this far. Malakai has always threatened to overtake Demon Control but it was always talk. I didn't think—"

"How long?"

He let out a short breath and spoke the next words in almost a whisper. "I figured it out when you identified Cesar Knight as one of your attackers from my database. I knew he was in Malakai's employ."

Before I could control myself, I lifted my hand and slapped him across his face.

"My, my," a strange voice came from the doorway. Startled, I jerked my attention from Siméon to a man with familiar silver eyes. He had platinum blond hair that contrasted against his golden skin tone. A heart-shaped face. Full red lips. Tall with broad shoulders.

My breath caught in my throat when the puzzle pieces matched up together in my mind. This had to be Malakai. The very demon who'd destroyed my home, car and all my possessions. He'd killed Lois and Christina, amputated thumbs and turned Denver Demon Control Angels' lives upside down. And now he was going to pay. I hoped.

I glared at him and took a defensive stance, preparing to fight.

The demon's lips curled up in an ungodly grin. Heck, every pore on his body screamed sacrilegious. Like a predator, he slowly stepped forward, staring at me as if I was his own slice of cheesecake. He spoke to Siméon through his perfect white teeth. "I didn't know you liked it rough, son."

"What do you want?" Siméon edged his body in front of me, placing himself between his father and me and I was relieved to be blocked from the pure evil the powerful demon exuded. "You have my attention now." Siméon's voice was calm and cool. "Say what you need to say and then leave."

Malakai let out a deep rumbling laugh and I peeked around Siméon to see that five or six demons, including Cesar Knight and Victor Adams, had poured into the room behind their leader. This didn't look good at all. My shoulder blades twitched uncontrollably, my wings begging to escape.

I was beginning to regret losing my temper and slapping Siméon. I could only pray he'd still be on my side. If he ever was.

"My son," Malakai began, "I'm afraid my craving to bond with you has passed. You've ignored me. You've embarrassed me. You've disappointed me. And now, as your father, I must punish you." He met my eyes. "Then perhaps the boys and I will have a little fun with your pet before we destroy her and the rest of her kind."

Siméon stiffened in front of me. "You touch her and you'll be violating the pact." His voice was a husky growl. "You'll be banished to Hell for eternity."

I gently patted his back, glad he'd stepped up to defend me.

Malakai chuckled. "Who's going to deport me, son? Angels have no control over me. Their MOG is powerless against finding me. Besides, the pact doesn't rule me. I rule myself."

"Then I'll kill you." Siméon hunched over then clenched and unclenched his fists. Every muscle in his body seemed to flex as he readied for battle. "You'll die at my hands if you or any of your minions lay a finger on her. How's that for disappointment?"

Malakai faked a yawn and the demons behind him laughed. "This reunion has been fun but it's time to move to the other location." He flicked a slender, clawed finger at his underlings and nodded toward Siméon and me. "Detain them," he said and disappeared, like a coward, into the hallway.

Siméon looked back at me. "Get in the bathroom and lock the door," he ordered through his gritted jaw.

Yeah, right. Like I was leaving him to fight on his own. He may have deceived me but I still couldn't help but care about him. Besides, I was sure a wooden door wouldn't stop these asshole demons from busting through. Before I had time to protest he turned and dove toward the enemy, throwing his body at them in full force. Cesar Knight and two other demons went flying into the wall, the drywall cracking behind them, with shocked expressions on their faces.

Yes! I wanted to clap and cheer but I knew I had to use that moment of surprise. I jumped onto the bed and used the bedpost to twirl my body around. My foot struck a demon who looked like a beefy Leonardo DiCaprio. He flew back and crashed through Siméon's closet door.

One point for the Angel.

Victor Adams grabbed for my legs when I landed back on the mattress so I leaped to avoid him. My wings burst free and I hovered as far as the ceiling would allow. Eight feet wasn't high enough apparently. He reached up with one hand, grabbed me by the hair and yanked me to the bed.

"Ouch, you jerk," I yelled, willing my wings back into my shoulders as I got to my knees. "No hair pulling."

Victor smiled and behind him I could see Siméon scrambling on the floor with three demons trying to pin him down. He wasn't giving up and neither was I.

I dodged Victor's next attack as he lunged forward onto the mattress. Then I brought my elbow down onto his back as hard as I could. Air gushed out of his mouth and I was certain I'd cracked one or two of his ribs.

"Take that, messenger boy," I said, ignoring the pain shooting up my funny bone. I felt quite proud of myself.

Until someone grabbed me from behind. Blond hair covered my eyes as a demon shoved me to the bed and pinned my hands down above my head.

"We meet again," Cesar Knight's voice growled into my ear.

I fought to push him off me but Victor had recovered quickly and was now restraining my lower half. "What should we do with her now, Cesar?" He gripped hold of my butt cheek and squeezed.

Cesar laughed into my hair. "Whatever the hell we want."

I don't think so.

I used the only body part I had that wasn't confined to give him a good old-fashioned head butt. Jerking my head back, I made decent contact with the demon's face. And then cursed under my breath at the amount of pain I'd caused myself. Thankfully, I knew it had done more damage to Cesar. Bones cracked and blood trickled onto and down my neck.

"You bitch," he yelled.

Great. Now I'd pissed him off. The two demons jerked me around until I was face up and splayed out on my back.

Cesar's nose was bleeding profusely but it didn't seem to stop him from wanting to kill me.

"Get her pants off," he said through a strained gurgle to Victor. "I'm going to teach her a lesson."

Oh crap. Didn't he want to kill me first? I struggled against their hold on me but I was completely restricted. Thick droplets of blood fell from Cesar's broken nose onto my cheek as he straddled my waist and held my wrists down. I hated this. I hated being under their control, being helpless to fight back.

I spat at Cesar. I jerked and wiggled. My wings burst free and I tried to hover up and away from them. But it was all futile. Victor had my jeans tugged down to my knees and of course I wasn't wearing any underwear. Damn it.

"It's time to see why the half-breed is so obsessed with you," Cesar said. His nose was healing before my eyes and the bulge in his pants told me he was getting his second wind.

Shit. Not this. Anything but this. I jerked around some more to let these demons know this wouldn't be easy. I'd die before I let them have my body.

Through all the noise of bodies struggling, slaps, hits and kicks, I heard a roar. A thunderous roar rose up and out, echoing off the walls of the bedroom.

Siméon.

It sounded like it was coming from Siméon. I tried to look past Cesar but he blocked my view. The next thing I knew, the two demons on top of me were swept to the ground by Siméon's forceful blow. He tackled them to the ground and swung and punched like a maniac.

Long scratch marks and welts covered his back and arms. His hair was soaking wet with both blood and sweat. I glanced on the floor and detected the demons he'd already fought and beaten begin to stir and rise.

Siméon had saved me. Again. But this battle was far from over.

I yanked my jeans up and zipped them, preparing to help Siméon. If I could only get my thumb on a few of them to even this out.

"Enough!" Malakai stepped into the doorway. His face was drained of color and his silver eyes were now a crimson red as he pointed toward Siméon, who continued to fight. "I said enough." Malakai's voice pierced my ears with only a whisper and I cringed. How did he do that?

He extended his arms in my direction and spread his long, clawed fingers. The air in the room grew thick with heat and the stench of sulfur. My skin felt as if it were being burned from the sun. My face flushed and my stomach turned. Whatever Malakai was doing made me weak, nauseous and lightheaded. And tired. So very tired. I slumped to the bed and struggled to keep my eyes open.

The fighting in the corner of the room stopped abruptly and Siméon looked back at me with wide eyes, his pupils dilated. "Leave her alone," he shouted and jumped to his feet. His body was bloodied and torn as he stalked toward the bed.

I sat up to meet him but a sharp, thudding pain in my head took the breath from me. I curled up in a fetal position and clenched my eyes shut.

"Abigail, stay with me," I heard Siméon murmur into my ear before I blacked out.

Chapter Twenty-Two

Heat surrounded me yet I was freezing as if ice water was running through my veins. I shivered and struggled to open my heavy eyelids. Too heavy. I needed more sleep. Just a couple of extra minutes, that was all.

"Abigail, are you all right?" Siméon was close. I felt his warm breath on my cheek and I instinctively inhaled it in.

"Mmm." That was nice. My tongue was stuck the roof of my mouth. I worked to fill it with moisture so I could speak. "More, please. So cold."

"I'm trying to keep you warm, sweetheart." Something soft and leathery adjusted against my shoulder. Something that smelled a lot like Judd's musky cologne.

"Abby, you up?" Judd's voice was a small distance away.

Siméon and Judd. Here together? My pulse sped up. Where the heck was I? I wrenched one eye open. Siméon was staring down at me with his eyebrows knitted together in worry. His face was a mess with caked-on blood. And I suddenly remembered how it had gotten there.

Malakai and his demons.

I tried to sit up and realized I was balled up in Siméon's lap. He encompassed me with his arms and legs. And this familiar jacket. Judd's jacket.

"Judd?" I scanned the dim room, only lit by a weak light bulb dangling from the ceiling.

He kneeled in front of me, his face streaked with blood, sweat and dirt. The injuries that had created that mess were mostly healed. "I'm right here." He shot an annoyed glance at Siméon. "He's just keeping you warm. You were trembling."

Siméon's fingers caressed my thigh underneath the jacket. "How are you feeling?"

My head was splitting in two, my mouth was parched and my entire body ached but I figured I had better not complain since I was the only one here not covered in blood. Well, my own blood. Cesar's blood was dried on my neck and clumped in my hair. "I'm fine. What happened? Where are we?"

Judd's chilled rough hand touched my cheek. "We're going to get out of here. Don't worry."

"Out of where?" I took in the surroundings for the first time. Red brick walls enclosed the small empty room and the ground was nothing but concrete. Only a trapdoor in the ceiling. Huh. Were we in a cellar of some sort?

Judd stood and started pacing. "The half-breed's daddy has us locked up. I guess he's been a bad boy."

The memory of Malakai's letter to Siméon popped into my head and I tensed. How could I trust Siméon when he'd lied to me? My sight focused in on a freshly scarred wound running from his ear to his bare shoulder. How could I not trust him? He'd fought for me. And he was here with me now. Not with Malakai.

"We were blindfolded on the way here," Siméon said. "But I have a good feeling we're high up in elevation. Somewhere in the mountains. There was snow on the ground when we were walked inside and the air was colder, crisper. No noise except the wind blowing through the trees."

Judd rolled his eyes. "Abby, you ready to get up and walk around? Get some blood flowing through you? Get away from Satan's little helper?"

Siméon tightened his grip on me.

A new throbbing sensation pounded in my head. "I'm not moving until someone tells me what happened. Last thing I remember I was being forced to go night-night by Malakai's magic fingers. What did he do to me anyway?"

"I warned you he's powerful, sweetheart," Siméon whispered, glancing up at the ceiling every so often. "The rumor is he'd learned some of his tricks from a coven of human witches. He might've even taken some of their souls as his own to make him stronger."

"Witchcraft? Souls? Never mind." I'd save that conversation for later. How had I been so naïve to think I'd known all there is to know about demons? Siméon and I were going to have a long talk after we got out of here.

We? What was Judd doing here anyway?

I rubbed at one of my temples and nodded to my best friend. "When did you come into the picture?"

"Right after Triple S knocked you out, I guess. I was driving by the half-breed's house to check on you when I heard the commotion. So I ran in and joined the fun." He ran a hand through his mussed hair and leaned against the brick wall. "It was stupid. I should've called for backup but I panicked."

"And then he was ambushed," Siméon added.

"Thanks to you. You coulda helped me out but you just sat there holding Abby."

"Why would I waste my energy on you? I care nothing about you."

Judd snorted. "Yeah and you didn't want to mess up daddy's maniacal plan to take over the world, did you?"

Siméon's heart pounded against my back and the testosterone filling the air was almost enough to gag me. *Here we go again.* I slipped out of his hold and settled into a spot against the wall, cuddling up into the leather jacket. They could argue all they wanted. I needed to rest my throbbing head.

"I didn't want Malakai to take Abigail's life," Siméon seethed, apparently forgetting all about keeping his voice down. He stood to his feet and faced Judd. "And he nearly did before you showed up with fists blazing and *no* backup. I thought Angels were supposed to be semi-intelligent. Or maybe it's the male Angels who don't have a clue."

"Right, right. And you keeping Abby in your home where Malakai knew where to find you was real smart, *half-breed*. What the hell were you thinking? Don't try to tell me you care about her when you're the one who put her life in danger in the first place."

"My home was more secure than your Demon Control building." Siméon gave me a quick glance. "I thought she'd be safe from the attacks if she was with me."

"You were wrong, chump. Now we're all screwed."

I rubbed at my eyes, trying to ignore the fact that they were talking about me as if I wasn't my own person and didn't make my own decisions. More pressing issues needed to be discussed. Like how we were going to get out of here.

The sound of footsteps on the ceiling made us all pause and look up. The trapdoor swung open and there was some murmuring and cursing before a body was dropped down. A man with long black hair and tattered, bloody clothes fell to his hands and feet with a thump.

A breathy moan pushed out of him as he collapsed onto his stomach.

"Kaleb." Siméon went to his nephew's side and, with Judd's help, propped him up against the wall in a sitting position. They pulled the blindfold from his eyes.

"Kaleb?" I forgot about my headache and forced myself to walk to where he slumped over, beaten badly but still alive.

"Who's this?" Judd asked, standing back.

"He's Siméon's nephew."

"Human?"

"Yeah."

Kaleb's bruised and swollen eyes met mine as I kneeled in front of him to gauge his injuries. Humans were so fragile and it was odd seeing someone as powerfully built as Kaleb in such a delicate state. He had a laceration on his cheek and his upper lip was cracked as well.

"He's bleeding," Siméon said, tilting up Kaleb's chin. "Right here." He pointed to two thin cuts under Kaleb's jaw. They weren't deep enough to reach a major artery but the amount of blood seeping out wasn't something to ignore. "And here." Siméon ripped open what was left of Kaleb's t-shirt to display two more slices across his abdomen.

Kaleb squirmed a little. "I just need to walk it off. Get out of my way."

"Don't move." I slipped out of Siméon's dress shirt, bunched it up and pressed it to his neck. "How did this happen?"

"Malakai's henchmen showed up at Naomi's house."

Siméon stiffened beside me. "Is she okay?"

"She wasn't there." His breathing was ragged as he spoke. "No one was. Everyone was at church. Those fuckers found me in the garage."

"Did they hurt the car?" I couldn't help myself. MOG forgive me.

Kaleb smiled then winced. "No, sugar, they didn't hurt the car. Just me. One of 'em slashed me with his sharp-ass fingernails. I didn't know some of 'em have claws."

"The older ones do," Siméon said, solemnly. "I'm sorry they went after you. I don't know why…" He let his words fade then turned to me. "Can you heal him?"

"Me?" I'd heard of rare occasions where Guardian Angels had licked their human's wounds to quicken the healing times. There was something in an Angel's saliva that could multiply a human's platelet count, speeding up the healing. But as an Angel who'd had very little contact with humans, I'd never seen it done or attempted it. I glanced back at Judd, who'd stopped pacing and was now giving me his full attention, his arms braced tight in front of him.

"Don't look at me, honey. My tongue is for women only."

"Tongue?" Siméon and Kaleb both asked at the same time.

I turned back to Siméon. "I'll have to lick the wound to heal him. I've never done it before so I'm not sure how effective it is."

Siméon drew out a breath. "That's the only way? Isn't there some sort of miraculous healing prayer you can say?"

Oh, geez. If there was, I sure the heck didn't know it. "It doesn't work that way," I said.

His red lips twitched up to a brief scowl. "Fine. Do it quickly. We need him strong enough to walk, at least and if he's lost too much blood he'll be nothing but deadweight." He shot up and walked to the other side of the room.

I rolled my eyes to the ceiling. Like this was *my* idea. Sheesh. Like I really wanted to lick Kaleb's nasty wounds and taste blood. I bit back a few curse words that were bubbling at my throat and turned my attention to Kaleb. "You mind?"

He grinned and winced again. "Hell no. Go for it, sugar."

I took a calming breath and then removed the cloth I had pressed against his neck. New blood immersed from the edges and trickled down his neck. Why did Dracula come to mind? Yuck. I definitely had no desire to suck Kaleb's blood. Quite the opposite, actually.

It'll be over with soon enough, I promised myself as I leaned over and closed my eyes. I pressed my tongue against his salty flesh and ran it over the deeper of the two cuts.

He hissed in my ear and gripped my hand.

"Sorry," I said, tongue still hanging out. I pulled it in and tasted the mixture of salt and copper run down my throat. It wasn't too horrible. It wasn't cherry cheesecake but it wasn't awful either.

More important, it seemed to be working already. The redness around the edges paled and the blood clotted.

"How's it look?" he asked.

"Better." I mentally patted myself on the back. Who knew I could heal people? Not me.

I went on to the next cut and got the same result. A burst of excitement rushed through me and I got the sudden urge to mend every laceration on the man's body. Eagerly, I moved on to the slices on his abdomen. Then his cheek. His lip...

Kaleb cleared his throat, breaking my concentration. "Is it wrong," he met my eyes, his pupils enlarged, "that I'm getting a hard-on from this?"

"Yes," both Judd and Siméon barked out.

"Very wrong," I said with a stern warning but couldn't help but smile.

Judd stormed over and kneeled beside me. "Are you almost done?"

"I guess." I shrugged. "What about broken bones? Do you have any?" I asked Kaleb.

He tried to sit up and cringed. "Probably a couple of ribs..." He lifted his hand. "And I think I broke a few bones in my hand when I got in a shot...But I'll be okay. Thanks."

I patted his knee, watching curiously as his bruised swollen eyes minimized and gained some normal color back. "Those bones should heal faster than normal since I'm in your blood system now." I turned to Judd. "Right?"

"The hell if I know." Judd got to his feet and started pacing again.

How long were we going to have to stay in this room until Malakai decided to finish us off? If that was his plan anyway. He'd obviously planned on killing off the Angels. But what about Siméon and Kaleb? Kaleb wasn't a threat to anyone but Siméon. He didn't seem to be on Malakai's good side, that was for sure. But could Malakai kill his own son? Was Malakai, Satan's Senior Servant, *that* evil?

I took another sweep of the room and the simplest thought occurred to me. The trapdoor appeared to be wooden and easily breakable by any Angel or demon. What were we waiting for?

I caught both Siméon and Judd's eyes and motioned them over. They huddled in.

"What's up?" Judd asked, sending an annoyed look at Siméon when their shoulders touched.

I grabbed Judd's shirt to warn him I meant business. "Why is it we're not breaking through that door and getting the heck out of here?" I kept my voice as quiet as possible. Didn't want to the bad guys to hear me.

Siméon chuckled. "Do you think they're going to make it that easy?"

"Why don't you tell us, half-breed?" Judd said. "It's your daddy who put us in here."

Ugh. "Listen," I growled. "What's our other choice? Wait for them to come to us? Why not take them by surprise?"

Kaleb braced his hand on my shoulder. "She's got a point. What's your plan? I don't have any of your powers but I'll do my best."

I thought it over for a second. "Siméon seems to be the strongest." I put my finger up before Judd could object. "He could climb up there, kick the sucker wide open. Judd can follow and you two can distract whatever guards are up there until I can hover up with Kaleb. What do you think?" I glanced from silver eyes to blue to brown and back again.

Siméon spoke first and I was glad since I'd given him the biggest duty. "I can do that. You know I'll do anything for you." He pushed a lock of frizzed out hair behind my ear.

I gave him a big smile. Then looked for Judd's answer. "Well?"

His mixed expression transformed slowly from irritation to acceptance. "Fine. Let's do it. But we need to keep the conversation going so whoever's up there won't catch on."

Before I could blink Siméon set to action. He gripped the wall and started climbing. "You're an imbecile, Judd," he said.

Judd smiled. "Me? You're the reason we're here in the first place, half-breed. If it wasn't for you and your daddy we wouldn't be locked up in this Hell hole."

Super. I guess conversation meant more insults.

Judd persisted. "What is that smell anyway? Is that what demon shit smells like? Damn. You smell that, Abby?" He didn't wait for me to reply because Siméon had reached the door, his entire upper body flexing as he held on. "Did you shit your pants, half-breed? Did your daddy scare you shitless?" he laughed.

I bit my lip. Maybe Judd and I could go to Angel therapy together. He really had a sick sense of humor.

Kaleb joined in. "I didn't know Angels were such assholes. Why don't you shut the fuck up, fairy boy?" He turned to me with a boyish grin, split lip gone. "S'cuse my language."

At least he was feeling better.

Judd spouted out a few more remarks while keeping his attention on what was happening above. Siméon looked down at me and mouthed, "Ready?"

I jumped to my feet and pulled Kaleb with me, then nodded to Siméon. He released one foot from its grip on the ceiling, bent his leg and kicked up with a swiftness I'd never witnessed before.

As I'd suspected, the door tore off its hinges and flew somewhere out of sight. "Go!" he yelled as he launched himself through the hole.

Judd went second. It had been years since I'd seen his wings spread to their full length and it was an amazing sight.

Glimmering, feathery translucence filled a good portion of the room as he flew up and out the trapdoor.

"Holy shit," Kaleb murmured, eyes huge as he witnessed the act. "You all really have wings?"

"You can see that?" Interesting. Not only was this human above a demon's influence, he was able to see Angels in action. But that was another discussion for a later time.

I heard a struggle above and wondered for a moment if my job should be to guard Kaleb below or join in on the fight.

Oh, heck. I couldn't let Sim and Judd do all the work. "Hang on to me, Kaleb. We're going up." I sprouted my wings and braced my hands on his waist. I'd have no problem lifting his weight but his height might make this awkward.

Once he seemed to get over the shock, Kaleb wrapped his arms around me. "No one is ever going to believe this," he mumbled in my ear.

Black locks of silky hair fell into my face. I blew it away from my mouth. "Don't tell them then," I said and willed my wings to flap, sending us up.

Chapter Twenty-Three

Kaleb's head hit the ceiling when we reached the top. Oops.

"Sorry." Okay, maybe it wasn't the best idea to try to fit us both through at the same time.

Kaleb didn't complain though. He grabbed hold of the frame of the small trapdoor and pulled himself up with my help. I followed quickly, maneuvering through the hole and onto the floor above, where I quickly willed my wings back in and situated myself in a defensive stance in front of Kaleb.

It was quiet. Too quiet.

I noticed the boys had taken care of two demons, one with his heart ripped out of his chest. The nasty looking organ was lying on the floor next to his limp body. Siméon's bloody hand told me he was the perpetrator.

"Little much, Sim. Sheesh." I wasn't sorry I'd missed that. I swallowed down the moisture filling my throat. I would *not* allow myself to vomit.

"Better him than you," Siméon said, throwing me a much needed grin.

The other demon was in a headlock via Judd's arms. "Do you want us to do the same to you?" Judd asked the demon, who I recognized from the attack at Siméon's house. He had spiky blond hair and large green eyes that seemed to be getting larger by the second. I decided to call him Spike. I would've tried to identify the other demon but I didn't want to heave and I knew I would if I took another look.

"Fuck you," Spike choked out.

"Where are the others?" Judd asked, his voice a deep growl.

Great question. Why would Malakai only leave two demons to guard us? It didn't make any sense.

I did a swift scan of the room. We were in some type of a cabin in the woods, maybe? A sheet-covered sofa sat in the middle of the one-room shack. A dusty bookshelf with a lit oil lamp on top was pushed up against the wall. Nearby, a wooden table and two chairs were knocked over, probably from the struggle. The windows were boarded up with plywood. And no light seeped through.

What time of day was it? I took a few steps toward the door but thought better of it. Who knew what would greet me on the other side. I turned on my heel and bumped into Kaleb's broad chest. I was about to apologize but figured it was his own fault for following me so closely.

"I've never seen a dead person before," he said. His face was pale and he looked like he'd had the same nauseated reaction I had.

"He's not a person," I said. "He's a demon." And I knew what would happen next. I pulled up a chair for Kaleb and faced it away from the dead body. "Here. Sit down and save your energy."

He followed my advice sans smartass remark. He *must* be feeling ill. "Listen," he said, grabbing my arm. "If we get out of here alive I'll give you my Citroën."

"Is that supposed to motivate me?"

"Hell, yes."

"I don't want to take advantage of you in your weakened state so I'll settle for weekend visits."

"You got it."

I heard the Hell Spirits coming and felt the gush of hot air so I decided to stand behind Kaleb and wait for them to take the body away. It didn't matter that the demon was lifeless, it was still an eerie sight. I could handle the heat and the sinister, black smoke but once they formed into hundreds of fingers and wrapped around the body, I refused to watch.

Siméon brushed by me and wiped his hands off on the sheet that covered the couch as if nothing had just happened. He didn't look at anyone as he spoke. "You may as well kill him or deport him, Judd. It'll be one less enemy to fight when the rest come for us."

I couldn't imagine what this could be doing to him. He was fighting for his life against his own father. No. He was fighting for all of our lives.

"Good point." Judd released Spike and threw him up against the wall. "How would you like to go home, demon? By my hands or by my thumb?"

I closed my eyes and braced myself for the sound of blood splatter.

"Wait," Spike cried out and I allowed myself to peek. "I'll tell you, okay. They're—"

Before he could say another word the door creaked open. I panicked and lunged for the lone intruder, tackling him to the floor before I could get a good look at him.

"It's me, Abby." Eli's voice in my ear was too good to be true.

"Eli?" I sat up on my knees and looked down at the Angel, goatee and all. He didn't look as tidy as he usually did but at least he wasn't covered in blood like the rest of us. "Holy cow. Eli! What are you doing here? Are there other Angels? Did you come to help rescue us?" My words slipped out faster than I could think.

Why would an Angel of Death go on a rescue mission? He wasn't mentally equipped.

Another question popped into my head. "Did they capture you too?"

"Sure," was all he said. He pushed himself to his feet and tucked a portion of his shirt back into his slacks.

"What the hell are you doing here?" Judd asked, still pressing Spike to the wall. "We've been looking all over for you."

I stood and gave Eli some space. He didn't look so good. Perspiration beaded his forehead and upper lip. His usual olive toned skin had drained to a pale yellow. His hands clamped and unclamped.

"Eli?" I gripped his forearm. "Are you okay? What's going on?"

"I, uh…" He gulped and pulled me to him.

I opened my arms to give him a hug but before I knew what was happening, he swung me around and held me tight to his chest with one arm. His other hand reached behind him and pulled out a gun. In a matter of seconds, the barrel was nudged against my temple.

Everyone in the room stilled, including me. Never in a million years would I have expected this. Not from Eli.

Was this a joke?

"Put it down, Eli," Judd yelled. "What are you *thinking*?"

Siméon took a step toward us and the gun cocked in my ear. "Stay back or I'll shoot her. I swear I will."

I wanted to form some words to reason with him but my breath caught in my throat. This wasn't the friend I used to joke around with while watching a ballgame. That man didn't have a mean thought in him.

Did he?

"Let Freddie go," Eli said to Judd. "Let him go or I'll shoot Abby."

"Dude, you gotta think this through," Judd said.

The barrel of the revolver pressed harder into my temple. "You listen to me, Judd," Eli said, his voice filled with malice. "You don't want to lose her, do you? I know how you feel about her." He backed up into the wall, taking me with him. "None of you want me to kill her so you'd better not try to pull any tricks on me."

"Eli," I gathered the courage to speak. "Don't do this. You know what will happen if you go through with this. You're already in deep shit for carrying a gun. Just put it down and we'll talk this through."

"Shut your big mouth," he growled into my ear. "I don't need some bossy bitch Angel to tell me what to do. Those days are in the past."

I gulped down the knot in my throat and centered my attention between Judd and Siméon, attempting to gain some sort of calmness. Judd looked furious, showing no effort to hide his new disdain for his former pal. Siméon was mostly expressionless, a hint of calculation behind his silver eyes.

"It's no use, Abigail," Siméon said. "The Angel has fallen. He's no longer one of you."

"What?" The words shocked me at first but it became obvious after I gave it a moment's thought. "You gave up your soul?" I asked Eli.

"I said shut up!" His body shook with what I thought was rage. Or maybe it was nerves?

"Relax," Judd said. "We'll do what you say. Just be careful with that gun." He released Spike-Freddie and put his hands up in surrender.

"Get over there and hold the human," Eli said to Freddie.

Sure. Pick on the weakest one. *Jerk.* I didn't like this new Eli at all.

The demon formerly known as Spike smiled as he crossed the room to Kaleb, pulled him to his feet and held his hands behind his back.

"Hey, watch it, man," Kaleb grumbled. "No need to get all frisky."

"You," Eli said to Siméon. "Open the door. We're all going to step outside. First you, then Judd. And don't try anything stupid."

"Funny you should use the word stupid," I muttered under my breath.

Siméon kept a keen eye on Eli as he walked to the door and opened it, revealing a thick wooded forest and a night sky, crowded with stars. Siméon had been right. There was a thin layer of snow on the ground and it appeared we were somewhere high up in the mountains with no signs of civilization in sight.

Judd followed him out the door, giving Eli the death glare as he passed.

Freddie pushed Kaleb by next. Kaleb gave me a weak smile. "Hang in there, sugar."

It wasn't until then that I realized my body was trembling and I was sweating bullets. No pun intended, trust me. This was ridiculous. I needed to get a grip. I needed to stop being the damn damsel in distress and find a way to knock that gun out of Eli's hand. As an Angel, he was just an AOD. His job was to come in *after* the violence had occurred. I was a Demon Control Angel. I'd been trained to kick ass and I could kick *his* newly demon ass across the Rockies and back again.

If only he didn't have a firearm pointed at my head.

He nudged me out the door and I got a good look at what greeted us. A large pentagram was painted in what appeared to be blood on the snow-covered ground. A demon stood at each tip, and Malakai stood in the center. His platinum blond hair hung low to his waist. He wore a long black robe and there was some sort of symbol painted on his forehead.

Cheesy son of a bitch. Could he be more cliché? And what was he planning? Some sort of a ritual?

He held out his arms, palms up and nodded toward us. "Excellent job, Eli. You've passed your test."

Eli stood tall behind me. "I am honored, your greatness."

Your greatness? I had a strong urge to jam my elbow into his gut. It might be worth it to get in one shot. One thing was for sure, I was never letting him watch my TiVo recordings ever again. Forget it.

"You've gotta be kidding me," Judd said. "You fucked up, Eli. You joined the wrong fucking side and you're going to fucking pay for this shit."

"Silence," Malakai warned.

"Fuck you, Satan's Senior Ass Licker."

Oh boy. Here we go.

Judd continued. "I was wondering what that smell was. I thought it was Siméon, here. But apparently it's coming from your mouth. Sorry 'bout that, Sim. Honest mistake."

"I said silence!" Malakai's voice boomed and echoed off the mountaintops.

Judd chuckled. "I thought I had anger management issues. Boy, was I—" He stopped mid-sentence, let out a whoosh of air and bent over.

I glanced toward Malakai to see his eyes glazed with red again and his hand was pointed toward Judd.

"Hey," I yelled. "Leave him alone, you jerk." I took a step toward Judd but Eli held me tighter and tapped the revolver against my temple, reminding me it was still there.

Screw this.

Instinct took over and I sprouted my wings. They whooshed up as far as they could, knocking the gun from Eli's hand. I hovered over to Judd, who had fallen to the ground. Willing my wings back in, I kneeled next to him. Thankfully he was still breathing. Just unconscious.

Eli ran toward me with the gun in his hand but Siméon grabbed him and threw him to the ground.

"How can you let them do this?" I yelled to Eli. "We were your friends. These guys just want to use you."

He got to his feet and looked to Malakai for instruction.

Malakai's eyes had transformed back to their normal color and he seemed to have gained his composure. "Just leave her," he said. "I'll take care of her if she tries anything." He swiveled on his heel and found Siméon. "Now we can get down to business."

Siméon crossed his arms in front of him and took on a macho stance. "I have no business with you. You're dead to me."

Malakai waved as if to dismiss Siméon's words. "I wanted the family reunion to be bigger than this but we'll have to make do."

"My family is not your family," Siméon said. "Leave them alone and let Kaleb and the Angels go. They have nothing to do with your anger toward me."

"Maybe but what better way to punish you? Torture your human relative and execute your Angel lover in front of your eyes. I think that would teach you a lesson, don't you?"

"Sir?" Cesar Knight spoke up from his spot on the pentagram. "Can we not just kill them all so we can move on? This is taking up precious time. And we must move to a different location soon before—"

"Shush, Cesar. We will leave when I say it is time and not a moment before."

Huh. Why the hurry? I wondered.

I held Judd's hand in mine and clamped my mouth shut, not wanting to draw any attention to us. He was here because of me and I refused to let anything happen to him. How the heck was I going to get him out of here?

I glanced from Siméon to Kaleb and found that I cared for their safety just as much as I cared for Judd.

How were we all going to escape?

Chapter Twenty-Four

At Malakai's command, Freddie dragged Kaleb to the middle of the pentagram and made him kneel in front of Malakai. I had no idea why. Kaleb was a harmless human. But these were malicious demons. There was never any rhyme or reason behind their evil.

Malakai pulled a dagger out from somewhere in his cloak and held it above Kaleb's head.

"Whoa there, buddy!" Kaleb struggled a bit but was held down by Freddie.

I jumped to my feet and moved to save him from whatever it was the demon was planning on doing. Siméon must've had the same idea. He moved beside me. But right before we reached the perimeter of the pentagram, a sharp pain pounded against my stomach and I flew back onto my butt.

Right. I'd forgotten about Malakai's power. I caught my breath and stood to my feet once more. At least it wasn't as bad as last time. At least I still had my wits about me.

Siméon stopped dead in his tracks and looked to me. "Abigail, are you okay?" He glanced back to Kaleb and to me again, probably deliberating which path to take next.

Apparently, Malakai's little magic trick didn't work on Siméon. Thank MOG.

"I'm fine." I took a calming breath. I was sure Siméon was strong enough to escape. If it wasn't for Kaleb and me, he'd most likely be long gone by now. He'd steered clear of Malakai for all these years. Heck, he'd even stolen money from him and survived. I was sure he could walk away now, if not fight his way out. He'd nearly beaten off all those demons at his home. If it weren't for me, he would've won.

And Kaleb. He was able to defy a demon's power of persuasion and view all our unearthly acts. As unusual as he was, could he also evade Malakai's power?

Could it be that Judd and I were the weak links here? Were we what kept Kaleb and Siméon in danger?

Kaleb looked over his shoulder at me. His arms were still clasped behind his back, held by Freddie. And the dagger Malakai grasped still angled threateningly above his head. Instead of fear, anger had formed on his stunning face. He was strong for a human, mentally and physically. He could survive this with Siméon's help.

"Save him," I said to Siméon, the words slipping from my mouth before I could stop them. "Save him and leave Judd and me. We'll be fine."

"I won't leave you, Abigail." Siméon's Adam's apple rose and fell.

Malakai chuckled and let the dagger fall to his side. "Therein lies the problem, my son. You've made the mistake of allying with the enemy. The enemy who will be extinct in a matter of months as far as I'm concerned. We are spreading the word of our plan and demons from all over the world are ready to join us."

That explained how Mikey Tyson in Golden knew about the rebellion. Damn. This wasn't good news.

Siméon shook his head. "Your plan is asinine, *Father*. The world would be chaos without the Angels. There is a reason for the Powers That Be Pact. The Lord of Hell, himself, realizes that. Without some sort of control on this Earth, there would only be pandemonium. And how could any of us benefit from that?"

Malakai's face lost its golden color and his eyes clouded over. "The Lord of Hell does not want us controlled by *them*."

He pointed the dagger at me and another shooting pain stabbed my gut.

I bent over but managed to remain standing.

"Do you see how weak they are, son? Who are they to think they can police us. We are above them. *We* are the superior beings. They are only pests to be exterminated. The leash will be shredded, son, and you stand there and tell me you would rather be on the other end of it." He shook his head. "I have no more patience for this."

What a freak of nature. How did Siméon grow up to be normal when he shared this guy's genes? Okay, maybe normal isn't the right term for Sim but he definitely wasn't the maniacal, I'm-going-to-take-over-the-world demon his father was.

I looked back at Eli to see if he was getting all this. Yep. He was. And he didn't seem to care. He stood lifeless with a big ole frown on his face. Not only had he given up his soul, he'd thrown in his personality as a bonus. I didn't know whether to cry or break out into hysterical laughter. It wasn't like I had friends to spare.

"It's true," Siméon said, glancing back at me. He was a striking vision standing there with the moonlight reflecting its glow off the snow and onto him. His upper body was bare and splattered with signs of brutal combat. His muscles flexed, ready for action at any given moment. "I'd rather live out my life in Hell than join in on your Angel hunt."

No. Those couldn't be the only two options. There had to be another way.

Malakai laughed. "As if I'd have you now. You are an embarrassment to me, Siméon. I'd had such high hopes for you. You were a miracle child, born of my seed planted in a human. It's a rare and splendid act therefore I was willing to ignore your weak human characteristics. I was willing to mold you and share my legacy with you."

Blah. Blah. Blah. No wonder Sim didn't want to have anything to do with him. He was bo-ring. Like pity-party-for-one boring. Like someone-pluck-the-feathers-out-of-my-wings-to-keep-me-awake boring. And he wasn't even done yet. I let out a sigh as he continued.

"You have failed me in so many ways over the years and I have turned the other cheek. But I can no longer do that. I—"

"Sir." Cesar lifted his hand cautiously.

Thank MOG somebody else stopped the insipid whining before I had to.

Malakai's eyes flared with anger. "Do you dare interrupt me, Cesar?"

"My apologies, sir but I believe it is of the utmost importance that we move on. Do you not smell them?"

Smell them? I sniffed the air, as did everyone else, including Malakai. The only scent I could pick up was pine and occasionally the odor of sweaty demon when the wind shifted in my direction.

"You all want to tell me what you're sniffing for?" Kaleb asked. "I can't smell a damn thing but B.O."

Siméon looked over his shoulder at me and grinned. "Angels", he mouthed to me.

Angels? They smelled Angels. A rescue team, maybe? I couldn't get my hopes up. How could they have found us?

I noticed Judd stir a little from the corner of my eye. Good. If there *was* a rescue team on the way then I wanted him to be awake to hold his own so we could get the heck out of here alive.

Malakai let out a low hiss between his clenched teeth. "Freddie, take the human away from me. There is a change of plans, I am afraid."

Freddie jerked Kaleb to his feet and pulled him out of the pentagram. Kaleb met my eyes and simply said, "Citroën."

I nodded. I loved the Citroën but my motivation to save Kaleb had nothing to do with a car. If anything, I could imagine a budding friendship between the human and me. We seemed to have a lot in common and I wouldn't mind hanging out in his garage, singing off-key right alongside him.

If we could just get out of this mess. I wanted nothing more than to have my normal life back.

"Siméon, my son," Malakai called. "Would you really like to be a hero for the Angels?"

"I'd only like you to allow Abigail and Kaleb to go free. That's all I ask."

"And Judd," I added.

Siméon let out a breath. "And Judd."

"I'll make you a deal." Malakai clapped his hands together. "You deserve to be punished and I have all the time in the world to kill off these Angels." He smiled an evil smile. "I'll agree to let them go...for now. We can consider it a head start, of sorts."

"And?" Siméon asked.

"Before they leave I would like to see your precious pet press a final thumbprint to your heart."

"I won't do that," I said. "No way. That's not going to happen." Just the thought of Siméon suffering in Hell brought stinging tears to my eyes.

"No?" Malakai chuckled. "Hell is where Angels believe demons belong, is it not? Are you telling me you don't agree?"

"Siméon is different."

Malakai lowered his head as if to consider this and then gave me his attention again. "Do you not know that being different will only get you in trouble?" He smiled again and let his eyes drop down and back up my body. "Maybe you do know that."

"I—"

Siméon put up a finger for me to wait. "And how do I know you'll stick to your word? If she deports me, how do I know you won't kill them anyway?"

Malakai shrugged. Locks of platinum hair fell across his shoulders. "There's no time to deliberate this, son. You know that. I can set you free and kill them all right now as your punishment, if that is what you wish. I will give you five minutes to make your choice. If the Hell Spirits haven't risen by then, I'll kill them."

"I've made my choice." Siméon marched over to me and grabbed my hands.

I jerked them away. "I'm not going to do it, Siméon. I can't."

"You must, Abigail. Think of Judd and Kaleb."

"That's not fair. What…" My voice broke in a sob and unexpected tears broke free and slid down my cheeks. I swiped them away and started again in a whisper. "What if you don't come back? What if I lose you forever?"

"Oh, sweetheart." He cupped my face and pulled me to him. "It makes me happy to hear you still want me despite all that has happened. I'll do everything in my power to come back to you. It won't be forever. A few months at most."

I rested my hands on his waist. Was he lying to me? I couldn't tell. All I read in his expression was a sense of urgency.

Malakai cleared his throat. "This is all very touching but the clock is ticking. Tick tock. Tick tock. It's you or them, son."

Siméon moved in closer and kissed my ear. "Trust me, love." He reached down with one hand and twined his fingers with mine.

"What will happen to you?"

"I'll be fine. When I come back you'll see."

I didn't believe for one second that he wouldn't suffer. What was Hell without misery? My heart pounded frantically and my entire body trembled. How could I say goodbye to him? What choice did I have? To die and take Judd and Kaleb with me? Or to deport Siméon and pray his trip wouldn't be fatal.

If there was a chance we could *all* live...

"Promise me you'll come back to me, Siméon. Please."

His lips traveled along my jaw and then pressed into mine. Soft and tender, he kissed me, calming me, giving me hope that everything would be okay when I knew down deep it wouldn't.

Not for Siméon.

He tugged my resistant hand up. No. I couldn't let him leave yet.

I forced myself to break away from his lips. "It wasn't supposed to be like this."

He gave me a weak smile and touched his forehead to mine. "I love you, Abigail. Remember that."

I wanted to say something in return. Anything to show him how much he meant to me. But all I could do was watch as he lifted my thumb to his chest...next to the other two thumbprints I'd branded on him. I had been doing my job, something I'd never thought twice about before. Now guilt ate at my gut. Now I regretted ever thinking the man before me was anything but good.

"Five..." Malakai started counting down. "Four... Three... Two..."

"Forgive me," I sobbed and pressed my thumb to his skin.

Chapter Twenty-Five

From yellow to a searing red, the tiny imprint on his chest transformed, telling me the process had begun.

Snow melted at our feet as the heat rose from the ground and wrapped around our bodies. I gulped down and looked up at Siméon. "I'm so sorry," I said.

"This isn't your fault, Abigail." I'd never heard him use that tone. Was it fear? Worry? "But please do me a favor and turn away. I don't want you to watch."

Oh, God. What had I done? I wanted to apologize again and again but what good would it do? The Hell Spirits couldn't be stopped once they began. Could they?

The smoky entity rose from the perfect circle of now dry, gravelly dirt and climbed our joined bodies. I refused let go. Despite his request, I gripped tightly to his forearms and pressed my lower half as close to him as possible. Maybe if I tried I *could* stop them. I hadn't ever attempted it before.

Maybe if I held on to him they'd take me too. We could go through this together.

And come back together.

The familiar swirling cloud tunneled above our heads, like a tornado. I'd seen it so many times. Never had it seemed this ominous and threatening. It whipped our hair around, black and copper twining together and blinding me at moments but I kept my attention planted directly on Siméon. He wasn't going anywhere if I had anything to say about it.

"Abby!" Judd yelled over the sound of the howling wind. He was awake. Good. He and Kaleb could flee and I wouldn't feel guilty for leaving them behind. "Let go of him!"

Siméon jolted forward, pushing up against me. I stumbled until I could grab his slumping shoulders and steady us both. It was apparent the Spirits had entered him. Veins of red crept over the whites of his bloodshot eyes and his breathing became ragged.

I held on to him but I worried I wasn't feeling the same effects as he was. Wouldn't they enter me too? This was my doing and I couldn't allow him to suffer on his own.

"Please, Abigail." Siméon's voice was strained. Painful. "Turn away." His face paled to a sickly jaundiced color before my eyes. Dark blue streaks zigzagged from his hairline, down his cheeks to his pursed mouth, where blackened blood seeped through.

Without warning, Judd grabbed my shoulders and yanked me back and away. "You have to let him go, Abby."

I struggled to squirm out of Judd's grasp as the Spirits disbanded from the funnel in the sky and fully encompassed Siméon with their fingerlike tendrils. He fell to his knees, a horrifying groan broke from his purple-tinted lips.

Judd jerked stubbornly at my arms. "Damn it, Abby. You shouldn't watch."

"I don't want to watch! I want to go *with* him, damn it. Let me *go*, Judd."

With strength I didn't know Judd had, he spun me around and wrapped his arms around me with an overpowering hug. "No fucking way are you going anywhere, honey. Not without me. You got it?"

A hot gust of air whipped through the sky and sounded like the snaps of multiple wet towels. Simeon's painful groan followed by complete silence squashed any hope I had left. He was gone. The Hell Spirits had taken him.

Because of me.

I collapsed against Judd. My lungs were heavy against my chest but I couldn't seem to relieve them. I couldn't breathe at all. What had I done? And how the heck would I fix it? There was no way I could sit back and let Siméon languish in Hell when he'd done nothing wrong.

Judd rubbed my back and kissed my forehead. "It's okay," he said. "Just breathe."

Malakai's evil snickers pulled me back to the situation at hand. Now we would find out if he would stick to his part of the bargain. Yeah, right. Siméon's deportation may have been for naught.

I finally released a breath, wiped any tears that had spilled and turned to face the demon. He smiled at me, his teeth entirely too straight and reflecting white against the moonlight. *Asshole*. I squelched the urge to run over to him and knock those teeth out of his skull.

"Amusing show, Angel pet." He clapped teasingly. The demon minions, including Eli, laughed until he put up a hand for them to quiet. "Siméon was a fool. Now maybe he will learn his lesson."

I dug my fingernails into the palm of my hand and burrowed my heels into the snow to keep from attacking. "You're the one who needs to learn a lesson, you *monster*. Siméon is your flesh and blood. How could you do this to him?"

"Whatever are you talking about? *I* didn't do a thing."

Kaleb, still held captive by Freddie, bent over and vomited. He must've watched his uncle's deportation. Shit. Freddie released him, allowing him to fall to his knees.

I started to go to him but Judd braced a hand on my shoulder. "You got what you wanted, Malakai. We'll take the human and leave now."

Malakai snickered again. "Angels never change. So trusting and so very naïve."

"Sir," Cesar said. "It's much too risky for us to stay here any longer. You should not have sent Freddie and Victor for the human without your protection. I warned you their MOG would find us."

My ears perked up. Why hadn't I thought of that? MOG surely would've been able to view Kaleb's capture without Malakai present. An Angel rescue squad was most likely on their way.

Way to muck up your evil fest, boys.

Hopefully we could outnumber the demons and overcome Malakai.

"Cesar, must you be so cowardly? Your whining is grinding at my last nerve. Leave if you must. I have business to attend to." Malakai's gaze drifted up and down my body.

Judd maneuvered in front of me and crossed his arms against his chest so all I could see was his broad back. Nice thought, macho man but I wanted to see what was going on. I stepped beside him and gripped his biceps. The show was just beginning.

Cesar ran a nervous hand over his blond mane of hair. It wouldn't hurt him to take a How to Manage Your Dumbass Leader 101 course. It appeared the Fabio look-alike was the brains behind the evil yet he had absolutely no control. "Sir," he began again. "I fear this mission has become too personal for you. Please take my counsel and—"

Malakai pointed his dagger at Cesar. "Siméon's insolence was contagious, was it?"

"No." Cesar held up his hands in surrender. "Of course not, sir."

"Then do as I say and shut up or I'll have the Angel deport you as well."

I'd gladly send all their sorry asses back to Hell. If only to even the score. What I wouldn't give to avenge Siméon and protect Judd and Kaleb.

Cesar lowered his head and cowered. Wimp.

"What now?" I asked. "An Angel rescue team is close. I can feel them," I lied, surprisingly well. "They're coming in a large group. Aren't you frightened? Don't you want to run before it's too late?" Again, I had no idea who or what was coming but I thought I'd give it a shot.

Malakai's lips thinned. "I suppose I'll have to hurry then." He waved his fingers, gesturing for me to come closer and damn it if my body didn't respond. My legs moved under me as if they had a mind of their own.

"Abby, what the hell are you doing?"

"It's not me." I tried to drop to the ground to keep from moving but my body stiffened up.

I heard Judd walking up behind me and I noticed Kaleb jump to his feet from the corner of my eye. "Stay back," I said. "I can handle this."

Just as soon as I get my body under control.

I should've guessed Judd would ignore me. He grabbed my arm to stop me and was greeted with the infamous stab to the gut. He keeled over, falling to his knees.

"Fuck. Shit. Fuck. Fuck. Fuck." At least he could still talk. "Goddamn you, Malakai."

Malakai laughed. "Believe me, Angel, God has been damning me for as long as I have walked this earth. Now silence yourself!"

"Fuck—" Judd's words were suddenly muffled.

"You'd better not have hurt him," I said, trying desperately to look over my shoulder.

"I have not even begun to hurt the Angel. However a muzzle will do him some good."

A muzzle. Okay. That wasn't too bad but it was probably infuriating Judd.

I stopped directly in front of him. Despite the cold air, sweat rolled off my temples and down my neck. I'd never worked so hard to fight back. And it irritated the heck out of me that my thumb was so close to his chest yet I was powerless to do anything about it.

He showed me his nauseatingly white smile again. Fine. As long as I didn't have to look into those familiar silver eyes.

"Honestly," Malakai said, brushing his smooth hand down my cheek. "I don't have a clue what Siméon saw in you. You aren't the least bit attractive."

"Thanks," I managed to say. Any insult from a demon was a compliment in my book.

"You seemed quite fond of him. He fucked you well, did he?"

I didn't bother to respond but Judd murmured loudly behind me.

Malakai ran the dagger along the strap to my chemise. "Siméon never had any taste when it came to women."

"Leave her alone," Kaleb said, fear clearly shaking his voice.

Malakai let out an annoyed sigh. "Silence him, please."

I heard a struggle to my right but I couldn't turn my head to see what had happened. *Please, God, just give me some movement back so I can send this Hell spawn back where he belongs before he hurts Kaleb or Judd. I swear I'll be good from now on. I'll even give up sex.*

Nothing.

And cheesecake?

Still nothing.

Damn.

Malakai jerked the dagger up, cutting the strap. Silk slinked down my chest. I couldn't see how much I was revealing but I could feel the cold air bite into my breast. He licked his lips and put his hand on me.

"Don't touch me," I warned. More murmuring from Judd.

He laughed again and pinched my nipple hard. "No, Siméon was blinded by something other than beauty when he saw you, of that I am certain."

My shoulders twitched. My wings were screaming to break free. Heck, every nerve in my body was working overtime just to move a quarter inch on its own accord.

He brought the dagger up to the strap on my left shoulder.

"Sir," Cesar said.

The dagger cut through the silk and my chemise fell to my waist. "But a pussy is a pussy and I cannot say I blame him for wanting to sample an Angel's."

Extra loud murmuring from Judd.

"Sir," Cesar said again. "They are close."

Malakai inhaled a breath. "Not close enough."

My pinky finger curled up in my hand and I realized I'd moved it. Yes! It was a small achievement but at the moment I'd take anything. Now to keep him busy until the rest of me decided to cooperate. "Has anyone ever told you you're creepy?"

The tip of the jagged blade slid slowly down between my breasts. "Handsome, charming, well endowed? Yes. Creepy?" He licked his lips again. "Never."

All five of my fingers were free. I squelched a smile. His little spell on me was fading and I was pretty damn sure he had no idea.

My wrist broke free next.

"Siméon must've avoided that gene," I said, feeling the dagger work its way back up. "He wasn't creepy in the least."

"Siméon was a pansy. He deserves whatever punishment the Lord of Hell gives him."

Two hands and an elbow were free. Should I use them to slap his smug face or wait to tackle him down and deport him? Shoot. A slap would feel great but I'd better be patient.

I finally gathered the courage to meet his eyes. "Siméon *is* what you could only hope to be."

"You talk too much, my pet." He traced the cold, steel blade along my lower lip and then sliced the corner of my mouth with it. Blood trickled down my chin and pooled by my tongue. "See what you made me do. I shall cut your tongue out next if you mention his name again."

Try it, asshole. Both my arms were completely mobile.

And Judd's murmuring was a little more discernible. I could make out every other curse word. Weird. What was happening?

"Sir!" Cesar yelled.

Malakai looked at something behind my shoulder and winced. He spun me around and held me to his chest, pressing the blade to my throat.

"Well hello, Isabelle. I wasn't expecting you."

Isabelle? All I could see was MOG. No Angel rescue team, no other Angels at all. Just MOG. She walked out from the thickness of the forest and onto the plain beyond where Judd knelt.

Wait. I guessed MOGs had first names too. I'd never thought to ask. My bad. Isabelle, huh? I always thought she looked like a Summer or Sunflower or some other hippy name. But Isabelle was cool too.

She had her usual tie dye t-shirt and ripped jeans on. Her cheeks and nose were rosy and strings of hair strayed from her bandana. She looked so tiny and harmless.

Not to mention fragile. Inadequate. Powerless. Pointless.

Shit. What was she thinking coming here by herself?

"Malakai," she said, perching her tiny hands on her waist. "I see you're holding a knife to one of my Angels. I don't like it."

"And?" Was Malakai shaking? He readjusted his grip on my shoulders, just above my naked breasts.

How humiliating was this?

MOG, er, Isabelle, rolled her eyes at him. "I see you haven't gotten any smarter over the years." She averted her attention to Kaleb, who was on the ground motionless. "You've harmed a human. I don't like that at all."

"Is he alive?" I asked. *Please let him be okay.*

MOG laid her hand on Judd's shoulder. "Go see to the human, please. The demons won't bother you."

Judd jumped to his feet and obeyed, his blue eyes slit almost shut, glaring at Malakai all the while. Sure enough, Freddie stepped back, allowing Judd to assess Kaleb. He checked for his pulse and breathing. "He's alive."

I blew out a gush of air and the tip of the blade pricked my neck. I stiffened. How quickly my life could be taken from me. Yes, superficial wounds healed pretty quickly. But a jab to the jugular would most likely do the deed. Who was I kidding? It would definitely kill me.

I wasn't ready to die.

I'll admit I'm not the best Angel but the little voice inside my head told me I had a lot to live for. And, damn it, I wanted to believe it.

Chapter Twenty-Six

"Drop the knife, Malakai," MOG said. She took a few steps closer and the blade pierced deeper into my skin.

I let in shallow breaths and didn't dare say a peep, knowing any movement on my part would mean certain death.

Any second now I was expecting an army of Angels to jump out from behind the hundreds of snow powdered trees that towered around us. The avenging Angels would bombard the demons and rip the knife from Malakai's hands and I'd be free.

Any second now. Yep.

Isabelle-MOG was deemed the Messenger of God for a reason, right? She was smart, right? She wouldn't come out here alone and simply demand Satan's Senior Servant and his band of idiot brothers to surrender. Cause that would be insane.

Right?

Someone would have to be high on dope to do that. Ha! What a jokester I was.

MOG's eyes—which seemed clear and sober, by the way—left Malakai and settled on me. She blinked and tilted her cute little head, as if expecting something to happen. As if expecting *me* to do something.

What? I was the one whose life was being threatened here. Didn't she see there was a sharp ass knife cutting into my neck, only a brief nudge away from ending my existence as an Earth Angel? Did she not know that this lunatic demon had put some crazy spell on me and took control of my body?

Which had started to fade but… I wiggled my toes a little. Hmm… I clenched my butt muscles. Yep. Those worked too. I already knew my arms were mobile.

What was I waiting for? Death?

I don't think so.

I watched Judd help a groggy and freshly bleeding Kaleb to his feet and another thing occurred to me. Why wasn't Malakai using his magic to immobilize anyone? And why hadn't he ordered any of his cowering minions to take MOG into custody?

And was it just a coincidence that Malakai's body-freezing spell had faded when MOG was near?

Duh. Why else would he be shaking in his tacky cloak right now, not saying a word when he was so confident and chatty earlier? It was so simple.

Malakai couldn't use his powers around MOG.

That had to be the case. Okay, it was possible I was wrong but that was my theory and I was sticking to it.

Maybe I should test it out.

My wings had come in handy when knocking the gun out of Eli's hands. And practice makes perfect so… I gave in to the urge and released them. With pent-up, boiling force they jutted from my shoulders and knocked Malakai away.

Yay! I was free.

I took that victorious moment to tie the straps of my chemise back together, knowing I wouldn't exactly look threatening with my boobs on display. But I faltered when a shearing pain ripped through my right wing.

Damn, that hurt!

I quickly assessed the damage. The middle of my right wing had been sliced halfway through. A clean cut. With that freaking dagger, no doubt.

Enraged and with only one strap tied, I spun around to face Malakai, Angel to monster.

A fight broke out around me, I realized just then. Judd had taken on Eli and Freddie. MOG had cornered Leo DiCaprio and another demon against the log cabin wall. Cesar and Victor were nowhere in sight.

But I couldn't concentrate on that now. Malakai was crazy-eyed and pointing that damn knife straight at me.

"You'll die one way or another today," he said, clearly his cocky self again.

I willed my wings to curl in, cringing at the pain it caused. They should heal internally, I hoped anyway. They'd never been sliced in two before.

"I wanted to cut them to pieces and have them as a snack," Malakai said. "I've heard they're quite delicious." He actually looked disappointed he hadn't had the opportunity.

I took a defensive stance, spreading my legs and readying my hands out in front of me. "You're a whack job, buddy. And you're going to pay for all you've done to the Angels and to Siméon. And to my *fucking* car, my home, my CD collection—"

He jerked forward and jabbed the dagger toward me. I slipped to the left and dodged it. He repeated the move, nicking my forearm this time.

It pissed me off a lot more than it hurt. "Ooh, you're gonna *get* it!"

"You okay, Abby?" Judd yelled. It looked like he'd deported Freddie already and was now wrestling with Eli. With *Eli*, for crying out loud. I still couldn't get over the fact that he was now the enemy.

I didn't know what MOG was doing behind me but there was an awful lot of demon screaming going on back there. Go Isabelle!

"Super," I yelled back.

I distracted Malakai with a front kick that barely missed his family jewels and then I pivoted and came around with my left leg, finally knocking the weapon from his grasp.

Go me! Look who was about to kick Satan's Senior Servant's ass. That's right. Little ole Abigail V. Angel.

Then he jolted forward and tackled me to the ground.

The back of my head hit the dirt hard. Thankfully it only shocked me and gave me a start of another headache.

We struggled on the ground. His hands gripped my throat. His claws dug into my skin. My hands made punch shots wherever they would reach. His gut. His ribs. His back. I ripped at his cloak and clawed at his undershirt. His chest was somewhere under there. If I could only reach it.

Panicked because I couldn't breathe, I wrapped my legs around him and squeezed. Air gushed out of his mouth and onto my face. Gross. Apparently white teeth didn't equal fresh breath in his case. All the more motivation to get him off me and—

"Abigail!" MOG yelled right by my ear. "Would you like some help or do you want to deport him on your own?"

If my eyes weren't bulging out of my head right then I'd have rolled them. I lifted my hand to give a thumbs up and felt something leathery and hard slip into it. I gripped and weighed it.

It was the dagger. MOG had handed me the dagger.

So MOGs were smart after all. When we got out of here alive, I was so going to give her a hug. Or a joint.

A new rush of adrenaline pumped through me and I pushed Malakai off me. I rolled with him, still in his tight grasp, until I was on top. With a weapon!

I lifted the dagger to show him I had it and intended to do some major damage if he didn't let go of my neck pronto.

"You little bitch." He grabbed for it with both hands.

I gasped for air but kept the dagger out of his reach. "You…" Cough. Cough. Deep breath. "You're going to go to Hell and you're going to tell Satan to let Siméon go. Got it?"

Malakai gave me a look of surprise and started laughing. Hysterically.

Whatever. I pressed the blade to his undershirt and ripped it open, revealing his chest. Then I threw the dagger across the open clearing and into the trunk of a tree at the edge of the forest. I was going to do this the right way.

"Malakai, you piece of shit. You've violated codes one thru seven, lust, gluttony, greed, sloth, wrath, envy and pride…on multiple occasions, I'm sure."

His smile faded fast. "Your fucking MOGs have seen nothing."

I shrugged and lifted my thumb. "Let's not play that game this time."

Panic finally dawned in his silver eyes. "Angels have no power over me. You will not prevail." He attempted to sit up and knock my hand away but MOG clutched his wrists and held him down.

She nodded. "Go on, Abigail."

Malakai squirmed underneath me and spewed out a string of words in a language I'd never heard before. As if that wasn't freaky enough, a thin reddish layer clouded over his eyes and his body heat rose about a hundred degrees between my thighs.

But nothing happened. His magic was useless.

I bent over him and met his sinister stare. "If you have an ounce of goodness in your soulless body, you'll make sure Siméon comes back home safely."

Then I pressed my thumb to his chest. Once, twice, three times.

Heat shot up through the ground with a violent force that knocked me off Malakai and onto the ground.

Damn. Someone in Hell was anxious to see him.

I stood to my feet and watched, no, *made sure* the Hell Spirits seized Malakai. I didn't want to take any chances. A demon this malicious didn't belong on earth. Ever.

Ten feet away, MOG had the same idea, her huge innocent eyes taking it all in. The deportation was faster than usual. The ground below Malakai groaned as it opened up, splitting in two jagged pieces. The demon met my eyes through the inky smoke. "You'll die, Angel. You'll all die," he said and then let out a horrendously painful scream as the tendrils of smoke clutched his body. They dug their fingers into his skin and squeezed him through the narrow opening.

The ground snapped shut. And it was over.

Instead of nausea assailing me, I was overcome with a strong sense of relief. Malakai was gone. With any luck, he'd spend eternity in Hell and no one would ever suffer from his evil transgressions again. I didn't even want to think about the damage he'd already done. The ideas he'd planted in other demons' heads.

"Good job, Abigail." MOG came up beside me and tied my other chemise strap. "Why don't you tend to Judd and your new friend while I go see if I can catch up with the demons who escaped?"

I tucked the chemise back into my jeans. "I can go with you."

"Not necessary. We'll locate them later if they're too far gone. They no longer have Malakai to hide behind." She grinned and squeezed my hand. "I think you're needed here anyway."

Needed here? What did I miss? I scanned the area but only saw Judd and Kaleb. Judd was breathing heavily, leaning against the cabin wall, his hands braced on his thighs. Kaleb was sitting against the opposite side of the wall, watching me. At that moment, I detested that he looked so much like Siméon. How could I miss him this much in the small time he'd been gone? It didn't help that Kaleb's presence jarred my guilt. Simeon would still be here if it weren't for me. How I was going to live with that, I didn't know.

A new knot formed in my throat. I gulped it down and wondered if Kaleb wasn't so thrilled to see me either since I was the reason his uncle was suffering in Hell.

How could he not hate me?

I avoided meeting Kaleb's dark eyes as I walked toward him. The least I could do was apologize.

He stood up, grunting a little from his new wounds. All that licking for nothing.

"Hi," I said and gathered the courage to make eye contact. "I'm so sorry about Siméon." I took a calming breath so I wouldn't start bawling. "I understand if you're angry with me. Heck, I wouldn't mind if you and Harley formed an 'Abby Sucks' club and charged admission. You could probably make a living off it."

A gorgeous smile spread across his face. "What are you talking about, sugar?"

I pointed over my shoulder. "I... Sim... You know..."

He brushed his knuckles across my cheek. "I know that you saved my life."

"Yeah but I sacrificed your uncle in the process. He's in Hell because of me."

"Nah. He's in Hell because of Malakai. And, well, for making all those bad decisions when he was with Malakai. None of that is your fault. I'm not angry with you, sugar. In fact, I believe I owe you a car."

"Weekend visits," I reminded him and couldn't help but get a little excited at the idea of spending any amount of time with that car. Darn, if Angels could get strikes for violating codes, I'd give myself a big fat thumbprint for Greed.

"You got it, sugar." He leaned over and kissed my cheek, his silky black hair falling across my face. "You did save my life," he whispered against my ear. "And I plan on making it up to you. That's a promise."

My cheeks blazed as my traitorous thoughts took a nosedive where they didn't belong. *Don't even go there, Abby.* Anything but friendship with Kaleb was only asking for trouble. Besides, he was talking about a car, not hot, sweaty sex in the back of a car. What was wrong with me? I backed up a few inches, gave Kaleb a *friendly* smile and went to see how Judd was doing.

Judd was walking away from me and over to where the trees began so I hurried to catch up with him. The sun was slowly rising, peeking through the forest and casting an orange glow on everything. As Judd turned to look at me, I noticed tiny flecks of amber in his blue eyes I hadn't seen before.

"I hear cars coming up the road down there," he said, frowning and pointing down the slope of the mountain at a windy road.

It was the first time I'd realized we were so high in elevation. Now that daylight was creeping in, I could see how just a quarter mile or so away, the land dropped significantly. And, like Judd said, a paved road swerved up the mountain.

"I wonder how MOG got here," I said. "She's one mysterious lady. Don't you think?"

"Abby?" Judd's hand slipped into mine. He angled toward me and cupped my face with his other hand. "I had to deport Eli, you know."

"Yeah, I know." I figured as much but I'd been trying not to think about it. "I'm sorry you had to do that. Eli made a huge mistake."

He sighed and wrapped his arm around me, taking my hand with his. He was bloodied and bruised, looking mighty gritty but he was still my Judd. "Forget about Eli. I'm pretty pissed at *you*."

I rewound through my mind all the reasons why Judd could be angry but figured I'd better not guess in case I picked the wrong one. "Why?" I asked and braced myself for the worst.

"*Why?*" He didn't look happy but he hadn't pushed me away either and I rather liked the comfort of his strong arms just then. "Abby, you tried to leave me. You wanted to follow that half-breed to Hell and leave me behind."

"Oh." I understood now.

"I don't get your fascination with him. I'll admit that it's grated at my last nerve but I never thought you would go that far to be with him. I thought he was something you needed to get out of your system. A little fling. Something to boost your ego. But I guess it was more than that."

"I guess so," I whispered the admittance. I couldn't lie to Judd by denying I had deep feelings for Siméon and how I hoped to God he would come back so I could at least know he was okay. "But…" But that didn't change my feelings for Judd and that I've always had an insane crush on my best friend. With all that had happened, how close we'd all come to death, I needed to tell Judd—to *finally* tell him—about how I felt about *him*. "You see…I…uh…"

A roar of engines gained his attention and he pulled away. "The rescue team arrived. Come on, Abby. Let's get out of here."

Chapter Twenty-Seven
Four weeks later

The new Demon Control building was going back up without a glitch. We'd decided as a whole to take the chance and re-erect it in the same spot. The high chance of being attacked again didn't outweigh the fact that Angels, Inc. was short on human funds. Well, that was MOG's reasoning.

I was going more with the *just try to fuck with me again* logic. That and the additions of the extra tight security, fire escapes, smoke detectors and sprinklers had me thinking staying in the same location was a great idea.

Whatever it took to get things back to normal, I was all for it.

Living at the AOD center, in Eli's old room, wasn't as awful as I'd imagined, mainly because I'd kept a low profile and had thrown myself back into my work.

Today was no different. I'd just gotten off a double shift and was about to fall face first into my tidily made bed. Pauline and I were roommates now and I was happy that, first, our paths hardly ever crossed because of our opposite work schedules and secondly she was a total Martha Stewart. I can't tell you how much I loved having clean laundry, lavender scented pillowcases and a stocked refrigerator. Talk about heaven on earth.

My head hit the freshly fluffed down pillow. I snuggled in and closed my eyes. Maybe I'd dream about Siméon again. I'd been doing that a lot lately. Not full-fledged dreams but tangible glimpses so real I'd wake up and look around to see if he'd come back and was here in the same room with me. Like the taste of his tongue in my mouth or the warm touch of his hand on my breast. The brush of his knuckles against my cheek. His arms wrapped firmly around my waist.

I know. My mind was screwing with me big-time. But I didn't mind. I kind of liked it. It gave me hope that he was okay. As long as he remained imbedded in my brain, he was a part of this earth. Call me crazy but I liked to think that Siméon was sending me these dreams somehow. Like an incubus, he came to me in my sleep. Was he reaching out to me from the otherworld of Hell? Could it be my dream state was his sanctuary?

I sighed and smooshed the pillow against my head. I was definitely going crazy. But at least the siesta visits saved me from feeling completely alone.

Judd had done a thorough job of avoiding me the past few weeks. Besides a smile or a wave in passing, I hadn't really had contact with him. No, I never had the chance to tell him how I felt about him, which I admit now would have been a monumental mistake. I could only imagine how much my confession would've scared him, a man whose single phobia was being committed to one woman. I couldn't blame him though. Heck, the whole *becoming human through marriage* idea scared me too.

He'd eventually get over being mad at me for what happened with Siméon. I was sure it was only a matter of time and I wanted him to feel comfortable in our friendship when he did. I *had* to believe we still had a friendship.

It was just past eight a.m. when I fell into dreamland and it seemed like only seconds later when something woke me.

A noise. The strike of a match, maybe. Someone was in my room. I opened my eyes and realized I was facing the wall. Not to panic though. It was probably Pauline lighting one of her scented candles. Yet another subtle hint for her roommate to hit the showers before hitting the sheets.

Nice try, Pauline. I admit I'd let myself go the past few weeks, showering less, shaving never. It'd take a rake to go through my hair on most days and don't even talk to me about makeup. Why? Who cared what I looked like? I didn't. I was too busy working to care. When I wasn't working, I slept.

I kicked the covers off me and grunted. I swore if she was lighting that fucking orchid candle again I was going to scream. Vanilla and fruit scents I could handle. Flowers, forget it. They gave me a migraine every time.

I waited for the smell to reach my nose. Sweet. Tangy. Way too pungent. Overwhelming.

What the hell?

I sat up to see MOG sitting at the end of the bed, puffing on a joint. Nice.

"Oh, Abigail." She shifted and faced me, her long straight hair flowing over one shoulder. "You're awake. Lovely."

"Please tell me you're not smoking a doobie in my room. Pauline is going to freak."

MOG waved away my concern. "Pauline doesn't freak. You know that." She took another drag and sighed. "You don't mind, do you? I haven't had one of these in almost a month. The AOD MOG tells me she's allergic. *Allergic.* Can you believe that? The poor thing."

I couldn't help but smile. "I don't mind, MOG."

"We're friends, Abigail. Call me Isabelle. Or Izzy. They used to call me Izzy when I was younger."

"Izzy? Okay. You can call me Abby. Some people call me Abby."

"Abby and Izzy. I like that. Do you want a drag?" She smiled and offered me the joint.

"No, thanks. But, I, uh, I've been wanting to talk to you. Ask you a few questions?" There'd been several things on my mind since the day Malakai was deported. Now seemed like as good a time as any to get some answers.

"Ask away."

I scooted to the end of the bed but realized the smoke was too much so I inched back and leaned against the wall. "Malakai was pretty powerful until you showed up," I said, trying to initiate the conversation.

She grinned and nodded.

"How'd you do it? How did you strip him of his powers?"

"You know that I'm a Messenger of God?" Her thin eyebrows scrunched together.

"Uh, yep."

"Well, there you go." She took another drag and tapped her foot on the ground.

"So what? All MOGs have powers like that?"

"Only when God grants them. I asked and I received. You see?"

Not really. I pushed a wild lock of hair behind my ear. "Well, why didn't you just ask God to evaporate Malakai and his crew to save all the trouble it took to deport him?" That seemed like the more logical thing to have done.

"Evaporation?" She giggled. "Well, that's something to think about in the future."

"I'm not kidding, Izzy."

"Honestly, Abby, leveling out the powers seemed to work well, don't you think? You got your revenge on Malakai and I got to see the look on his disgusting face when the Hell Spirits yanked him to his demise. I have to tell you, I've been waiting years for that to happen. Besides…" She shrugged her dainty shoulders. "A good fight never hurt anyone."

"'Cept I almost had my jugular sliced and my right wing cut off."

"Right. Right. How is that, anyway?"

"Better." I would've been angry at her nonchalance but it felt so good to have a conversation with someone who didn't think I was dirt. Her friend, she called me. Huh. That was nice.

"Good. I'm glad to hear that. I'm stocking back up on my herbs and potions so in the future…" She let the rest of the words fade away and a deep frown formed on her pixie face. I knew what she was thinking. Cesar Knight and Victor Adams hadn't been brought to justice yet. For whatever reason they'd slipped off the radar. Well, off MOG's radar anyway. The demon revolution hadn't been nipped in the bud just yet. I imagined another uprising would explode any day now.

I was ready for it.

"Anyway." She stood up and disappeared into the bathroom. I heard the toilet flush and then she stepped back out without her joint. "Thanks for letting me stay awhile." She gave me a weak smile.

I smiled back. "Anytime." And I meant it. "See you around."

I waited for Isabelle to leave before I hopped into the shower. I had a few hours before my next shift started and I was too hyped to go back to sleep. Talking to a friend had raised my spirits and I had to admit I'd been acting like a big crybaby lately. Maybe if I got my head out of my ass I could work in a visit to see the Citroën. And Kaleb. He called me occasionally to tell me the car wanted to see me. But, I don't know, I hadn't felt up to it until today.

Yeah, I'd been really pathetic.

I shampooed and conditioned my hair, shaved my legs—not for Kaleb—and used Pauline's scrubby cucumber watermelon body wash all over. After ten minutes with the hair dryer, I threw on some makeup—seriously, not for Kaleb—and then pulled on some jeans and one of Pauline's sweaters. And a dab of her perfume.

Did I mention how much I liked having her for a roommate?

I was about to dial Kaleb's number when someone knocked on my door. I threw my cell on the bed and went to answer it. Isabelle hadn't knocked the first time so why would she make the effort now? Pauline had her own key. And although the other Angels had been sort of nice to me since I'd deported the enemy, they still kept their distance. Who the heck was it?

"Who's there?" I asked.

"It's me, Abby. Judd."

"Oh." My heart did a thumpity-thump in my chest as I turned the lock and opened the door.

He had one hand stuffed in his faded jeans pocket. In his other hand he held a plastic grocery bag. A mustard stain took center stage on his white t-shirt. And his hair needed a comb.

I couldn't remember the last time he'd looked so good.

"Hi." I gestured for him to come in.

He brushed past me and stopped in the middle of the living room. Like my dearly departed apartment, the living space was small. It was a studio, all in one but there was no half wall separating the bedroom in this apartment. I watched as Judd's eyes did a quick scan of the area and then landed on me.

"What's that smell?"

I sniffed and then remembered. "MOG was here."

"Oh. That makes sense. Everything okay?"

"Yeah. Everything's great. Do you want to sit?" I pointed at the floral couch smothered with way too many throw pillows.

He picked the pillows off, sat and patted the seat beside him. "You look good, Abby. You weren't leaving, were you?"

"Not just yet." I sank into the couch and faced him. He'd stretched out his long legs and leaned toward me with a curious expression. "What?"

"We got the results for Piper's bug back from the lab."

"Yeah?" I'd nearly forgotten about that little detail. Judd had been sure Siméon had been behind that whole scheme. I hadn't believed it for a second. "And?"

He rolled his eyes to the ceiling and I could've sworn his cheeks turned a little pink. "Turns out it wasn't really a bug. It was just a watch battery."

I bit back a laugh. "Really?" That was interesting. If it wasn't a bug then... "Then how do you think they found Demon Control?"

He frowned and shrugged his shoulders. "Eli, maybe."

"Ah." Well, that bit of news sucked. If it was true, not only had Eli turned his back on the only people who'd ever cared about him, he'd thrown us to the wolves, as well. "I'm sorry, Judd. I know he was your best friend."

"You're my best friend, Abby," Judd said. For that I was grateful but I knew he was still hurting inside. "Don't look at me like that, honey. I'm fine. Besides, I've been hanging out with Felix lately since I don't have a car. He's been pretty cool."

"Huh. But don't his constant Yoda impersonations bother you? I think it's kind of annoying." Not to mention Felix had called me easy at one point.

Judd chuckled. "Yeah, it's pretty irritating but he only does that when he's nervous."

I raised my eyebrows. "I make him nervous?"

"Guess so. Most females do, so don't let it go to your pretty little head." He skimmed his fingers down a lock of my hair.

"Course not." *Sigh.*

He smiled, showing me his teeth. "You know Pauline isn't so bad either."

"Pauline? You like Pauline?" Should I hit him now or later?

"Why not? She's fairly harmless."

I fisted my hand. "Are you going to ask her out?"

He leaned in closer. "Would that make you jealous?"

I just stared at him. Silence would be my only answer.

"No, I'm not going to ask her out. I've got more than I can handle dealing with you."

"What is *that* supposed to mean?" He was *dealing* with me?

"All I was trying to say was it wouldn't hurt you to have a friend besides me. And Pauline might be a good match for you. You should give her a chance."

"I've got other friends."

"Siméon, you mean?"

"Yes. Siméon and Kaleb. In fact, I'm meeting Kaleb later today."

He pulled back and narrowed his eyes at me. "What's wrong with having a female friend? Why do you have to hang out with these big, blockheaded men?"

"I happen to *like* big, blockheaded men."

"I bet you do."

"Jealous?"

He jetted his hand through his unruly hair and sat back against the cushions. "Maybe. A little."

I leaned forward this time, loving that he still cared. "You're a big blockhead and I really like you." *More than you know.*

"Yeah?" His lips tipped up to a half grin. "Listen." He reached for the plastic grocery bag he'd thrown on the floor and handed it to me. "I thought you might want this, to, you know, start growing your collection again."

Intrigued and slightly ecstatic, I ripped open the bag. I *never* got presents. Then I saw it. An *Ultimate Aerosmith Hits* CD. "Holy shit."

"I thought you would like it. It has that *Angel* song on there you used to listen to all the time."

I fought back the tears burning at my eyes. Our spending allowance was close to zero until Demon Control was up and running again. "You shouldn't have, Judd. This is so sweet."

"It was no big deal. Really. The demon who works at the store gave me a good deal."

Uh-oh. That didn't sound good. "Tell me what you did."

He chuckled. "I told him I'd ignore the fact that he'd just sold an adult movie to a kid if he'd give me a store credit."

"Judd! You're going to lose your Angel status again if you abuse your power. You know that."

Judd angled toward me again and cupped his hand to my cheek. "It'd be worth it to see a smile on your face again. Abby…" He drew in a breath. "I'm sorry I haven't been around the past few weeks."

The seriousness of his voice was making me uneasy. "It's okay."

"No, it's not and I want to explain." He edged even closer and was now only inches from my face. "When I kissed you. Remember? In the closet?"

"Yeah?" I bit into my lip. How could I forget?

"It changed things between us."

I didn't like where this was going.

"I've always been attracted to you," he said. "You know that."

"I *didn't* know that." Was he kidding?

"Well, it's true. I've had the hots for you since I laid eyes on you. But I never acted on it because you've been the only person I can hang with. You know? You don't mind when I cuss. You don't get all superior when I make a mistake. You don't judge me."

I blinked. "You have the hots for me?"

"Yeah." He grinned. "And the kiss didn't help much."

"It was a great kiss. Although you turning the light switch off on me kind of ruined the moment."

"Sorry. I got nervous."

That made sense. "So?"

"So I'd like to kiss you again sometime, if that's all right. No pressure. No strings. Just a kiss once in a while."

"*Just* a kiss?"

He lowered his blue eyes to my lips and back up again. "Once in a while."

"I, uh." I cleared my throat and crossed my wobbly knees. "I don't see anything wrong with that if you don't. I mean, if you don't think it'll harm our friendship."

"That's what I've been thinking about the past few weeks. I was worried I'd fucked up by kissing you. I thought maybe I'd opened Pandora's Box and there was no going back. But we're reasonable adults, right? And we both want to remain Angels, right? It's not like I'm asking you to marry me. We're not going to take the plunge and join humanity with a simple kiss."

I shook my head, maybe a little too hard. "Good point."

He lightly brushed his thumb over my lower lip. "Abby, if I ever do or say anything that makes you uncomfortable all you need to do is say so and I'll back off. Your friendship means more to me than anything."

Aw! He could be so sweet when he wasn't being a putz. I let my gaze drift down to his mouth. "When's this kissing affair going to start?"

"How 'bout right now." He closed the distance between us and started with a slow lingering kiss. His taste was familiar. His scent felt like home. I nearly moaned as his tongue slid seductively alongside mine. This was much different from our intense tango in the janitor's closet. I guessed he'd gotten that out of his system. Or maybe he wasn't angry about Siméon anymore.

Siméon.

Here I was making out and having a grand ole time when Siméon was suffering in Hell. Because of me. I braced my hands on Judd's shoulders and eased away. We had eternity to continue this…this kissing game. A game I looked forward to playing but not when guilt ran like tar through my veins.

Judd slowly opened his eyes, most of the blue had disappeared. "What's wrong, honey?"

"Just a kiss, remember?" I played it cool. Or tried to anyway. Judd always knew when I was lying.

He grinned and I noticed his cheeks grow pink. "Right. Well, I see I'll have to do some negotiating in the future." He let out a nervous chuckle and stood to his feet. "I better go. I, uh, have to meet up with Felix. He wants to start going to the gym with me."

"Really? Good for him."

"Not like he has a choice. The streets haven't exactly been kind to him since we gained our Angel status back. Three demons have slipped away from him because he can't catch his breath." Judd pressed a hasty kiss to my cheek. "See you soon," he murmured into my ear and then walked out the door.

That was interesting. I brought my fingers to my lips and stared at the door he'd just closed. I'd always known he'd be a good kisser. Lord only knew what he could do with his lower regions.

My cell phone started ringing, thankfully, pulling me out of the gutter where my mind was swimming. I ran for it, checked the number and felt my heart pang against my chest when I saw who was calling me.

Siméon. How could he be calling? Was he back?

I quickly answered. "Hello? Sim?"

"It's me. Harley." Her voice was a whisper but I could still make it out.

"Why are you calling me from your uncle's house? Is he there? Is he okay?"

"Listen. He didn't want me to call you so I'm trying to keep it down. He came back early this morning and I don't know what to do." She sounded like a teenager, panicked and unsure, rather than the adult she pretended to be.

"About what? Is he okay?" Why wouldn't she answer me? And what did she mean he didn't want her to call me? God, he must hate me.

"He wasn't this bad last time he came back. Last time he healed pretty quickly and my Nana was here with me. I don't know what do." She sniffed into the phone. "Kaleb told me how you fixed him up. Can you help my uncle?"

I actually felt bad for the little snot. She must really care about her uncle. "Yes, I'll be right there," I said, even though I had no idea how badly Siméon was hurt and if I could help him.

All I knew was I'd give everything I had, my last breath, to keep him on this earth.

Chapter Twenty-Eight

༄

I pulled Eli's stupid Geo Metro into Siméon's driveway. MOG had given the car to me since my VW had been barbecued in the fire. I'd felt a little sad and mournful about taking it at first. Now that I knew Eli had been the one to give Malakai Demon Control's location I didn't feel so bad. In fact, the first chance I got I was going to sell the damn thing and buy a car that didn't make me nauseous every time I turned on the engine.

I had no clue what had pushed Eli to give up his soul. So what if he'd felt emasculated when his Angel status had been taken from him? Did he really think becoming a demon would give him that power back? I shook the thought of him out of my head. He wasn't important anymore. And for the pain he'd caused I wouldn't doubt he'd learn his lesson in Hell and come back begging for mercy. Too bad for Eli clemency had never been given to a fallen Angel. Not once in the history of Angels, Inc.

Not my problem, I thought as I walked to the front door. Harley opened it before I had a chance to ring the doorbell. My heart dropped at the sight of her. Her eyes were puffy and black lines of mascara trailed down her cheeks.

She closed the door behind me and grabbed my arm before I could make my way to Siméon's room. "Wait," she said. "Just so you know, I didn't want you near him but it wasn't like I had another choice."

I straightened my shoulders and met her glare. "Just so *you* know, Siméon means a lot to me and I'd do anything for him." I blew out a calming breath. "So I'm glad you called me."

She swiped at the fresh tears rolling down her blackened cheeks. "I almost didn't. You're the one who did this to him. If Kaleb hadn't insisted on the phone…"

"I'm sorry." What else could I say? She was right, I had done this to Siméon. "Believe me, if I'd had another choice—"

She put up her hand to stop me. "I know. Kaleb told me everything. Just go fix my uncle, okay?"

I ignored her bossy tone and headed down the hallway. It wasn't until then that reality struck me like a fist between the eyes. Siméon had come back. I hadn't lost him. I was so close to seeing him again. So close to finding out if he ever wanted to see me again. If he had any brains in his glorious head, he'd tell *me* to go to Hell.

I prayed he wouldn't.

An unusual odor met me at his bedroom door, along with a cloud of warmth, easily detectable when the rest of the house was freezing. I gripped the doorknob. It rattled underneath my trembling hand.

Get it together, Abby. He needs you.

Gathering courage, I pushed the door open. The smell immediately hit me. It didn't take long to recognize the source. Siméon was curled up on the bed facing the battle-battered wall. His naked body was covered in blisters and what could only be dried-up vomit. His hair was mostly gone. Singed off. His skin was no longer the golden tan but a sickly yellow.

He was still, lifeless.

Oh, God. "Siméon?" I jolted forward, taking hasty steps to the side of the bed and felt relief when I noticed his lungs expand.

He clasped his hands and moved them from in front of his eyes. What I saw raised gooseflesh all over my body. Gone were the sparks of silver, the shiny confident glints in his eyes. Instead, a dull gray peeked up at me.

"Leave me." His voice was so hoarse I barely understood.

I tried not to take it personally. He wouldn't get rid of me that easily. My ego could take a nap for the rest of the day as far as I was concerned. Siméon may not have wanted me here but he certainly needed me. I leaned over and touched his cheek. It was feverish, even for a demon. Dangerously feverish. "You won't heal unless you're hydrated," I said. "I'll get you some water."

"No, Abigail," he croaked. "Please, just go."

"I'm not going anywhere." Hiding the hurt, I stepped out into the hall where Harley was waiting. "He needs water," I told her. "And new bed linens. I'll get the water if you know where to find the linens."

She gulped and nodded. "I do."

We separated, each on our own mission. I hurried back to Siméon with a tall glass of room temperature water, not wanting to jolt his system.

Slowly, he propped himself up on his elbow while pulling a bile stained sheet up to his waist. He took the glass but didn't look at me. "I still don't want you here," he said and gulped down the water.

Okay, that was it. I'd had enough. "I know you're mad but you'll just have to put up with me until you're well."

He shook his head and pulled the sheet up farther to his chest. "I don't want you to see me like this. I'm repulsive."

Ah. He was embarrassed of his appearance. But what he didn't he realize was all I saw before me was a loving and generous man who'd risked his life for me. More than once.

"Siméon Keller." I kept my voice even. "Not one part of you is or ever has been repulsive. Okay, maybe you smell a little bit right now but I'm going to help you into the shower and you'll be back to a burning hunk of man in no time. Got it?"

"Stubborn," he simply said. His eyes were already gaining back their shine as they rolled up at me.

"Yep, that's us. Stubborn. Come on. Let's get you cleaned up." I lent him a hand but he ignored it.

"I can manage," he grumbled but wobbled unsteadily as he stood.

"I know you can, Mister Man but I can't seem to keep my hands off you." I wrapped an arm around his waist, avoiding the fresh scars that trailed across his back and together we made our way into the bathroom.

He slumped down on the toilet seat as I turned on the showerhead and let it heat up from cold to lukewarm. "What are you doing?" he asked when I kicked off my shoes and started to unbutton my jeans.

"Undressing." I waited for him to argue but he only watched as I stripped off the rest of my clothing. Perhaps I should have felt self-conscious under his attentive stare but I figured he'd seen me naked before and he hadn't complained then so why not now?

Not to mention he looked like he was going to collapse from exhaustion at any second. Sexual thoughts were probably the last thing on his mind. I tossed my bra and panties to the floor and held a hand out to him. This time he didn't protest.

He stepped into the shower before me and gripped the handrail, letting the water beat down on him. His sallow color seemed to wash right off his body, yet it didn't tint the water as it rushed down the drain. Weird. It was as if it simply evaporated or sank into his pores. It was amazing what a little hydration will do for an immortal.

Siméon rested his head against the shiny black tiles and closed his eyes. I grabbed a fresh washcloth and a bar of soap and started scrubbing the crusted vomit and bile that had somehow made a scattered path from his mouth to his thighs. All the while, I took an inventory of the wounds and scars that were disappearing before my eyes. And took note of how much weight and muscle he'd lost. According to the ribs defined against his skin, at least twenty pounds.

"This is humiliating," he said but didn't attempt to stop me.

"Consider it foreplay." I winked up at him.

He didn't look amused. In fact, there was a darkness in the back of his eyes that told me a thousand unimaginable stories of pain and anguish. Unimaginable to me, that was. He'd lived through nearly a month of it. I remembered MOG's description of Hell and shuddered. It was like living your worst nightmare and not knowing if you'd ever wake up.

I finished quickly, not bothering to wash what was left of his hair. Considering there were several bald spots, I figured he'd have to shave it off and start from scratch. I shrugged to myself. Might be kind of sexy.

After wrapping a towel around him, I guided him back to the toilet and made him sit. "I'm going to change your sheets. I'll be right back."

"Abigail," he started to say but I left him before he could continue. If I stopped to think too long about how much he'd suffered, I'd break down. If I stopped to listen to him protest about my presence, I'd break down. I had to keep moving. I had to keep telling myself that he needed me here.

I grabbed his silk robe from the hook on the door, tied it around my body and went back out into the hallway. Harley was sitting against the wall with the fresh linens in her lap. When she saw me, she jumped to her feet. "Here." She pushed the sheets into my hands. "How is he?"

"He'll be fine. You can go on home. I'll stay with him tonight." The other Angels would just have to take on a few more cases to cover my shift.

"You sure?"

"Positive. And Harley, thank you again for calling me."

She lifted a shoulder. "If you send him there again, I'll kill you," she said and turned on her heel.

"Okey-doke." I didn't have a comeback for that one so I went back into Siméon's bedroom and changed the sheets. I heard him brushing his teeth and then gargling mouthwash. Good. He was feeling better already, I thought, until I walked back into the bathroom and saw him staring into the mirror with wide-eyed horror. He was trembling and white knuckling the side of the sink.

"Siméon," I whispered carefully but he still jumped. I didn't waste time apologizing. I pulled him to the bed and drew out the blanket for him. I'd comfort him the only way I knew how.

Wearily, he dropped the towel on the floor and eased onto the mattress. I slipped his robe off me and curled up next to him. His eyes were still red-rimmed and I knew it wouldn't take much for him to fall into sleep.

I pressed my cool body to his feverish one and trailed my fingers gingerly across his shoulders and chest. Up and down and from side to side. If I'd had any kind of a voice, I'd have sung him a calming lullaby. But God hadn't blessed me with that talent so I continued to soothe him with my hands.

The quivering settled, as did the temperature of his body. And when I laid my head against his chest I listened as his heartbeat grew steady.

"I missed you," I said. *Please don't hate me.*

"Oh, Abigail." He cupped his warm hands to my face as his lips pressed to my forehead. "My Angel," he whispered. "There are no words to describe how much I missed you."

"Really? You're not angry with me?"

"I love you, sweetheart." He kissed my cheek and pulled me closer to him. "The vision of you in my head was my only refuge. You gave me a reason to survive, to come home. I swear I'll do everything in my power to never go back there again. Never."

Hot tears burned my eyes and the tarry guilt that slugged through my veins thinned, freeing me. The man in my arms wasn't a demon. I knew that now. Demons couldn't love, couldn't *be* loved. No, there was no doubt in my mind that Siméon didn't belong anywhere but on this earth with me.

I found his hand and twined our fingers. "I'll see to it that you never ever get deported again," I said. "I promise."

Then I prayed to God that I could keep that promise.

About the Author

Multi-published author, Viola Estrella, loves a story with humor, flawed characters, paranormal elements, and romance. She tries to include these aspects in all that she writes and loves every minute of it. When she's not reading, writing, or watching her share of reality TV, she's spending quality time with her husband and sons in their Colorado home. To read more about Viola, visit her website.

Viola welcomes comments from readers. You can find her website and email address on her author bio page at www.cerridwenpress.com.

Tell Us What You Think

We appreciate hearing reader opinions about our books. You can email us at Comments@EllorasCave.com.

Why an electronic book?

We live in the Information Age—an exciting time in the history of human civilization, in which technology rules supreme and continues to progress in leaps and bounds every minute of every day. For a multitude of reasons, more and more avid literary fans are opting to purchase e-books instead of paper books. The question from those not yet initiated into the world of electronic reading is simply: *Why?*

1. *Price.* An electronic title at Ellora's Cave Publishing and Cerridwen Press runs anywhere from 40% to 75% less than the cover price of the exact same title in paperback format. Why? Basic mathematics and cost. It is less expensive to publish an e-book (no paper and printing, no warehousing and shipping) than it is to publish a paperback, so the savings are passed along to the consumer.
2. *Space.* Running out of room in your house for your books? That is one worry you will never have with electronic books. For a low one-time cost, you can purchase a handheld device specifically designed for e-reading. Many e-readers have large, convenient screens for viewing. Better yet, hundreds of titles can be stored within your new library—on a single microchip. There are a variety of e-readers from different manufacturers. You can also read e-books on your PC or laptop computer. (Please note that

Ellora's Cave does not endorse any specific brands. You can check our websites at www.ellorascave.com or www.cerridwenpress.com for information we make available to new consumers.)

3. **Mobility.** Because your new e-library consists of only a microchip within a small, easily transportable e-reader, your entire cache of books can be taken with you wherever you go.

4. **Personal Viewing Preferences.** Are the words you are currently reading too small? Too large? Too... ANNOYING? Paperback books cannot be modified according to personal preferences, but e-books can.

5. **Instant Gratification.** Is it the middle of the night and all the bookstores near you are closed? Are you tired of waiting days, sometimes weeks, for bookstores to ship the novels you bought? Ellora's Cave Publishing sells instantaneous downloads twenty-four hours a day, seven days a week, every day of the year. Our webstore is never closed. Our e-book delivery system is 100% automated, meaning your order is filled as soon as you pay for it.

Those are a few of the top reasons why electronic books are replacing paperbacks for many avid readers.

As always, Ellora's Cave and Cerridwen Press welcome your questions and comments. We invite you to email us at Comments@ellorascave.com or write to us directly at Ellora's Cave Publishing Inc., 1056 Home Avenue, Akron, OH 44310-3502.

Cerridwen Press
Monthly Newsletter

News
Author Appearances
Book Signings
New Releases
Contests
Author Profiles
Feature Articles

Available online at
www.CerridwenPress.com

Cerridwen Press

Cerridwen, the Celtic goddess of wisdom, was the muse who brought inspiration to storytellers and those in the creative arts.

Cerridwen Press encompasses the best and most innovative stories in all genres of today's fiction.

Visit our website and discover the newest titles by talented authors who still get inspired—much like the ancient storytellers did...

once upon a time.

www.cerridwenpress.com